Praise for
BEARING SECRETS

"An intense, can't-put-it-down read."

—Janet Evanovich,
author of *Two for the Dough*

"A fast-moving rollercoaster ride through three bizarrely linked generations: Barre doesn't let up until the disparate plot pieces come crashing in to a surprising center."

—*Santa Barbara News-Press*

"As good or possibly better than his first . . . Ample evidence that the PI novel is still a viable commodity and that the PI of the '90s is definitely a new breed."

—*Mystery News*

"A solid, intelligent mystery . . . A Ross Macdonald-like tale in which the past never lets go and families are the source of both our greatest pain and our greatest joy."

—*Booklist*

"Good narrative, inventive plot, striking characters, and psychological depth make this a keeper. Recommended."

—*Library Journal*

"[A] complex drama . . . the links . . . keep the reader enthralled."

—*Publishers Weekly*

"Hardesty is one of the more appealing personalities making up the new crop of PIs, and Barre writes a very smooth brand of prose, with believable characters and dialogue."

—*Mostly Murder*

"Leanly written, carefully plotted and very, very intense . . . *Bearing Secrets* will reward you in full."

—*The Mystery Zone*

continued . . .

THE INNOCENTS

"A truly powerful and moving novel . . . an intriguing world of mystery, deceit and murder. Richard Barre is a skilled writer and *The Innocents* is a gripping story."

—Michael Connelly,
author of *Trunk Music*

"The book's strength comes from the chances it takes . . . Add some fresh characters, a couple of clever plot twists and you have an auspicious debut."

—*Chicago Tribune*

"Barre delivers . . . An engrossing mystery that moves quickly in prose that is as sleek and muscular as its protagonist. This first outing easily handles, then transcends, the genre requisites for a lively, intense read. Reserve a long evening for this one . . . It delivers the tension and pace that mystery readers demand, but Barre goes beyond that. Hardesty is no cardboard cutout. He and several others pop into 3-D and transcend the posture of their own drama."

—*Santa Barbara News-Press*

"A powerful novel . . . a violent novel of action and suspense that is, in the end, a voyage of self-discovery."

—Michael Collins,
author of *Crimes and Misdemeanors*

"There's much to admire in this first Hardesty novel: crisp, street-smart dialogue; a likable protagonist; and very nasty villains. A solid debut."

—*Booklist*

THE GHOSTS OF MORNING

"Barre has tapped into the psyche of a generation; *The Ghosts of Morning* is a ride as wild and exhilarating as the California surf. History, nostalgia, and gritty human realities hooked me so deeply into the world of Wil Hardesty . . . the plot grabs, the characters seduce, and the pace never lets up."

—Nevada Barr,
author of *Endangered Species*

"Wil Hardesty is a new private eye whose destination may just be the pantheon of great ones who followed tough clues before him."

—Michael Connelly,
bestselling author of *Trunk Music*

"No smart-mouthed wiseguy or lady-killing swinger, Hardesty could be you, me, or a neighbor, a person trying hard to survive a few of life's dirtier tricks."

—*Cleveland Plain Dealer*

"Barre is a skilled writer, an uncanny observer and comes equipped with an uncommonly good ear for dialogue. His investigator, Wil Hardesty, is a most welcome addition to the pantheon of private detectives."

—Ross Thomas,
author of *Ah, Treachery*

"Barre is on my short list of must-read authors."

—Janet Evanovich,
author of *Two for the Dough*

Berkley Prime Crime Books by Richard Barre

THE INNOCENTS
THE GHOSTS OF MORNING
BEARING SECRETS

BEARING
SECRETS

RICHARD BARRE

BERKLEY PRIME CRIME, NEW YORK

BEARING SECRETS

A Berkley Prime Crime Book / published by arrangement with
Walker and Company

PRINTING HISTORY
Walker Publishing Company, Inc. hardcover edition / 1996
Berkley Prime Crime mass-market edition / December 1998

The Penguin Putnam Inc. World Wide Web address is
http://www.penguinputnam.com

ISBN: 0-425-16641-4

Berkley Prime Crime Books are published
by The Berkley Publishing Group,
a member of Penguin Putnam Inc.,
375 Hudson Street, New York, New York 10014.
The name BERKLEY PRIME CRIME and the BERKLEY PRIME CRIME
design are trademarks belonging to Berkley Publishing Corporation.

PRINTED IN THE UNITED STATES OF AMERICA

10 9 8 7 6 5 4 3 2 1

To my father, Benjamin Alfred Barre
How fortunate I was . . .

ACKNOWLEDGMENTS

As always, much love to Susan, who made it possible.

Many thanks to Special Agent Thomas P. Griffin, Federal Bureau of Investigation, and CPI Jim Rochester for their answers to my questions. Thanks also to Shelly Lowenkopf, Leonard Tourney, and Fred Klein for their input; Philip Spitzer, Michael Seidman, and George Gibson for their faith; Marlene Tungseth for her supervision; Krystyna Skalski for her jacket design; Susan, Mary, Ruth, and June for their usual superb effort; Laura Hendricks for her assistance; the Santa Barbara Public Library (and all libraries) for being there; and the friends, relatives, readers, and bookstore folk who gave their support and encouragement.

May 1974

He was lost, flat-out lost—somewhere over California in the miserable goddamn dead of night. He banged the compass, watched it spin slowly. Useless piece of crap . . . Fear was replacing annoyance now; it had been too long since the last lights.

The Piper bottomed out suddenly, then steadied; lightning strobed a horizon thick with storm clouds and horsetails of rain. Clayton waited for the squirmy feeling to leave his gut, then swore. Some fucking pilot: Dead reckoning was going to get him killed at this rate. He felt better at the joke. What the hell, there was bound to be something before long. He knew the route like the back of his hand, just like he'd told the guy with the ten grand and the strange eyes. Change of plans? Your dime, pal—consider it delivered, whatever it is.

He reached under the seat and felt the hard metal skin and combination lock under the plastic handle, felt the man's look again at his suggestion of curiosity. Covering: relax, just joking; it's as good as there—my word. The man loosening his coat then, casually showing him the gun, serious shit.

"Radio silence, of course," the man said.

"Silence," he'd agreed. "Here, look—the damn thing's not even working."

He shook the man's grim face from his mind and took a drag on the hand-rolled cigarette—product testing, he rationalized; besides, it was pretty good shit, hybrid strain he'd pol-

linated himself. He felt the package beside him. Ten K, counted out while the man fidgeted. He thought about spending it, about Lacey's face when she saw the money. Ten thou for a few hours' work; Christ, then, what was in the hard case? For a second, temptation gripped him.

Wind shear brought him back.

Fucking idiot is what he was. A daylight cowboy, follow-the-highway-there-it-is navigator; not something he admitted to—he still had his pride. But how often did somebody ask for a night drop? Hell, who remembered? For ten thousand, not him.

Dark, a sliver of moon lost in storm shroud: the moon and him. Some dumbshit move this, the fear coming again with the buffet of wind. He felt the drift, compensated for it. Time maybe for a closer look, reckon it out from the topography. Hell, it beat running out of gas—where he was headed if he didn't find a bearing before long.

Last toke, then flaps, the descent as gradual as he could make it. Something's out there—come on! He cracked the window and felt the cold touch his sweat.

Any second now . . . There, ahead. My God, he was low.

Water? He strained to see. What water, for crissake?

Too late he saw it: dead tree right side, a looming scarecrow. He felt the impact, saw the wing separate past the middle rivets and spin away. The plane sloughed sideways, banking, shattered side leading the plummet, metal groaning, control irretrievably gone, though he fought it awhile, strangely calm.

Just before the plane hit—when he knew he was in for it, water coming up fast—the thought formed. Something half-remembered he'd heard once as a kid and puzzled over, then twisted around occasionally to suit the joke he was making. The foolishness brought a half-smile: If no one was there to see or hear him fall—like the tree that made no noise in the forest—would he?

ONE

May 1991

Tahoe peeked through breaks in the green, then above it as he climbed. Puffs of dust rose around his boots, graying them; currant bushes and manzanita thinned out. Breath came quicker now, despite his climber's shape.

Midway up, Max Pfeiffer paused. Silence save for the jays and a boat, its razz carrying miles in the morning quiet. His time: He couldn't recall a morning he'd slept in up here, no matter how much he'd put away the night before. The air was like heaven's hand, slapping you awake, showing you things you'd seen a thousand times and never before: trees, lake, rock, sky—beauty like no other. Even Nam couldn't compare, uncut emerald that it was.

Max Pfeiffer shifted his pack and scraped through a patch of buckbrush, its blooms hiding thorns that went unfelt, even in shorts. On his legs, thin red lines formed and began to weep lightly as he climbed.

This morning he'd picked a particularly hard route, one that brought him face-to-face with the lichen-crusted rock. Eagle Rock, his rock. Let the tourists follow the power-line trail in comfort. As in most things, they missed the point.

Two-thirds of the way, the trail left him to footholds and weathered spurs in the mottled lava. Not many knew the rock was old volcano core, he thought, breathing fast. Placid old Tahoe, wind-in-the-pines Tahoe. Not back then.

Hard minutes passed, and then he was on top, steadying a moment, taking it all in: Hurricane Bay, Sugar Pine Point, Mount Tallac farther south showing late snow. He could see the boat now, pulling its wet-suited skier, a far-below dot trailing silver wake. He checked his watch.

Six-eighteen, right on schedule.

Max Pfeiffer walked to a south-facing promontory and sat on a ledge above the sheer drop. He slid the pack off, fumbled inside it, unsnapped the container top, and ate. He'd added honey to the yogurt before leaving, swirling it in carefully like chocolate marbled through a cake. Tart-sweet, it was, just about perfect, if he thought about it.

But his thoughts now were tight frames of Holly, random recollections back and forth across time that seemed terribly compressed. Birthdays, braces, outings, little incidents, how good she'd been about everything—little girl to woman in what seemed like two blinks. His knowing this moment would someday come, the time merely borrowed.

After a while, Max replaced the container and spoon, watched the sun emerge from yellowish glow over the east-side mountains: first rays like God streaming through a hole in the sky, touching his face, his hands, the hooded dark parts under permanent shroud. Soon it was so bright he no longer could look directly at it, and for a moment he closed his eyes, let it all go.

Ashes in the wind.

He blinked open, spent the next twenty minutes watching the new day unfold and drinking coffee, sweetened with the same honey, from a small vacuum bottle. Far below, green spires bowed in the breeze that ruffled his hair and cut through his sweatshirt.

Max shivered as he drew out the newspaper and scanned it again. There was no mistake, no chance for reprieve:

DROUGHT SOLVES
SEVENTEEN-YEAR MYSTERY
Lake Isabella Yields Plane, Missing Aviator,
Clues to Disappearance.

Bakersfield. County sheriff's deputies today were examining the contents of a watertight case thought to contain clues to the disappearance of Clayton Lee Jones, who vanished with his plane the night of May 15, 1974. The discovery was aided by California's drought, which brought Lake Isabella levels to record lows and revealed the wreckage to a local fisherman who reported it. A sheriff's spokesman, while declining to specify the contents of the case, said the department was working closely with federal officials to determine its origin. The plane, a single-engine Piper aircraft without markings, was traced from engine serial numbers. Jones's remains were identified from dental records. As to why Jones . . .

Max released his grip on the pages; they were immediately stolen by a sweep of wind. He watched one spread settle a quarter mile to the south, toward his house. The other drifted more vertically, spiraling into a spruce near the car pulling in beside his own parked in the turnout.

He watched the occupants get out and look upward, followed them until they disappeared into the trees, shaking his head at the way they were dressed for the climb. He pictured them sweating already, tearing hell out of their cheap suits. The thought brought a thin smile.

Max Pfeiffer waited until he figured they were about halfway up. He stood slowly and stretched. Then, without looking down, he took a deep breath and stepped off Eagle Rock.

TWO

Wil Hardesty turned off the electric sander and rubbed resin dust from a spot where his mask didn't fit quite right. He touched the just-roughened fill coat.

Should about do it.

Steadying the longboard on the shaping rack, he examined the ding crater—no worse than the dozen or so she'd picked up over nearly thirty years of surfing. *Southern Cross* he'd named her, after blue and red stripes that intersected aft of center; a Hobie clone he'd made when he was, what—seventeen? He shook his head, positioned the fiberglass patch. He was spreading resin over it in the area he'd taped off when he heard the phone, then Lisa at the window.

"Wil, it's for you, a Holly Pfeiffer. You know her?"

"No," he said, pulling down the mask. "And I can't leave this right now."

"Well, she knows you." A pause. "She mentioned the Innocents."

Over a year now and he was still getting calls, most of them morbids. He cursed this one silently, knowing how Lisa would be. It was always the same. "Some reporter, likely. Get her number, will you?"

"I made the mistake of telling her you were home. She said she'd wait."

"My luck." Hardesty turned back to the laminating resin; already the stuff was getting tacky. He carefully squeegeed the goop around, then inspected his work: An hour's sanding and a final coat of gloss would finish it. Back in business. He crossed the carport and headed up the stairs, opened the door.

Lisa looked up, then went back to slicing bell pepper as he picked up the receiver. "This is Hardesty. You know me?"

He caught the caller off guard. "No—yes. I saw a story about you. About the child murders. You, um . . . killed . . ."

The voice was youngish, twenties maybe. He waited.

"You're still a private investigator?"

"Off and on. How can I help you, Miss Pfeiffer?" Her uncertainty indicated she was probably not a reporter; they went right for the jugular. Like you owed them a pint.

"It's Ms., and I'm not sure I can afford you," she said. "What do you charge?"

Good question, he thought, save us all some time. "That depends, Ms. Pfeiffer. Fifty an hour, three-hundred day rate for most things. What did you have in mind?"

"Three hundred?" It was said with heat. "You should be ashamed, Mr. Hardesty."

"That right? Ashamed of what exactly?"

"Greed is out, in case you hadn't noticed."

"I take it you disapprove."

"I thought you helped people," she said. "Instead you're just another damn . . . *capitalist*." The phone was hung up abruptly.

Wil rubbed his eyes, replaced the receiver. He looked at Lisa working: indigo tee worn loose over white jeans and pink-swooshed Nikes. Usually she was curious. He walked over and rubbed her neck.

She stiffened. "I'm fine."

He dropped his hand. "No," he said. "Not fine. You want to talk?"

She shook her head slowly. "About what? It's still there for me, Wil. You know that."

"Yeah." He said it gently, conscious of the irony in all this: their nearly splitting up over his not wanting another child; her engineering a pregnancy; his finding out only when she miscarried after the beating she took from Guerra. Of Wil suddenly feeling the need, as she had then, only to be told after months of trying that the damage to her system was most likely permanent.

This time there was only so much he could do. Her scars, like her condition and the reasons for it, like her rising anger, could not be masked by time. Like infected wounds that weaken and kill long after the skirmish, they were the Innocents' final casualties.

The Innocents: He'd taken bad risks, lied to her, buried two friends, put her in the danger that resulted in the miscarriage and left them with this hollowed-out shell of a marriage—pain driven home by the occasional call, the well-intentioned re- mark. New pain for her, old for him; twenty-four years of marriage on the line.

The sound of the phone dispelled their awkward silence. He moved to get it as Lisa went downstairs for something.

"Wil Hardesty."

A sigh. "Nobody else will even talk to me." Holly Pfeif- fer's voice.

"Wonder why," he said finally. "You want to start over?"

"It's just that my father always warned me about being exploited."

Something clicked. *Pfeiffer*: somewhere recent. "*Max* Pfeif- fer?"

"That's right. You saw the story, then."

"Yes."

They killed him, Mr. Hardesty, the fascist FBI. He was the most wonderful, loving man, my father, and they killed him, hounded him all his life because he fought for justice, and now he's dead. My father—" She fought for control.

"Ms. Pfeiffer, if I remember correctly, the paper called it suicide."

"Suicide—" Holly Pfeiffer sniffled sharply and exhaled. "They threw him off Eagle Rock. Murdered him. And if they didn't, they might as well have."

Wil settled against the chair facing the window. Traffic

streamed left-right on highway 101; just beyond it waves rolled up on La Conchita's broad beach. Two miles north, the Rincon entertained a few diehards and grommets, though surf conditions were poor, he knew, two-footers at best.

He gentled his tone. "Ms. Pfeiffer, can I help you with something?"

"Now they're trying to blame that horrible kidnapping thing on him. It's so unfair—" Her voice broke, then steadied. "I want you to help me stop them, but I have very little money, and I refuse to go to *her*."

"Her . . . ?"

"My grandmother—his mother, I mean. One of them."

"What about your mother?"

"She died a long time ago. It was just my father and me."

"Where are you calling from?"

"Lake Tahoe, the west shore. Where our home is."

Wil thought, seeing a possibility in it for *them*. "Listen, it might work for my wife and me to take a few days and go up there. Since we'll be at the lake, I could come by. No charge for the visit and we can discuss money when I see you. Sound doable?"

The change in her tone was like sunlight parting clouds. "Yes—that would be—please. Let me give you directions."

He reached for pencil and pad, wrote as she spoke. She concluded with "Mr. Hardesty, I'm . . . Can you come soon?"

"I'll check flights and get back to you. What kidnapping?"

"That awful thing with Angela DeBray. I don't remember the year."

Angela DeBray. Click: seventy-something, Wil just back from Nam. Taped demands, media circus, ransom fiasco, ultimately the little girl found dead. Click-click: gunfire, flames spewing, urban terrorists incinerating. Front row center via TV. Final body count: seven, eight, ten? He couldn't recall.

"I'll do some reading," he said. "D-e-B-r-a-y, right?"

"Right," she said. "I'll be expecting your call." The dial tone returned.

As he hung up, he heard Lisa on the stairs, watched her

come in, put a jar of chutney on the counter. Her eyes still glistened.

He came over and leaned against the countertop. "An idea . . ."

She looked up.

"Couple of days at Tahoe. You, me, the lake. No phones, just us."

For a moment there was a gleam, then it faded. "I'm booked solid, Wil, you know that."

"Let Bev handle it." Dismissive and impatient sounding, it came out not as he'd intended. Her accounting practice was her; *LISA CPA* on the plates of her brand-new Infiniti. Though things had been somewhat better for him, she still brought in the bulk of their income.

"I only mean she's good, Leese. Capable."

"She's also working on extensions. It's not fair to pile my stuff on."

"Good chance to heal up a little."

"Damnit, don't put that on me. And which part was going to be my healing, the time when you'd be around or the time when you weren't?"

He shook his head. "The girl needs help. I just thought we'd—"

"—combine business with pleasure," she finished for him.

"Thanks, but you do your work and I'll do mine." She twisted the jar violently, spilling chutney. "*Goddamnit.*"

Wil moved off toward the bedroom, paused at the door. "I'll call her back, tell her I'm not coming. We'll do something here."

Lisa looked down at her hands, then up at the ceiling. "No, don't do that. A break might be good for us both."

"Come on, Leese."

"Just go," she said quietly, still not looking at him. "Please."

Hardesty kicked a rock, watched it skid down the tunnel and out the beach end. Then he was clambering over rocks that supported the roadway and heading down hard-packed sand toward Mussel Shoals. Late, afternoon sun threw his shadow toward the revetment; gulls pecked through washed-up kelp. Four pelicans squadroned out toward the offshore oil rigs, horizon-outlined.

He fiddled with the coins in his pocket. Hell, maybe what they needed was just to chuck it, start over with new people, new lives. How many friends were helping themselves to thirds—forty-something fantasies?

He thought again of how Tojio Shigeno had reacted—Tojio's beautiful almond-eyed daughter taking up with a blond, six-two, surfer college boy with no prospects save Vietnam duty. A Samurai with hemorrhoids; if Tojio'd had a sword, he'd have fallen on it. As it was, he retired to his orchids and left his only flower to a justice of the peace and Wil Hardesty. To this day they barely spoke.

He turned at the Shoals and started back, squinting into the sun. God, Lisa had been gorgeous then; not that she'd lost much. Maybe they'd just grown in different directions since the miscarriage, the finality of it like some vault door closing—common enough, according to the therapist they'd seen. Harder to accept when the statistic was you.

He thought about ways to talk her into Tahoe, giving up finally—better to not push it. He shielded his eyes toward the Rincon: surfers gone now, sun descending on the incoming sets, impossible not to think of what happened there. The bright bloom of blood, Gringo lolling in the swells, Wil carrying him up the beach, his friend's blood streaking off the longboard. The sirens.

Over a year it had been. Five since Devin.

The tip of a wave hissed over Wil's bare feet, then receded. He watched it go, chucked a rock at it. Then he started back up toward the house.

THREE

Wil timed a gap in the traffic and hit the accelerator, a throaty roar the payoff. Nearly restored now, the '66 Bonneville, awaiting the scratch for a new paint job, looked like a patchwork quilt from the color-mismatched body panels he'd scrounged to replace the ones with bullet holes. Still, it flew, no dropoff there. Still swallowed the longboard through the panel he'd cut in the rear seat.

The *Southern Cross* hadn't been out much since Gringo; twice, maybe—way down for him. Occasionally he'd run into some other surfing graybeards and they'd ask, wondering about one of their own. Some even remembered him from the sixties, from Newport Beach days: dawn patrols and thermosed coffee, doughnuts you never got completely free of sand, the sunny pre-Vietnam insouciance—days that had stayed with him for thirty years. In time he'd be back; he always was. Even after losing Devin to it.

Beyond finding a house he and Lisa could afford then, surfing was how they wound up in La Conchita—not much for size, but hard by the best winter swells in California. Every now and again they were tempted to move closer to city conveniences. Then they'd go for a walk on the beach.

Heading north, he passed the Rincon, noticed the surf unimproved over yesterday, the usual optimists riding out the glass-off. Lisa was gone when he got up; an early client meeting the note read—sorry about Tahoe. He was, too. After a shower and coffee, he booked a flight for the following day, secured a car and a westshore room through the travel agent, thinking maybe Lisa was right. A little distance just now wasn't such a bad idea.

Wil exited the freeway; several more minutes and he was pulling into one of Santa Barbara's elevated parking structures. From the top floor, he took in red tile roofs, the harbor, Channel Islands caressed by a finger of haze reaching up the ninety miles from L.A. He descended, entered the library, stopping first at the newspaper index file; downstairs then, to microfilm. After some noisy scrolling, he found what he was looking for.

It came back quickly enough.

Two months the drama had played out, beginning March 23, 1974, with the kidnapping of Angela Justine DeBray, thirteen days after her third birthday. She'd been abducted from the Atherton home of her parents, Elden and Collette DeBray, he of the publishing and media empire. An employee, Thomas Littlefield, was shot to death by the intruders; other shots terrorized the help, who remembered nothing beyond the masks and guns, the militarylike precision of the grab.

Wil scanned a grainy photo of the little girl: big eyes fixed on something out of frame, smile showing even baby teeth, wisps of hair touching her Peter Pan collar, a face that tugged at the heart. The parents too: Elden DeBray pleading into a bank of microphones, Collette DeBray, younger but aging, a handkerchief to her lips. Anguish the collective facial feature.

Three days later, Field Marshal Z of the Army of Revolutionary Vigilance claimed responsibility for the kidnapping, denouncing DeBray's crimes in a tape delivered to a San Francisco radio station along with one of the child's shoes. The ARV: known wanteds for a series of Bay Area bank robberies, ostensibly to finance the coming revolution. Field Marshal Z: self-styled urban terrorist, aka Cleon Lamar Chapman, violent recidivist and paroled felon.

The governor, in advance, rejected any kind of capitulation to terrorism. The FBI took over the Angela DeBray case.

Two more tapes, rambling diatribes about the impending

massacre of rich by poor and the unification of revolutionists under ARV leadership, were broadcast on April 8 and 20. Wil read the transcripts, recalling the stilted bullshit from before. As yet no ransom set by the kidnappers.

He recalled his revulsion as the case unfolded: Wednesday, May 1, the ARV demanding $2 million, further instructions to be sent later. The DeBrays and their repressive allies were to move quickly if they were to see Angela alive. For effect, her screams had been tacked on to the end of the tape.

Seventeen years and he still could hear them—scrolling, focusing, scrolling; knowing the outcome yet fixed by a growing sense of horror. Tuesday, May 14: The ARV instructed a watertight case with the money in it be left under an overpass in a wide spot off the southbound James Lick fast lane, 10 A.M. the next day. Any attempt to interfere, Angela would be fed to the traffic. 10:16, May 15: A Chevy sedan, windows smoked, slowed and picked up the case. At 10:35 the car suddenly veered off into the ramps and caverns of San Francisco International Airport. Fearing an incident, the authorities closed in, sealed the airport.

Too little, too late.

Three minutes it took to locate the car; arriving units ordered a terrorist to halt. The terrorist, masked and shoving black coveralls into the car's trunk, resisted and was shot four times by the agents. Barely alive: Deborah Ann Werneke, parolee in a campus bombing rap. Firearms analysis matched her weapon to one fired during an ARV bank holdup, a B of A in the Marina.

Angela Justine DeBray was not in the car. Nor was the money.

About an hour later, Field Marshal Z's angry call—too brief to trace—directed authorities to a shallow grave off Skyline Drive. She'd been killed by a crushing blow to the head, the weapon a Dom Perignon bottle later ID'd from the DeBrays' trash. The note said: *Die, then, by the blade of your own sword. Field Marshal Z, Army of Revolutionary Vigilance, Day 1, World War III.*

She'd been dead almost from the beginning.

Thoughts of Devin flashed, the familiar ache. Where the miscarried fetus had also been a boy, it was still more abstract to Wil than flesh and blood. Devin, forever ten going on eleven, was no abstraction. Wil thumbed aspirin from his pocket pack and went to wash them down.

Back at it, feeling for the DeBrays as he hadn't in 1974, he scrolled further. Based on a tip, law enforcement units had closed in on a prefab in L.A., the Pacoima area of the San Fernando Valley. A hundred lawmen were in no mood: After automatic rifle fire responded to their surrender demands, they'd cut loose.

Newspaper pictures triggered Wil's memory of the coverage—ugly house squatting in a lawless yard, bullhorned voice demanding surrender, tear gas cannisters shattering window glass. Gunfire taken and returned, the bullets like firecrackers popping, scattering the crowd. Smoke appearing—puffs at first, then a horrific black column rising from the inferno toward helicopters circling like scavenger birds.

Nine dead, it turned out: three of gunshot wounds, six of smoke and burns, anyone watching awed by their decision to die that way—Field Marshal Z and his martyrs to the revolution. Deborah Ann Werneke, miraculously, lived to be the only ARV survivor.

Next editions were predictable: photos of Lincoln Stillman with the forearm crutches, half-glasses shoved back on his forehead, face frozen in midobjection. Deploring the use of excessive force, demanding an investigation. Stillman the Mamba Negra legal counsel, defense attorney for the Atlanta Seven, Raymond and Ella Robbins, the Liberty Ship bombers, the Berkeley Eleven. Name it, Wil thought, wondering what became of the wild-maned defense attorney with the polio-weakened legs.

Something flashed: back to the indexes, to the Berkeley Eleven trial, 1969 microfilm—and bingo.

Max Pfeiffer as one of the Eleven: Tonkin Gulf Patriots they'd called themselves, an SDS spin-off group, arrested in a violent counteroffensive to retake the UC chemistry building, seized initially by the TGP to make some point about Vietnam. After a week, campus police stormed in. Result: one officer killed, hammered with his own nightstick.

The Patriots were tried for murder.

Lincoln Stillman entered self-defense.

Wil recalled Stillman's critics later asserting that Max Pfeiffer had more to do with the acquittal than any of Stillman's maneuverings. Reading Pfeiffer's testimony, it was hard to argue. The protest of an immoral, unjust war was what was really on trial, he'd said. To a person, the Eleven regretted the cop's death. But it was the inevitable result of the assault—political repression of their right to protest—not murder. Pfeiffer, his arm broken in four places during the melee, then asked the jurors which of *them* would hesitate to intervene to prevent genocide.

Cheers from the packed gallery, the judge clearing the court, the jury finally deadlocking. The prosecution declined to retry, in part because no one actually witnessed the policeman's death. The other part was Max Pfeiffer. The final article included a photo of Lincoln Stillman, braced up and wearing his trademark bow tie and sandals with ragg socks, his arm around Max's shoulder.

Wil looked more closely at something in Max Pfeiffer's eyes, a vulnerable quality, enhanced by nearly toneless pupils. The face was handsome enough, though unsmiling. Lincoln Stillman's was jubilant.

Wil cross-referenced, found another entry. Three years later, Christmas Eve, 1972:

Berkeley. Paulette Miles Pfeiffer, wife of prominent anti-war activist Maxwell Pfeiffer, Jr., was killed by a car bomb while driving home from a candlelight vigil at the Naval Weapons Station, Concord. Mrs. Pfeiffer, a long-time advocate of antiwar causes, had been arrested numerous times. Her death represents an escalation in the

*number of violent incidents concerning Vietnam within
the last twelve months.*

Wil searched for the rest of the article.

*With Mrs. Pfeiffer at the time of the 12:30 A.M. incident
was her daughter, Holly, age one. Miraculously, the
child was found unhurt in bushes near the burning au-
tomobile. Mr. Pfeiffer, legal representative for many local protest groups, accused the FBI of murder. Pending
his wife's funeral services, he was unavailable for further comment.*

Holly Pfeiffer—*fascist FBI*; he checked further, but it was
the last time Max Pfeiffer made news until his obit.

Wil called Holly Pfeiffer from the library. Getting her machine, he left the approximate time she could expect him tomorrow. For a while he turned his imagination loose on what
her life had been like in the interim, what she was feeling
now, the tough-hurt quality he'd heard in her voice. Then he
picked up his tickets from the travel agent, retrieved the Bonneville, and hit the freeway south.

Lisa's note said she'd be late—midnight oil for an impending
IRS audit. After some debate, he decided on taking a weapon,
packing his shoulder holster in the suitcase, rebuilt .45 automatic in the airline shipping container. Calming a paranoid
girl seemed no cause for armament, but since the Innocents,
he'd taken to having the gun along when he traveled.

Following microwaved leftovers, he went for a walk on the
beach. Moon sent shimmers up the wet sand; an offshore
breeze carried inland warmth and the fragrance of something
blooming. He remembered the Berkeley Eleven, the trial happening as he recovered in an Oakland hospital from three
rounds taken during the attack on his eighty-two-foot patrol
boat. Hurting, he'd followed it everyday in the papers. Exer-
cising their rights, they'd been; a shattered building and a dead

UC cop so much traded coin to protest an evil war fought by evil exploiters for evil purposes.

Stillman; Pfeiffer; Berkeley Eleven.

He'd wished them straight to hell.

Even better: proximity to the Viet Cong ambushers who'd used a mother and her three kids to bait the *Point Marlow*, everything but their own cause expendable. They had a lot in common with the Eleven, he'd thought then. Not much since had changed his mind.

Still, he was intrigued by Holly Pfeiffer's call, her link to all that. As if an echo had finally returned from some distant canyon.

He sat awhile, absorbed in the ocean's pulse, the rumble-hum of traffic on the highway. Then he walked back to the house, climbed the stairs, let himself in, and went to bed. For a while he drifted, random thoughts coming in bright snatches like fast-burning flares. And later, time-disconnected in the hospital room, holding Devin's ice-cold hand while the sound of his son's flatline cut through him.

At some point, he was vaguely aware of Lisa getting in beside him. Waking up late to pale light and overcast, he wasn't sure he'd dreamed it or not. At any rate, she was gone again.

FOUR

The 3:18 hop from San Jose descended, gave a couple of air-pocket lurches, then picked up a blaze of afternoon sun reflecting off the gambling casinos. Stateline, Nevada—monument to something-for-nothing, Hardesty thought. A big empty, cast down among the pines.

Still, Tahoe looked enticing from the air, a good place to get a feel for the lake's size, twenty-two miles by twelve, running north-south along a slight dogleg to the California side. Cobalt depths, splashes of green for the shallower parts, water so clear you could see a silver dollar at fifty feet—something he'd read once. He looked again at the development below, wondering if it still held. Hoping so.

The small airport was efficient enough; twenty minutes later he had his luggage and the rental car and was crawling past the "Y" on his way up the lake's west side. Traffic thinned out as Highway 89 narrowed. Wil opened the window, gulped in mountain air crisped by snow still lurking under the high cornices. At Emerald Bay he stopped at the view overlook. Cameras on either side of him clicked rapid-fire, camcorders panned robotlike, tourists smiled dutifully. Far below, late-afternoon sun lit the boat wakes and the little stone tea house on the little stone island. Beyond the inlet and the deep green undulating sweep of conifers, whitecaps and a few sailboats patterned the lake.

Later, from a newish Old Tahoe-style lodge and marina, he

called Holly Pfeiffer, asking if she wanted to meet there. No, she told him, I've cooked something—whenever you're ready.

Following her instructions, Wil backtracked a short distance along the lake, then turned off into an expanse of ponderosa pine mixed with spruce and fir. In a bit he spotted it, a peeling brown A-frame set well back from the road. Decking circled the house as did bush dogwood and wildflowers, small white daisies and such; in the middle of the turnaround, rocks bordered a grouping of young aspens. Wind shook dry needles from the pines.

He was savoring the whispery sound when the door opened.

The girl was pretty, somewhat on the intriguing side. Hair kind of reddish, cut utilitarian and banged across a smooth forehead; nose lightly freckled, attractively so, cheeks flushed as though she'd just finished working out. Closer to the light he saw nicely spaced green eyes—suspicious eyes that regarded him sharply. Microscope eyes.

"Wil Hardesty," he said. He extended his hand.

She gripped it and released. "I'm Holly." She wore a faded Cal Berkeley sweatshirt over sand-colored cords. "You're, um, tall."

"Helps me peek into windows. Shall I come in?"

She stepped aside. "What about your wife?"

"Not able to make it, unfortunately. Her work." Wil handed her his card. As she scanned it, he looked around at cedar paneling that needed stain, comfortable clutter, stairs that dipped down. The room was large and undivided, the kitchen to his right. A serape-draped sofa faced floor-to-ceiling glass that looked out onto the deck and, through breaks in the trees, to the lake. Behind the house the sun was setting, tinting the mountains on the Nevada side a warm shade of pink.

She put down the card, saw him admiring the view. "We'll sit outside, if you like. You want some wine?"

"Something without alcohol, please. I like your place."

"My father bought it when I was young." She saw the question in his glance. "I'm twenty now."

"I'd have guessed older," he said, hoping to elicit response.

"Like what?"

"I don't know, couple of years."

"Is that good or bad?"

The edge in her tone, tilt of her head—or was it him? "Fine by me." He watched her crack open a mineral water, add a bit of lemon and hand it to him, then pour herself a glass of jug Chianti. Something simmered on the stove and she stirred it.

"We're having pasta. That okay?"

"Smells good," he said, following her through sliding glass out onto the deck. They settled in weathered chairs, sipped their drinks. Wil undid the button on his shetland sportcoat, loosened his knit tie.

"It's private here," he said, looking around for neighbors. "Quiet."

"We have an acre, bigger than most of the other lots. Especially the newer ones with their city houses and phony yards."

He let it pass; beyond the deck, bats skittered after insects. Holly Pfeiffer began picking at a fingernail.

"How did you, um, get into your kind of work?" she asked.

"Doing similar things in the military," he said. "When I got out, I got a license."

"You were in Vietnam?" The edge hardened.

"Yes," he said.

"Drafted, I suppose."

"Volunteered. I was with the Coast Guard."

Her eyes narrowed. "I thought they saved people."

"Among other things."

"War things?" Tempered steel.

"During wartime, yes. Port security, patrolling for contraband, things to support the Navy."

She watched the bats a moment, started on another nail, unconscious of it. "You were lucky to come back okay."

Smothering heat and river stink, mortar bloom swallowing up four small figures waiting for rescue; flashes then, the whine of bullets. Brown water closing over his scream.

"You did, didn't you?"

He realized he'd been staring. "More or less."

"You were wounded?" The nail gave a little snap and she stopped, curled her fingers under.

"One time out. That was during the first tour."

"You actually went back after you'd been wounded?"

"That surprised my wife too," he said.

Holly Pfeiffer reddened. "Then you're one of them."

Nothing he hadn't heard for years and shined on; despite it, her tone was starting to annoy him. "If by that you mean I was one of the ones trying to make a difference, yes. Is that a problem?"

"It means you condoned it," she said.

"I guess I did," he said evenly. "Didn't much like the way it was run, but so what?"

She snorted. "I wish my father were here to tell you so what. The war was everything he hated."

"I know. I read about him."

"And you came up here anyway? I must seem like a soft touch."

"Hardly," Wil said, appraising the green eyes. Heat lightning seemed to dance behind them; already he was regretting this petty confrontation, letting her push familiar buttons.

"I loved my father more than anything," she said. "He was a great man. While you were fighting poor people trying to free their country from imperialism, he was fighting the pigs and the fascists who were fucking up *this* country." She paused to let the storm pass. "They finally got him, but not what he stood for. Not while I'm here. Please leave now, Mr. Hardesty."

She reminded him of Scarlett O'Hara facing down forces beyond her control or comprehension. Wil leaned forward. "What about dinner? Even enemies have to eat—you know, the Geneva Convention?"

She looked across at the mountains, vague silhouettes now, her jaw set. "God, I wish he were here," she said.

•   •   •

They ate off plates chipped around the rim. In the sink, inter-mittent drops splashed in the pot Holly Pfeiffer had put on to soak. Moths buzzed the deck light.

"This is good," Wil said at length. "Capers and what—leeks?"

"My father's recipe," she said, regarding him. "You don't want wine?"

"No, thanks."

She poured herself more Chianti. "My father didn't believe in arbitrary laws. He let me drink when we agreed I was ready. What about you—you don't drink at all?"

Wil twirled spaghetti around his fork. "Not anymore."

"Not even tempted?" A flush was beginning to bloom at her throat.

"Ms. Pfeiffer, you mentioned the FBI had come. Why now?"

She took an exaggerated pull on the Chianti.

"Couldn't we at least talk about it?"

"They were here to arrest my father, all right? Because of the plane."

"The plane."

"Don't you read? The plane they found in the lake."

"Tahoe?"

Her look was patronizing. "No, Isabella—three hundred miles south. The plane was discovered because of the drought. The FBI got involved because of what was in the plane. I'd show you, but I can't find the newspaper."

"I read an article on his death, that's all."

She took another gulp of wine. "My father was very upset. Next morning he was gone and the fascists were here, two of them. They took his note, but I memorized it. It said"—she took a deep breath—" 'I'll always love you. Trust me now.' I told them I didn't know where he went. 'Blue BMW,' one of them says, then they tore out of here. In a couple of hours they were back—after they'd killed him."

"When they came back, what did they say?"

"That there was new evidence linking him to the Angela DeBray thing. It was horrible."

Candlelight picked up the red in her hair, the shine in her eyes; Wil let a moment pass, then: "They tell you what it was?"

"No, but they asked questions, mostly about money. You'd think they could see that we don't have any."

"A BMW?"

"God, it was almost as old as I am."

"How did they know about it?"

She shook her head. "I have no idea. No one knew our real name. Not even the neighbors."

"How come?"

"Oh, *please*. The FBI killed my mother. My father always said they'd kill *us* if they could find us."

Wil put down his fork. "Forgive an observation, but they go here quick for not knowing where you were."

"Meaning what?" she said sharply.

"Meaning it sounds as though this thing in the plane was what prompted them to act. That they knew all along where you were."

"Sons of bitches."

"They leave a card?"

She stood up, spilling wine on her place mat, and fished a card off the counter near the phone. She handed it to him, then swiped angrily at the spill.

Wil read, *Federal Bureau of Investigation, Albert R. Vega, Special Agent.* He copied the name and Sacramento phone number in his notebook, then watched her empty the bottle into her glass.

Wine-bright eyes caught him looking. "You disapprove, don't you?"

"Not yet. Would you have a recent picture of your father?"

The distraction worked; he could see her thinking. "One," she said. "He was very paranoid about photographs." She went downstairs and came back to the table with a color snapshot. "Eagle Rock. We used the timer."

Wil took it, saw the two of them, backlit and happy in hiking shorts and T-shirts, the lake spreading out below. Max Pfeiffer was as Wil saw him on the library microfilm, but less pinched, less stressed. His hair, bleached by the high-altitude sun, was wisp thin, the peak much receded. He was smiling, a red bandanna around his neck, glints reflecting off round steel-rimmed glasses. Max's arm was around his daughter's shoulder.

Holly Pfeiffer passed him another photo; this one was dog-eared, the color faded. The woman's hair was auburn, her face delicate. Her eyes, however, challenged the camera. She wore an embroidered peasant blouse and long skirt, and she leaned against a dinged-up VW squareback. Despite a directness that bordered on chip-on-the-shoulder, something else shone through, a luminosity.

"Your mother?"

Holly nodded.

"I can see where you got your hair." He anticipated the reaction, intercepted it. "That's a compliment, Ms. Pfeiffer. Incidentally, I read you were with her the night she died."

"Murdered, you mean. Regular FBI family, we are." She tossed off half her remaining wine. "She took me everywhere. My father always said I turned out more like her than he could have hoped."

"He never remarried?"

"No. He was always afraid."

"Of what?"

"Shit, where have you been? Afraid of subjecting a wife to more fascist harassment." Her words were beginning to slur. "I didn't even go to school." She pointed to a wall of books and a PC. "That was my education. And no kid had a better teacher."

"What about friends?"

"Who needs friends, I had him. He knew so much. He'd traveled—Europe and . . ."

Wil waited.

"Vietnam." She said it softly, looking into her wine.

"How about some coffee, if I make it?" he said.

They faced each other over a homemade coffee table, Wil on a vinyl recliner split in places, Holly Pfeiffer on the couch, hands cupped around her mug. Bugs still hurled themselves at the outside light; occasionally one buzzed the glass.

"Military advisers, they called them," she said. "It wasn't even a war yet. But he was drafted, so he went."

Wil sipped coffee. "He wasn't in school?"

"Only on the dean's list at Boalt is all." There was a hint of a smile. "He refused to fight for a deferment. Said he'd be damned if he was going to let some poor man take his place."

"Army?"

"*Fucking* army, he called it." She set her mug on the arm of the couch, watched the steam rise as she talked. "He saw what was happening, how corrupt the South Vietnamese were, the politics and torture. Civilians murdered."

"One man's civilians, another man's Cong."

"Are you going to listen or argue?"

She had a point. "Go on," he said.

"He questioned things, so they gave him this lousy duty— latrine, KP, late watches. Then they had him walking point, hoping he'd get killed. Still he questioned what was going on. So the army held an inquiry. It was a joke, my father said." She looked up at Wil, her eyes boring in.

"They decided on a medical discharge, instability or something." She pointed to a frame on the wall behind him. "That's how unstable he was—magna cum laude."

Wil looked; the degree read 1969, University of California, Law. "That's when he met your mother?"

"No, before. They were married that year."

"How did they meet, do you know?"

"At an SDS meeting. She was older and very political."

"And attractive," Wil said.

Her gaze broke, drifted downward; she started in on her nails again.

"Tell me," he said. "The FBI ever find out who planted the bomb?"

"Haven't you been listening? They did. They killed her."

"Your father told you that?"

"Yes, my father told me that, and unlike you, I believe him. And now I'm tired, Mr. Hardesty."

Wil stood up. "On the phone you mentioned your grandmother."

"His mother," she said, "never my grandmother. I've only seen pictures of her. All she needs is her money, my father said."

He set his mug on the table; the room had cooled markedly, but Holly Pfeiffer seemed not to notice. "Where does she live?"

"I don't know. San Francisco someplace."

"And his father?"

"Dead. Don't you ever get tired of asking questions?"

"Sure," he said, conscious that the wine had left her tone. Without the edge, her directness was not unappealing. "What about your mother's parents?"

"They disowned her before I was born. Her lifestyle didn't suit them."

"I can imagine. Well, thanks for dinner," he said. "Any idea what you'll do now?"

She shook her head. "Maybe they'll kill me too. It won't be easy, though."

"No kidding. They'll probably have to draw straws."

"Don't patronize me, Mr. Hardesty. Just go, please."

"Okay," he said. "If you'll have breakfast with me. We'll expense it and serve the government right. Deal?" Wil wasn't sure, but it looked as if she was masking a smile as she closed the door behind him.

FIVE

Lincoln Stillman watched the gate swing shut behind them. As he turned and faced forward, the seat made a rich leathery sound. He watched Behr glide the Rolls up beside the steps. Behr set the brake, got out, opened the door for his employer.

"Thank you, Behr. Park it, then join me in the study."

Lincoln Stillman swung his legs out of the car, then stood. Bracing himself with the forearm crutches—glorified canes, he always told people—he mounted the shallow steps, walked past Henning holding the door open for him, and entered the foyer. Highlights danced off the crystal chandelier; his crutches squeaked on the hardwood. On his way to the study Stillman did not even glance at the Vermeer, spotlit as it was to emphasize the girl playing her lute.

Once inside, he closed the double doors and faced the room. The study was large; during the day, it looked out on flagstones and beyond that, making him crazy every time he saw it, an ocean of lawn. Water overages were costing him a fortune, but Monika liked it, so it stayed lush. Luckily he couldn't see it now; instead he caught his own reflection in the French doors: My God, had he really gotten that fat? He sucked in hard, smoothed down hair that still drove prosecutors to drink; nearly white now, but unvaried in length for twenty years. And the face, reminding him of bread dough unrisen in spots. Unfortunately, as much as the hair and the canes, it was what people remembered.

Stillman tossed his suit coat aside, unclipped the bow tie, made himself a drink. Downing Wild Turkey, he looked around. Every piece of furniture brought back some snub he'd received in law school. He'd made a list, about a hundred names. Every time he won a case, every time he made news, he'd disseminate it to the list. Much to his delight he was still disseminating, though the list had shrunk some. He raised his tumbler to the Whistler or John Singer Sargent or whatever it was on the wall, big son of a bitch, Monika's anniversary present to him. He tossed off the rest of the bourbon, poured two fingers more. Careful, he thought—got to outlive all the bastards.

He wondered how his friend the ex-champ was doing tonight. Now there was a *man*, God love him, stuck it to them and still came out the most respected figure in the world. He made a mental note to have Monika's art buyer watch for something appropriate—whatever you gave a punch-drunk heavyweight. Gladiator sculpture, maybe.

He set the canes aside, sat heavily in the desk chair.

Behr knocked softly and entered, the door frame emphasizing how huge he really was; any bigger and the Kraut would have to turn sideways. Plus Behr's salt-and-pepper brush cut always looked stiff enough to wash vegetables. Appropriate metaphor, Stillman thought, considering the number of messes he'd cleaned up. Over time Behr was the best thing about the Monika deal, no argument there.

Stillman waved his glass at the florid round face. "Help yourself to schnapps, you want it," he said. "Monika around?"

"I've not seen Mrs. Stillman," Behr said with only the slightest of accents. He poured the liquor, drained the glass, looked expectant. "You wished to see me?"

Lincoln Stillman tapped his fingers lightly, the maneuver designed to upstage prosecutors. So polished was it, so innocently soft-loud-soft, he hardly noticed when he was doing it anymore.

"You read the newspapers, Behr?"

Behr shook his head.

"Wise man, only give you ulcers. Still, sometimes it can be valuable." He reached into his desk and brought out a section of the *L.A. Times.* Handing it to Behr, he allowed the man time to read, then cleared his throat.

Behr looked up.

"Kind of makes you wonder what was in that case, doesn't it?" Stillman said.

Behr blinked wide-spaced eyes. "You think it fits?"

"I do."

"Not much hard information."

"That was two days ago. Things change. Nothing surer than that."

"And you're thinking it would be wise if I started reading the newspaper."

"Behr, with your powers of deduction, you could have been a lawyer."

Behr smiled politely. "Does Mrs. Stillman know of this?"

"No. And I thought it best not to trouble her—if you understand me."

Behr nodded; Stillman poured him another schnapps. "Could be nothing," he said, setting down the bottle. "Then again it might be the news we've been waiting for."

The big man nodded, rose. "Tomorrow's still on, I assume."

"To my knowledge, yes, but check on it with Monika. She was working out some new twist, a guy in a wheelchair or something." Lincoln Stillman paused. "And Behr? For this other thing? Keep a bag packed and your mouth shut."

SIX

The phone caught Wil in deep sleep—pulse racing, not yet comprehending where he was; grasping it then, reaching for the sound, the air in the room chill on his arm. He opened his eyes to semidark. "Hardesty . . ."

"All right," Holly Pfeiffer said.

He lay back on the pillow.

"I'll have breakfast with you," she went on. "If—"

"If what," he managed. He raised his wrist up to his eyes and blinked: 5:20 A.M.

"You come with me to see where they murdered my father."

"Eagle something."

"Rock," she said. "Eagle Rock. You'll pass it on your way to pick me up. In a half hour."

Wil expelled a breath. "You *are* aware of the time?"

"Stop bleating, he was up there at sunrise. I'll bring coffee. Just hurry up." The line went dead.

Trying to recall what it felt like to be twenty and not getting it, Wil eased out of bed and into the shower. Afterward he dressed in jeans and a sweater, tossed his notebook in the rental and headed south, the road at this point near eye level with the water. Tahoe's calm mirrored a few clouds turning faint yellow as the eastern light intensified; exposed rocks marked the years of drought. Except for a couple of trucks, the road was nearly empty.

Two miles up, he saw it, a darkly weathered hulk that rose straight up from the mountain side of the highway. Wil craned, guessing its height at well over two hundred feet, then continued on to the A-frame.

Holly Pfeiffer was waiting on the steps, wearing khaki shorts, boots, the faded navy and gold sweatshirt from last night, and a blue kerchief. Around her waist was a small pack. She rose as he leaned over and opened her door.

"I've got it," she said abruptly. "You're late. We're going to miss sunrise."

"Good morning to you, too," Wil said.

They drove in silence back to the wide spot under Eagle Rock; Holly ran a hand through her hair. "This is where my father left the Beemer." She got out of the car, started up the trail.

Wil locked the rental and fell in step beside her. "Nice day—brisk. Good to start early, don't you think?"

She stopped abruptly. "Look, I'm finding this hard enough. Do me a favor and be quiet. Listen to the forest. Maybe it'll tell you something."

For a while they walked, dust rising with their steps.

"It has birds."

"What?" she said.

"I hear birds. And a pleasant sound—wind, I think, in the trees."

She said nothing. The incline steepened.

"This the path he took?"

"I doubt it," Holly said. "He'd have chosen one of the verticals. He was a good climber despite his arm."

"Broken when the cops retook the chemistry building."

She stopped again, her curiosity apparent. "You know about that?"

"I told you I'd do some reading. His testimony was impressive. And Lincoln Stillman defending, no less."

As they cut through chest-high manzanita, a jay dove at them, squawking. Breath came faster with the steepness.

"My father hated Lincoln Stillman, used to call him an

opportunist and a glory hound." She paused. "He made a pass at my mother once."

"Did your parents know him before the trial?"

"They met during another case. After my mother died, my father worked for him awhile. But then he quit."

They stopped a moment, continued on.

She said, "You ever hear of the Citizen Defarge Committee?"

Wil's eyes searched for the summit. "After the character who knitted while the guillotine lopped heads off the French nobility. Sure."

"My mother was a founder—this is her sweatshirt I'm wearing. My father saved it for me."

"You wear it well." He watched a flush spread up her face. "Does no friends mean no boyfriends either?"

She kept her eyes on the trail. "I've seen them, in their pickup trucks and baseball hats. They bang nails and drink beer and drive like fools and use women like . . . garbage cans."

"My word."

"Don't be dumb, Mr. Hardesty. I have more important things on my mind. You can understand that, can't you?"

"Uh-huh." Wil led the way up a steep part, then looked back, extending her a hand that she waved away. With that they were on top, the lake almost entirely in view. Patches of snow dressed the tips and some shaded portions of the surrounding mountains. Sparkle danced on the water, so bright it made them shade their eyes.

"Damn, we missed it."

He gulped air. "My fault. I owe you a sunrise."

"Feeling the altitude?"

"Not bad," he said.

She looked skeptical.

"I run at home. Surf when I can," he said.

"Blond hair, the shoulders—I should have guessed."

"Not a big surfing fan, I take it."

She shrugged. "Rich-boy sport. Tell me it's not."

"Didn't used to be," he said. "If you were good with your hands, you could make your own board. Get a little gas money together, bum a ride—nobody much around then. Like everything else, the good things get overrun."

She softened. "Skiing's like that. My father could recall when Squaw was twelve bucks for all day. We had to quit going finally." Her eyes scanned the lake. "Do you know that Tahoe never gives up its dead?"

"I haven't heard that one."

"They become a part of it, all the people who've gone out and not come back. Boats too, I've seen pictures—steamships that used to visit the resorts."

"Plenty of room out there, I suppose."

"It's deep, over sixteen hundred feet in places. The cold water preserves things." She stepped over to the edge.

Her tone brought a chill; he eased in that direction, eyes fixed on her.

She said, "I think he'd like it out there, don't you? When the leaves are gold and the surface is warm from the sun." She turned to face him.

"I do, yes. Did they find anything of his up here?"

She swallowed hard and rubbed her forehead. "They found his pack and thermos, an empty container and spoon. As though a man who kills himself would eat first."

"Happens sometimes," he said, relieved. "Any signs of a struggle?"

"You think they'd say anything about it? They even had the nerve to tell me he looked peaceful."

"You mentioned coffee."

Holly sighed, unzipped the pack, fished out a blue vacuum bottle, and poured the contents into coffee-stained Melmac cups. They sat on an outcropping of rock.

"Oh that's good," he said after drinking some. "French roast?"

"His favorite," she said. Suddenly she began to cry. Wil studied the lake: early boats, their hum muted by distance, wood smoke curling up from cabins, sunshine lighting the trees and the rock and her face. After a bit she stopped and wiped her eyes. "It's just so *unjust*."

He said, "I'll do what I can, if you like."

"Then you think he was murdered, too?" Her voice was damp.

"I didn't say that. But I will agree to help you complete this. It's your call."

"What about your fee? Unless I can prove he was murdered, I won't even be getting the life insurance. Not that it'd be much anyway."

Wil thought about the way he'd left it with Lisa, tension that might run itself out if he held off a little longer. "Tell you what," he said. "Long as I'm here already, I'll see what I can turn up in a couple of days. Pay me what you can afford, if you think it's worth it. Fair?"

She thought a moment, then sniffed and nodded, sun picking out the red in her hair. Her eyes still glistened, but hope lit them now.

"One thing, though," he said as she looked at him. "We lose the Ms. Pfeiffer."

This time she didn't try to hide the smile.

The man in the wheelchair was doing his best with the heavy glass door, but was having his problems. The edge kept hitting the metal ring on the big wheel and slipping from his gloved hand.

The bank guard let it go for three attempts, then stepped forward. Best not to be too eager, he thought, disabled vets resented being treated as helpless; much as possible you had to let 'em do it themselves, something he'd learned on the job. Not this one, but a lot he knew by name. Came here to cash their checks in army fatigue jackets and surplus boots, hard-set faces. Whenever he had the chance, he'd jaw with them, see if they'd been any of the places over there he'd been. Break down the walls a little, let 'em know they weren't alone.

Some appreciated it, some shied away. Never stopped him

from trying, though—there but for the grace and all that. Besides, he'd made some friends that way.

"Morning," he said to the man as he swung the door wide.
"Think they'd invent some'n better, wouldn't you? Things
weigh a damn ton."

The man regarded him long enough for the bank guard to
see his reflection in the man's mirrored sunglasses. Beyond
that there was no response. With a hard thrust he wheeled into
the lobby and took a position behind the rope.

Nothing personal, the bank guard figured, probably be a
little bitter at life myself. It was the Beverly Hills types who
snubbed him that were the real cripples—plenty of those
around. Still, this beat a lot of work hands down: nice decor,
pretty people, air-conditioned—rare you ever broke a sweat.
After the buckets he'd sweated in Nam, that was fine by him.

The bank guard rubbed an itch where he'd Velcro'd the
backup gun to his ankle, then adjusted his holster belt. He
nodded to the younger guard standing by the flag at the other
end of the lobby. Younger every day, he thought—this kid
looked barely old enough to shave. Nineteen he'd been when
his number came up in the lottery, twenty when his plane left
Fort Bragg. He shook his head. Added security: Heaven help
us if the kid ever had to fire his Smith & Wesson in anger.

The bank guard checked his watch: early yet for the ar-
mored transport people. His eyes followed a brunette in tight
jeans, then two men who entered, the bearded one queuing up
behind the vet in the wheelchair. The other, heavyset and
wearing Wayfarers, started in on some paperwork at the far
writing stand. The bank guard saw his young counterpart use
the water fountain, then his gaze drifted to the teller line,
where the bearded man was becoming increasingly agitated at
the wheelchair vet.

Yet another, he thought. The bank guard watched a suit
leave his desk and approach, which only started the other two
yammering at *him*. The bearded man shoved the suit. Wheelchair rammed his chair into Beard. Beard took a swing at

Wheelchair and missed. At that point the bank guard stepped between the two.

"Cool it now," he said to the short man. "Enough's enough."

"Please," the suited official added. "This *is* a bank."

The guard watched the bearded man's eyes dart right. From behind him there was a sound he knew all too well: the bright metallic snick of a shell being jacked into a shotgun chamber. He turned to face a pump Winchester. Slowly the man in the wheelchair rose from the chair and smiled.

"Get his gun," he said to the bearded man.

The guard felt his holster lighten. "Gotta be a better way than this," he said. His eyes scanned Wheelchair's face, seeing his own again in the glasses. "Talkin' federal time here, man. You thought this through?"

Wheelchair turned and triggered two rounds at a pair of CCTV cameras, exploding them off their wall mounts. The sound ricocheted against the bank's hard surfaces; a woman at the desk screamed, another wailed. Wheelchair's voice then: "Everybody down, nobody gets shot. On the floor. *Now!*" He turned to the bank guard. "That answer your question— *man?*"

The bank guard had time to see the heavyset man club down the young guard, tight jeans bounding over a teller's station with a bag in her hand, and then he was prone with the half-dozen others who'd been in line. Through a rift in the bodies, he could see blood on the young guard's face.

"*Come-on-come-on-come-on-come-on . . .*" Screams from in back where the vault was, then running feet. Off to his right, the short man's voice again: "*Fuckin' A, people. Speed it up!*" Then: "*Jesus Christ, look at this. Bo-fucking-nanza.*"

The backup gun felt useless at his ankle; no way to quick-draw from spread-eagle. There was another scream and this time the sound of impact. "*Goddamnit, I said down.*" Another scream. The bank guard calculated his chances even if he could get to the Walther: seven rounds, four of *them.*

The Jean girl's feet hit the marble in front of him and ran across his field of vision. As they passed, he focused beyond, to where his partner was rising up haltingly, blood streaming, his gun coming up to parallel.

Shit, man! No way in hell.

But the younger guard was up now, wiping away blood, aiming the S&W and firing. There was a grunt as the rounds impacted and the heavyset man hit the writing stand and spun off onto his face. The shotgun cut loose then.

Lord God, here we go.

The bank guard reached down and palmed the Walther. From near the door, he saw the bearded man aim a handgun across the room at the younger guard. As the man opened up, the bank guard triggered three rounds, saw the man pitch through plate glass. Formica disintegrated above him then; he dove behind the counter and rolled to his left. Another shotgun blast; the bank guard felt a ripping in his leg and then the Smith & Wesson was firing again, the young guard stumbling toward Wheelchair.

As he struggled up from the floor, the bank guard could see Wheelchair swing the pump gun, heard empty clicks from the young guard's revolver. Then there was an explosion of red and the young guard's body was flung backward onto a screaming woman customer.

The bank guard was balanced on his good leg now; coldly, carefully, he put the remainder of the clip into Wheelchair as the man was bringing the shotgun back around to fire. Heavy buckshot tore off acoustic ceiling tile; dust rained. Wheelchair's body came to rest across a PC workstation.

For a moment nobody moved.

The bank guard looked down at blood pouring from his leg, then at Wheelchair. He heard someone shouting, *"My God, look out!"* something like that, but shock was starting to blur things. He was turning to see where the girl had gone when he heard the sound again, the metallic *click-click.*

He saw a huge man pointing a pistol-grip shotgun at him. Where the man had come from, he didn't know. Nor could he make out the man's face behind the nylon stocking pulled tight. As the bank guard dropped his eyes to the weapon's bore, it seemed to grow larger, as big now as any of the field pieces he'd fired at Khe Sanh, and in that instant he was strangely resigned to how it was going to end.

Wil got them a deck table overlooking the marina as Holly went inside to find a newspaper. The waitress filled their mugs, then moved off to coffee other tables; beyond the log railings, Wil could see a young girl in wet suit and water skis struggle up behind a red Donzi amid much cheering from the group on the boat. Four men wearing bicycle gear argued over leaving a tip, then clacked off across the decking.

Holly sat down, her face ashen. She handed him the paper:

NEW EVIDENCE LINKS TAHOE
MAN TO DEBRAY KILLING

Suspect in 1974 murder of Atherton girl a suicide.

Sacramento. FBI agents and sheriff's deputies presented evidence they say wraps up one of the state's most infamous murder cases, the 1974 kidnap-murder of Angela Justine DeBray, abducted from her Atherton home by masked gunmen seventeen years ago last March 23. The child was found bludgeoned to death in a shallow grave May 15, 1974. Some authorities had speculated that the ransom money, which was never found, burned in the savage fire that consumed nine ARV (Army of Revolutionary Vigilance) members after their shoot-out with lawmen in a Pacoima safe-house two days later.

In a statement yesterday, FBI Special Agent Albert Vega revealed that the money, specially marked before the ransom was paid, was found in the watertight case discovered in a small plane in Lake Isabella, east of Bakersfield. Also in the plane were the remains of pilot Clayton Lee Jones, who took off May 15, 1974, near

Santa Cruz, and was reported missing later by his wife, Lacey Louise Jones. Contributing to the discovery is California's multiyear drought, which has dropped lake levels to historic lows.

Vega said the money was found with a note linking Maxwell Pfeiffer, Jr., well-known antiwar militant in the late sixties and early seventies, directly with the crime. Missing from the $2 million ransom was an amount believed to be Jones's fee. Undissolved pieces of marked bills were found in the cockpit. Vega also disclosed that fingerprints lifted from the note and the inside of the case matched Pfeiffer's. The suspect, 51 and a resident of Lakebridge, West Lake Tahoe, leaped to his death from Eagle Rock just as FBI agents were closing in. Pfeiffer, who went under the name of Edmund Maxwell, leaves a daughter, Holly Rose, also of Lakebridge.

Vega indicated Pfeiffer's role in the kidnap-murder may never be fully known, but speculated that he acted as a go-between for the ARV, picking up the money at San Francisco International Airport, where one terrorist was captured. For a cut of the ransom, Pfeiffer is thought to have arranged for the money to be flown to Los Angeles, where the remaining ARV members had fled. Vega said the discovery has enabled them to conclude their investigation, once the largest manhunt in California history.

Head shots of Max Pfeiffer and Angela DeBray appeared between the story and one about a $2.5 million L.A. bank holdup in which five died. Holly Pfeiffer's skin seemed too tight for her face.

"Fascist press, it's all lies." Other tables picked up her tone; people stared openly.

"Come on, let's get out of here." Wil dropped a bill and touched her arm.

"Forget it. Let them hear what kind of thugs do their dirty work." She waved the newspaper at the starers. "You're not safe, you know. They lie and murder and invade your privacy and tear apart your life, and none of you has the guts to fight back. Well, I have the guts. *I have*—''

He muscled her past the gapers, past the hostess stand, and out into the parking lot. As he let go of her arm, she swung at him, connecting with a smack that surprised and stung. With effort, he got her into the car. As he drove, he rubbed his cheek.

''Don't expect me to apologize,'' she said.

He nodded; neither spoke the rest of the way. Before he came to a stop, she was out the door and into the house. Wil picked up the newspaper, scanned it, found nothing else relevant, and followed her inside. As she sat on the couch, feet drawn up, he made two instant coffees and handed her one.

''Leave me alone,'' she said with eyes straight ahead. ''You're as bad as they are.''

''Back to that, huh? Burn the bridges, scorch the earth. You need me, I'll be at the hotel, provided they haven't thrown my clothes out on the street.''

''Don't ever manhandle me like that again. Is that clear?''

''Clear,'' he said. ''And now a little advice for you: Swing at me one more time and you're on your ass. Believe it.''

SEVEN

Behr moved slowly into single whip. Discipline, of course, was everything. Form too; none of his teachers had expressed much optimism at his being able to master it, a man his size. Which only enhanced the feeling of calm as he eased into White Crane Spreads Wings. Knees relaxed, weight shifting, arms floating into the postures, head centered correctly on the spine. Balancing the chi. Behr felt his breathing step up in tune with his warming inner state, the sensation of parting the air as though it were water. Continuous, flowing movement: Intercept and Punch, Cross Hands, Embrace Tiger and Return to Mountain, Step Back to Drive the Monkey Away.

The telephone.

Behr let it ring a half-dozen times before picking up.

"Interrupt your chi-chi?"

"T'ai chi, Mr. Stillman, a form of martial art. Very beneficial. You—"

"—should try it? Now *that* would be something."

"I didn't mean—"

"Don't sweat it, Behr, keeps your edges honed, I know. Speaking of which, did you read what I left you?"

Behr lit a cigarette, exhaled smoke. "Very involving."

"Then you took note of the details."

"My plane leaves in a few hours."

"Just so you know, I'll be in Washington, arguing my nuts off in front of the Supreme Court on behalf of some misbegotten Popsicle jockeys. Have fun up there—I'm jealous.''

I'll bet you are, Behr thought; even *he* knew of the exploits with Capital Hill hookers. Idly, he wondered how Stillman's legs behaved in bed. ''Thank you, Mr. Stillman,'' he said. ''I'll be in touch, either directly or through Mrs. Stillman.''

''Make that directly. Reminds me—any of that brouhaha from yesterday traceable to us?''

''No,'' Behr answered. ''The woman is out of the country. The dead men were loners, veterans with robbery records and antisystem histories.''

''Bleeding-heart fodder with built-in motivations—*sounds* like something Monika'd think of.''

''Credit where it's due, Mr. Stillman.''

''Some haul, two-and-a-half mil.''

''Undeserved in light of our sloppiness. Some transfer of currency or something.''

''No looking a gift horse. Still, that's a tad close for my taste.''

''Rest assured, I've heard from Mrs. Stillman on the subject.''

''Enough said, then. And don't sweat driving me to the airport, Henning can do that. You skedaddle.'' Lincoln Stillman hung up.

Behr replaced the receiver, shook his head at the phony twang, the man not knowing when to turn it off anymore. He eased his six-feet-seven into the recliner, amused himself by separating Stillman myth from Stillman fact. Apart from the bio they kept ready for media inquiries, what he knew for *certain*: Stillman *was* the son of a Washington State tenant farmer, he *had* been offered a WSU wrestling scholarship. Polio *had* struck him down, and a law school in Spokane *had* considered him after a newspaper story showed Stillman reading encyclopedias of evidence as he recuperated. Those things he knew because he'd seen the framed clippings on Stillman's wall. Whatever else he took with a grain of salt.

Meeting him had been an experience in itself. Behr recalled their shaking hands as Stillman cozied up to Monika, his surprise at the crutches when Stillman walked to the bathroom, the wad of cash Stillman used to pay for room service. Behr had both hated and liked him, feeling guilty at first about the hate. Until he realized *that* was Lincoln Stillman—no one stayed neutral. Which was exactly as the man liked it, courtroom-clear, for or against—against if *he* had any say. Behr had never seen anyone who so much loved a fight. He took a final drag on the cigarette.

Like the time Stillman wasted the drunk.

It was just after they'd arrived and were celebrating, Stillman buying. Behr knew Monika had probably started it; not knowing American customs, she'd tried staring down the man at the next table who was staring at her, a tactic that only encouraged him. Behr was about to break the man in two when Stillman tapped the pocket with their papers in it, waggled his finger in warning. He bought the man a drink, invited him to join them. Behr remembered the look in Stillman's eyes, the whiskey untouched from then on, the four doubles he bought the man leaning lower and lower over Monika's bodice. Stillman's hand on hers, squeezing it every time Monika looked ready to kill.

They'd left the bar then, gone outside to the man's car, Stillman leering, "Go ahead, show him your titties, dear." Monika, wooden, not comprehending, but complying. Stillman handing Behr the crutches, his stiffened fingers striking with blinding speed. Stillman's muscular forearm around the sightless drunk's neck, the twig-snap crack of vertebrae.

They Dumpstered him nearby, Behr parking the man's car alongside. Stillman gave Monika the pleasure of reporting two black men attacking a lone white guy, her screaming for the cops to hurry. The man's money he gave to Behr.

"Good for business," Lincoln Stillman said as they drove home later. "Might wind up defending whoever it is they arrest."

Behr had never forgotten it. Welcome to America.

He'd learned quickly from Stillman: how to confuse, then strike; how to find weak spots; when to appear vulnerable, when not. The thing with Monika, he'd simply buried.

Well, almost buried. Behr lit another cigarette, knowing the time even before checking his watch. From his second-story window over the garage, he saw Henning ease the Rolls under the portico. Lincoln Stillman came out and got into the car; Henning brought the man's briefcase and overcoat, then two suitcases. The familiar profile was outlined briefly as the Rolls drove away.

Across the courtyard, curtains parted in an upstairs window, revealing for a moment an entirely different silhouette. Such a waste, he thought, her belonging to Stillman—blond Monika, sculpted ice. Behr sat down, smoked the rest of the cigarette, barely conscious of it. Then he stepped over the black leather softcase packed earlier, opened his door, and closed it softly behind him.

EIGHT

Lisa answered on the second ring. Reviewing P and L's, she told him. "How's it going with you?"

"Not good," Wil said. "There's evidence her father was involved in the Angela DeBray thing."

"I read about it," Lisa said. "What now?"

"She's convinced he was murdered. I said I'd give her a couple of days, see what turned up. Looks pretty much of a lock, though."

"How's she doing?"

"So-so. We had words."

"Poor Wil, twice in the same week. I'm sorry about the other day."

"No big deal."

There was a pause. "Yes it is. I've been thinking about everything. About Devin. What it was like after the Innocents. What it's like now."

"Lisa . . ."

"It's not just you. I don't like myself much."

He twisted the phone cord, tried to ignore the elevator-drop feeling. For a beat there was nothing, then:

"I'm thinking about separating. I want you to do the same."

He exhaled sharply, fought breathlessness, tried to unscramble his thoughts without success. "Christ, what's driving this? My coming here?"

It was as though he'd flipped a switch.

"How much are we together anymore, really together? I work to avoid, you work to avoid. But it's there, like the elephant in the corner, all this guilt and accusation—Devin, the miscarriage, you name it—whenever we talk, we end up fighting. So we don't talk, just work. Sublimate. What kind of life is that?"

He said nothing, stuck between denial and damage control. It was true yet untrue, a reach at the extreme. Nominally committed to rebuilding since the Innocents, they'd drifted, swept along by schedules, demands—things that had sucked in so many of their friends. Already he was feeling as if he should be feeling more.

"God, how can I explain this," she went on. "Maybe I'm finally getting that what we both need comes more from things other than us."

"Any chance you're exaggerating?" he finally said.

"Is Holly Pfeiffer paying you?"

He exhaled slowly.

"Does she even *have* money, Wil?"

"You encourage me to leave, to stay away, then question why I'm here?"

"My point exactly. Don't you see the irony? I feel guilty just bringing it up."

The feeling in his gut was slithering toward his throat: no way to break even, let alone win. "I love you," he said. It sounded hopelessly inane, like a child arguing with elders.

She took a breath and went on: "After you left, I realized this thing cuts two ways. My work feeds *us*, like yours does, but it also feeds *me*. It pays attention, it's there when I need it. I know that sounds stupid, but—"

"No, it doesn't sound stupid." His eyes were out the window on some kids playing. Images came: Devin on his tenth-birthday surfboard, *"Watch me, Dad,"* as he ripped toward the Picketline; kids on the beach shouting after the wave hung his son there like torn green and black overalls.

She was saying, "All I can think about is whether it's good for me to be married to you anymore."

"I can be home tonight, Leese."

"And do what? Fight? Make love?" Her voice held an edge now. "Wil, I've been seeing Dr. Marsh, and—"

"The marriage counselor with the ex-husbands."

"*Please*. It's her opinion I should use this time to think about living apart. You think, too. Let's figure this out, because I hate it the way it is."

"Lisa—"

The line clicked off. "Later," he said to the buzz.

For a while he just sat, separation thoughts filling the room, making it hard to think, chaotic jazz riffs from a tilted stage. There must be a way to get back what they'd had: everything, it seemed in retrospect—nothing some cold-eyed academic and her marital quota system would get. Give Lisa a day, then grab a flight, that was it. Meantime, handhold this—throwback. Not that there was much he could do. Paulette Pfeiffer would be proud, all right. *And thanks a lot, Max.*

He called room service, then dialed the sheriff's office in Tahoe City. In a few minutes he had the contact he needed, an appointment, and directions. By the time he changed clothes, his lunch had arrived, but he felt nothing like eating.

Ward Delbaugh leaned back in the chair; Wil rested a desert boot on his knee and brushed at dust left over from the hike up Eagle Rock.

"Private eye," Delbaugh said. "Don't get many up here. The occasional convention."

Wil nodded at the tall man: outdoor face, dark hair, rangy frame, working eyes under a laid-back appearance. "Sergeant, your deputy said you responded to the Pfeiffer suicide. I was hoping to ask you some questions."

"On behalf of?"

No reason not to say. "Max Pfeiffer's daughter. My client."

Delbaugh sat up. "Client?"

Wil nodded. "She's got this idea her father didn't jump. I told her I'd talk to you about it."

"Uh-huh. Pretty girl—sure gave those FBI guys a hard time." He grinned at the thought.

"She thinks they pushed him."

Delbaugh straightened a stack of papers. "So I gathered. Got some mouth on her, I'll say that. Sure wouldn't have figured the father for all that stuff—neighbors said it was like he wasn't there. Wasn't for the business I'm in, I'd be kind of shocked."

"No trouble with the law, then?"

"Not unless you count the daughter not attending school, which I don't."

"How about the scene?"

"We talked to some people on the trail who remembered the FBI fellas because of their suits. They also remembered hearing Pfeiffer hit the ground. If the Feds did help him over—which I hope you consider as unlikely as I do—they'd have needed wings to do it."

Wil thought a second. "Autopsy?"

"Broken neck, limb trauma, internal injuries—normal jumper stuff. No drugs. Definitely alive when he left the rock."

"She said the FBI agent mentioned he looked peaceful."

Delbaugh shook his head. "Yeah, well—I wouldn't go quite that far." He opened a cabinet drawer and pulled out a file, laid a photo on his desk. "Being polite, probably."

Wil leaned over for a better look: Max Pfeiffer's head was angled sharply to one side; considering the height from which he'd fallen, he was surprisingly unbattered, except for the left eye protruding. Wil noted no terror, no evidence of struggle in the expression.

"Satisfied?"

"Thank you, Sergeant." Wil stood, shook hands.

"You're aware of the arrangements, of course," Delbaugh said.

"Arrangements?"

"Disposition of the body, his mother taking it for burial. I thought you'd have heard by now." Delbaugh picked up the phone. "Excuse me," he said, then, "Doc—Del here. When's the Pfeiffer body due out? All right, thanks.

"Max Pfeiffer left at noon today. Gladding Brothers Mortuary in San Francisco. Doc said a Mrs. Maxwell Pfeiffer accompanied the van."

"His mother?"

Wil was sure the neighbors heard it.

"How *dare* she!" Holly Pfeiffer went on. "By what right? He hadn't seen her in years, her and her damn money."

"And she didn't consult with you, and she didn't consider your feelings. Calm down," Wil said. "Maybe she couldn't. Or maybe she just didn't think. People grieve differently."

"He couldn't *stand* his mother. *Damn her!*"

"She have a name?"

"Yes she has a name—Rose Lorraine Pfeiffer, Bitch Queen of the Bay."

Wil came over to where Holly was on the couch and sat down close. She looked startled; good, he thought. "Look, I know you're upset. But think about this: You're alone now and it wouldn't hurt to make a few friends, me included. You keep going like this, nobody's going to give you the time of day, let alone care how hard you've got it. Clean it up. You're too sharp and too pretty to let your mouth keep making a fool of you." He stood and walked to the sliding glass door, keeping his back to her. "Now—what exactly do you know about your grandmother?"

From behind him, a long sigh. "What I told you. She has money and lives in San Francisco."

"Where?"

"Near the Golden Gate, I think. The address is in my father's book."

"Get it, please," he said, still not looking at her.

"Regular Dirty Harry." She left the room, went downstairs, and was back in a minute. "Okay?"

Wil followed her finger to the listing: 844 Camino del Playa. There was no phone number.

"Thank you," he said. "Now what does she look like?"

"My father threw out her pictures. He hated her, I told you."

"You never saw *one?*"

Holly hesitated. "She has gray hair, a domineering face. My father said she bossed *his* father into an early grave. He was this famous attorney, water rights or something, Maxwell Bennett Pfeiffer. He expected my father to join his firm. But he died."

"This was before your father went on trial?"

"After."

"So Max was welcome there even after the trial?"

"Not when *she* was there," Holly snapped. "Besides, my father wanted nothing to do with either of them—exploiters, he called them. And now she has him. *God . . .*"

"Holly, he's not her property, he's her son. How about a little compassion."

She looked out the window, then back at him. "Did you mean what you said?"

"What?"

She picked at a fingernail. "You know . . . about being pretty."

Wil smiled slightly. "Sure, and not just me. Delbaugh, the sergeant you talked with? He thought so, too."

"He's old."

"So am I. Almost your dad's age."

"You don't look it, though."

"Don't look too close. Listen, I want you to call your grandmother."

"*Ha,*" she shot back.

"Or I will."

"Be my guest. She has no interest in me." Holly concentrated on the light leaving the deck.

"Give her a chance," Wil said. "Maybe she thinks you're the reason her son stayed away."

"Get real."

"Things get magnified in people's minds, sometimes beyond recognition." He picked up the phone, dialed San Francisco information; a moment later he had the number. An oriental-sounding voice said the missus was due back later. Wil left his name, said he'd call again, that it concerned her granddaughter. He noticed Holly watching him, though her eyes darted away as he hung up.

"How'd you like another crack at the lodge?" he said.

Fired by sunset, the clouds glowed and pulsed like hot coals. Music played on the deck, and under it the gentle lap of water on beach stones. Gas heaters hissed softly above the tables.

They watched the lake for a while. Finally she said, "My father loved it up here. He said it felt like the top of the world—all the bad stuff far away down below."

"And what do you think?" he asked. The waitress came with their drinks and the fried zucchini he'd ordered.

"What do you mean what do I think?"

Wil bit into a battered spear; it was hot and he set it aside to cool. "I mean all I've heard from you are your father's observations, never yours. I mean what do *you* think?"

She took a swallow of her drink. "I like it. Especially when the aspens turn and the tourists go home. I like early mornings, the way the water changes color. When a thunderstorm hits the lake—usually they come in from Reno, the big clouds do, then the wind picks up and makes the sailboat rigging sound like wind chimes. It's great to watch the rain sweep across the water, build a big fire. Hear the hush after it snows . . . What?"

He hadn't realized he was smiling. "I like hearing you talk," he said. "Go on."

She flushed. "I like it, is all."

The waitress came for their order; after she left, Wil said, "Kind of quiet without friends. What about other stuff—TV?"

"What about it?"

"Just wondering. I didn't see one."

"That's because it's broken," she said sharply, "and we never had it fixed. Besides, I have better things to do."

"Right. So you'll be staying up here, then?" Seeing her hesitate, then well up, he wished he could take it back.

She swiped at her eyes. "I don't know. I don't even know what we owe on the house. I'll have to get a job."

"I'm sure your grandmother would help."

"I won't ask."

"She's your father's mother. She'll figure it out."

"Let her—who cares? Not me."

"Look, everybody needs help one time or another. You don't have to decide right now."

Their food came. Lights gleamed around the shoreline now, and the night air smelled of fresh water and cooling earth.

"What does your wife do?" Holly asked.

"She has her own accounting business."

"My father had a name for accountants—moneychangers in the temple. I don't think he—"

"Give it a rest, huh?"

She looked at him. "Jeez Louise. Just kidding."

"Listen to yourself sometime. Not everybody fits your idea of how the world is. Or his."

She poked at her dinner, washed a bite down with coffee. Wind soughed lightly in the pines surrounding the lodge.

"I talked to her today," he said. "Things aren't so swell right now."

Green eyes came up over her mug.

"Fact is, she wants me to think about a separation." It came out in a rush, his own frankness surprising him.

"My big mouth," she said. "How many years?"

"Too many." He looked at the stars.

"Kids?"

"We had a son. He died."

She searched his face. "I'm sorry. What was he like, can you talk about it? I mean has it been . . ."

"Never long enough not to hurt," he said. "But it's okay. His name was Devin. He died surfing—with me." Wil touched the scar between his eyebrows, flashed on the surge heaving him into the jagged piling as he fought to free his son—barely feeling it until a girl's eyes widened in horror at the blood on his face. "Someplace we shouldn't have been."

He gulped coffee and told her about it, omitting the guilt he still felt, the depression afterward, the booze and pills that nearly spiraled out of control; about staring once into the black muzzle of his .45, one round and out. "Five years it's been. Odd to think he'd be sixteen now."

She was quiet for a bit; across the lake, moonrise touched the jagged black rim of the Sierra Nevada. "And you never had any more?"

"Lisa miscarried a while ago. We can't."

She nodded. "What's she like, your wife?"

"Dark hair. Easy on the eyes. Nice. You'd like her—everybody does." He fingered a pattern in some spilled sugar. "She can cut ahi thin enough to see through," he said, not knowing exactly why.

"Ahi?"

"Japanese for tuna. Lisa's Japanese."

Holly stared. "Then you *do* know what it's like to live in a racist society." She sounded impressed.

"Here it comes."

"They're forcing you apart, aren't they?"

"Her old man wouldn't mind. Nobody else seems to care."

"Says you. My father—" She saw his look. "*Damn*. What did you get from what's-his-name, Delbaugh. The official line, I suppose."

Wil expelled a breath slowly. "He didn't put much stock in your theory, no." He told her what Delbaugh said as she stirred more half-and-half into already tan coffee, stared at the mug. She was still staring when he'd finished, the spoon making repetitive little tinks.

"I understand how you feel, Holly, but did your father have any reason you know of to do what he did?"

"No."

"He wasn't ill or depressed? Worried about money?"

"No." Sharper this time.

"Recent letters or calls, anything other than the newspaper article that might have upset him?"

She banged the mug down, splashing coffee on the table. *"No!"*

Wil waved for the check; neither one said anything while it came and he signed for it. Their silence lasted all the way home, until he pulled into the drive and levered out of gear.

"People make mistakes, Holly. Let it in."

"What are you talking about?"

"Nobody's perfect, not even him. Wouldn't kill you to cut the man some slack. Might even help."

"Help how?"

"Right now it's tough to separate grief from denial. But you need to. Grieving heals, denial only prolongs the misery."

She looked away. "The voice of wisdom and truth."

"Whatever." Wil tightened his grip on the wheel.

"And I should just behave and be nice, right?"

"That's not what I meant."

"To you he's guilty, isn't he? Done deal. *So who needs you?*"

Holly slammed the car door and ran up the steps. For a moment he just sat there, peaking and coming down as lights went on in the house. Then he eased out the lane and drove slowly back to the highway. Waiting to turn onto 89, he punched up the car's cheap radio, scanning through dead air and weak signals to a station with a weeper country song playing. He jacked up the volume; empty road led him too fast into the curves. The music—something about sweet love going sour—did nothing for his state of mind, but he left it on anyway.

NINE

Wil was on the road by seven, peeling a bran muffin as he drove. He followed the river to Interstate 80, then over the hill past the lake where the Donner Party endured their frozen hell, his ears popping with the altitude. Through granite outcrop, then pine forest and iron-red earth, trees with leaves, and finally, Sacramento Valley flat. At nine he was brushing crumbs from his tie, telling a thin woman behind thick glass he was there to see Special Agent Vega concerning the suicide of Max Pfeiffer. He was midway through a month-old *Newsweek* when a man opened the door to the outer office.

"Al Vega. You wanted to see me?" He accepted Wil's card. "La Conchita—where's that?"

"South of Santa Barbara. Don't blink, though."

"Ah," Vega said. "Nice area, the coast. I'm from San Diego. Come in, Mr. . . . Hardesty."

Wil entered a small office. PC terminal, metal files; on a desk two teenage kids and a smiling woman posed in front of an oak tree.

Vega said, "There's coffee, if you'd like some."

"Please." In a minute he was sipping from a foam cup, taking in Vega's short-sleeved blue shirt, red-patterned tie, stocky frame, dark mustache. Hispanic eyes trying to decide about him.

"You have something to add to the Pfeiffer case?"

"Questions, if you don't mind," Wil said. "I'm helping Holly Pfeiffer get straight on some things."

Vega's expression was part grimace, part grin. "Not sure what I can add, except that it isn't what she thinks. Which she's doubtless told you."

Wil hoped his smile looked more knowing than it felt. "She's good that way, all right. I was hoping you could give me your perspective, something I could take back to reason with her."

Vega nodded. "First off, climbing that thing wasn't my idea of fun. We acted to apprehend after our lab matched Pfeiffer's prints on the case they found in the plane."

"Some break, that. Okay if I hear about it?"

"No harm now, I guess." Vega reached for the phone and spoke into it; moments later the thin woman dropped a file on his desk, then departed. Vega took out a stack of eight-by-ten photo enlargements, pointed at the first. "The plane," he said, and as Wil nodded, turned to the next one. "Cockpit, the pilot's remains—you can see where he crunched the panel. That's the case there, amazing it hadn't been breached. Being under the seat helped." More shots: the case shown closed, then open.

Wil took in the stacks of hundreds, eight rows by five. Vega flipped to another photo. "The note," he said, handing Wil the glossy.

Wil took it. The writing was hurried, scrawly: *Change of plans. Don't try to find me. Max.*

Vega said, "Even without it, we'd have made him from the prints. Look here." He passed Wil two blowups, one faint but visible, one carefully laid down on a fingerprint card. "This one was taken during Pfeiffer's Berkeley Eleven bust. You can see how it matches the one we lifted inside the case."

Wil looked closely; the two left little doubt. He said, "Could I get copies of at least the note and the prints? My client won't like it, but it might do something for her peace of mind."

Vega nodded. "Lemme ask," he said. In another minute he

was off the phone. "Okay—under the circumstances. Far as we're concerned, this thing's a wrap. I feel sorry for her, but there you are."

"Thanks." Wil looked at the photographs again. "And the pilot?"

"Clayton Lee Jones, small-time marijuana grower, made him from dental records. Had a P.O. box in Santa Cruz. His wife reported him missing—took her time about it, but apparently his being gone wasn't too unusual. He flew out from near there. Cash-crop country."

"Any idea where he was headed?"

"Not Lake Isabella, it's safe to say—gas gauge showed damn near empty. Weather records from that night noted big westerlies and thunderstorms. We figure he drifted, then lost his bearings—easy to do with the garbage he was flying by."

"Which would have put him on line for L.A.?"

"Most likely," Vega said. "That's where the ARV was, and he'd have needed someplace to refuel. We had alerts at all the airfields, even the small strips, so I figure he was aiming for the desert. There's places everywhere to land, and they could have met him with gas."

"You believe they were expecting him."

"Wouldn't you be expecting two million bucks?"

"Then what was the change of plans referred to in the note?"

"Jones's wife said he'd set it up to fly some dude. Since none of the locks busted in the crash and no other bones were found—presto, change of plans."

"His wife describe the guy?"

"She said Jones never told her what he looked like."

Wil drew out his notebook. "Her name is Lacey, right?"

"It *was*—Lacey Louise Jones. Year or so later she was killed in L.A., a bus accident." Vega put on glasses and thumbed the file. "She had family in Santa Cruz, a sister, Paula Anspeth. Nothing to add."

"Any address on her?"

He checked again. "Eight-seven-five-seven North Sorrel.

Number four. It's seventeen years old, though.''

Wil wrote it down. "Mind one more thing?"

"Shoot."

"You guys got there pretty fast."

"You could say that."

He smiled. "Could say more, too."

"Sure we knew about him, it was our business to know," Vega said. "Berkeley was an armed camp then, and we looked in on a number of radical types. You have to admit Max Pfeiffer qualified."

Wil said nothing.

"What we had going ceased after DeBray because we needed the manpower. When the ARV burned up, we naturally figured the money got torched—case closed. Then we found he'd split."

"But you did find him."

"We were curious," he said. "Sometimes when they bolt it means something. Took us a while, but we traced him— him and his daughter, assumed name, the whole Garbo bit. Our South Shore people watched him. Got to be almost a game."

"How so?"

"We knew about him, he knew about us—even flipped us off one time, seventy-eight I think. I went through about a ton of stuff on him recently, with the money and everything. Figured there'd be a trial, but he saved us the trouble."

"So he did," Wil said. "What happened at SFO?"

"You referring to the money?"

Wil leaned forward on the hard chair. "Just wondering how it got from the airport to Jones's plane in Santa Cruz."

"Zero on that," Vega said. "The terrorist we nailed had time to pass it on to somebody, but she never admitted knowing who. We just figured it was Z."

Checking his notes again. "That was Deborah Ann—"

"Werneke. Her pseudonym was on a passenger list headed for L.A." He removed a speck of something from the tip of

his tongue. "With her we got lucky—a minute later, she'd
have been gone. We about done here?"

Wil wastebasketed his empty cup. "Really appreciate it,"
he said, standing. "Can't say my client will, though. Maybe
in time."

"How's she doing?"

"Not great," he said. "All her life she idolized Max Pfeiffer, believed in him. You can imagine how she feels now."

Vega looked at the family picture on his desk. "Too bad
Pfeiffer didn't think of that," he said.

Wil thumbed Vega's envelope with the photocopies in it, trying to pick the best way to tell her. Direct, he figured at length;
she'd smell an end run otherwise and hate him for it. Probably
hate him anyway. He thought of Lisa. Great month he had
going so far.

Donner Lake came and went, then the long grade to the
turnoff. Too weak from drought to support the rafts that always seemed suspended on it, the Truckee River seemed lifeless, a slim shadow between banks. After a while Lake Tahoe
appeared, blue-blue through the trees, then he was turning the
rental car into Holly Pfeiffer's drive, parking alongside the
house.

He knocked, heard light footsteps, and gave her a shot of
him through the glass eye in the door. She opened it, wiping
her hands.

"Where were you?" she asked, returning to her dishes.

He leaned against the couch. "Fact finding," he said.
"Your favorite organization."

A snort. "Facts and the FBI are mutually exclusive," she
said. "What kind of crap did they feed you?"

Wil said nothing, just looked at her. Outside, a chain saw
razzed and reverb'd.

"Well?" she demanded.

"Maybe you should sit down."

She rinsed a plate and started on another. "Don't tell me:
Max Pfeiffer, kidnapper and child killer. And you bought it. I

can tell by your face." She put the plate in the drainer, then came up with a handful of soapy flatware. *"Didn't you!"* She stood as though frozen, the water running, chain saw buzzing. Slowly she dropped the utensils in the sink and walked over to face him.

"I lived my whole life with him, damnit. Don't you think—"

Tilt. Game over. "So long, Holly. End of the line."

"What?"

"You heard me. I told you I'd do what I could. Well, consider it done." He touched the envelope inside his sportcoat, then changed his mind. *Enough is enough; cut your losses.*

"Find the truth if I remember."

"You wouldn't accept the truth if Moses brought it down the mount and handed it over. Some chance I have."

"So that's it?" Something like shock was beginning to dawn and settle in her tone. She put a wet hand to her throat.

"You got it. *Sayonara.*" He moved toward the door.

"What about me?"

"Good luck. And don't say it hasn't been fun. I already know that."

Color rose in her face and her eyes showed liquid fire. "Hey, nobody's begging you to stick around."

For a moment he hesitated, wondering at all of it: the train-wreck suddenness. Whether between them they could scrape together even one mature adult.

"Go."

Fuck all, who needs it! He turned away, had his hand on the knob when the chain saw cut in again. Wil concentrated on it; something disquieting about the noise. He knew the sound a chain saw made when cutting: muted as it bit into wood, louder coming out. This one simply revved and revved, a drag racer waiting for green.

"You expecting cutters?" he asked.

"What do you care?" She cocked her head, listened. "Probably just county people clearing dead trees. Damn drought . . ."

Revving again, closer now—almost loud enough to cover

the sharp tinkle, the thump from downstairs. Everything went slow motion then: picking her up under his arm, the race for the screen door, crashing through it—out of time if his take on the sounds was correct. Her yelling, flailing; his stumbling with the load, cracking his shin against one of the chairs, knocking it over. Then off the lip of the deck and rolling, pine-needled, just ahead of the explosion.

He looked back at fire shooting up, hot on his face as he pulled her away wide-eyed. There was another sheet of flame, this time reaching the treetops.

They were ten yards and running when pine bark on the tree ahead dissolved into chips. Wil turned as he dove, caught a large form sighting down a gun barrel off to their left. He put a big cedar between them and the shooter, looked around in time to catch a secondary explosion: the rental car.

Another burst raised dirt; three rounds pocked against the cedar. "Where's this creek bed go?" he shouted at her. She froze; he grabbed her arm. *"Where?"*

"Neighbors below us. Then the lake."

"All right," Wil said, watching the man-form dart tree to tree now, attempting to cut them off. "When I say move, you go and keep going. Got that?" He saw her nod.

Wil picked up a broken branch, snapped it to pistol size, then whipped it around the tree, his arm extended.

The figure jerked behind cover.

"Over here," he yelled, hoping to freeze the figure an instant longer. *"Move."* And as she did, he dashed after her, hightailing it down the dry ravine. More rounds, angry air and rocks flying, Wil ripping through branches that lashed and stung. He caught up to her about the time they heard voices coming up the rise toward the column of black smoke.

"Hold it," he whispered, and she stopped with him. No sounds yet behind them, just the voices in front. Wil crouched, yanked her down. "Stay quiet. He'll smoke them too if he has to."

Footsteps joined the voices:

"... *hope nobody was in there ...*"

"... *that guy's house, the one in the papers.*"

"... *anybody call the fire people?*"

Gradually the voices faded. Wil looked to see how Holly was doing: some scratches reddening, dirt in her hair, shock. "You okay?"

It brought her back.

"My house—the fucking FBI. What did I tell you?"

"Any neighbors away that you know of?"

She blinked. "The Slaters come after Memorial Day, so what? My house ..."

He pulled her to her feet; a hundred yards of hard going and they passed a retaining wall that Wil vaulted, then helped her over.

"Here?"

She nodded.

"All right, pray," he said as they circled a stone two-story with a sloping roof, empty patio, shuttered windows. With his folding knife he carefully loosened a shutter. The interior showed dim light, shrouded furniture. Wrapping the shetland around his fist, he broke the window inward and then they were standing inside.

"Why are we here?" she asked accusingly. "Why aren't we going for help?"

Wil found a fireplace tool, hooked the shutter closed as tight as it would go, then braced it. "Because us out there favors him. Find the phone. See if it works, then come tell me. And whisper—we aren't out of this yet." He edged to each of the windows and peered out the slats; in a moment she was back.

"Phone's working."

"Probably too much trouble to turn it off," he said. "Keep praying." She was about to say something when he held a hand up, motioned her back from the window, and dropped to one knee.

He was edging around the side of the house, delicately for

such a big man: salt-and-pepper hair closely cropped, checked shirt, suspenders over twills, tan leather work boots. Against his leg was a submachine gun, suppressor mounted with a skeleton stock. Wide-spaced eyes scanned the house and yard. His hands were the largest Wil had ever seen.

Two windows down, the man rattling each shutter; one window and he was checking theirs. Wil tightened his grip on the fireplace tool, cursing himself for not having worn the .45. There was a rattle at their shutter, then quiet. Wil gave it fifteen minutes, checked his watch: 3:49. A second wave of sirens sounded.

White-faced and breathing rapidly, Holly emerged from behind the couch. "Can't we go now? *Please*?"

Wil shook his head. "Keep watch while I use the phone. You see him, point—no talk, okay?" He slipped over to a chair near the kitchen, pulled the phone down beside him, dialed Los Angeles County Sheriff's and asked for Homicide, Lieutenant Epstein.

Fingers tapping, then: "Mo, it's Hardesty . . . No, I can't speak up. Listen, I need a huge favor, help from your database . . . You tell *me* which one. Here's the deal: big man, around six-eight, fiftyish maybe, crewcut . . . Yeah, the Lakers, right. Guy carries a sub—silenced, curving magazine, triangular stock. Got a way with explosives, too. I *know* what I'm asking . . . Yeah. No, thanks, I'll hold."

"Is that long distance?" she whispered as he waited. "The Slaters will kill me."

"Could be worse," he whispered back.

Ten minutes they waited, twenty, twenty-five, Holly glancing over to roll her eyes occasionally, then out the window. He watched her, thinking she was holding up better than he'd have expected. Then Epstein's voice in his ear: "You still there? . . . Okay, Weapons says it sounds like one of the MP5s: Heckler and Koch, German-made, nine mil, not to get on the wrong side of. Usually winds up with law enforcement types. Nothing on the shooter, but I've got some places left I can check. Where can I call you?"

"Nowhere," Wil said. "I'll get back to you later."

"You need the cavalry?"

"Don't think so, thanks. If something happens, though, find the big guy."

"Tell you what," Epstein said. "You phone before midnight or I'm sending out the troops. Where are you?"

Wil gave him the lodge, then hung up and dialed it, requested they switch him to another room as far as possible from the old. A surprise, he told the clerk, nobody supposed to know, and had anyone been asking. Not that he knew of, the clerk said, Wil telling him he'd be in late. He hung up, then joined Holly.

"Anything?"

"Nothing," she said. "Are we okay yet?"

"I'd say his window on us is about closed. But we'll—"

"What about my house?"

"Don't worry, what's left isn't going anywhere. You know a way to the lodge without using the highway?"

She ran a hand through her hair. "If you don't mind a hike."

They left the stone house at nine, the now-chill air still acrid with smoke from the explosion and fire. Thin clouds hung around the moon, which threw a pale shimmer off the lake. Dogs barked occasionally as they passed, the sound picked up and thrown back by others before dying off. Avoiding lights, following cover, they made the lodge by eleven o'clock. Holly skirted the lobby as Wil traded keys and asked for messages. There were none. Inside the new room, he went to the gun case, unpacked the shoulder rig and put it on, worked the Colt's action, loaded a clip plus an extra round for the chamber. He ordered up food and they ate hungrily, saying little.

Finished, he checked in with Epstein, then called Delbaugh: not in, the dispatcher telling him they'd have to page Sergeant Delbaugh. In a few minutes he came on, listened as Wil went through it.

"Seeing her house, we wondered," Delbaugh said. "You people all right?"

"Hanging in," Wil answered. "Any way we can handle the paperwork in the morning?"

There was a pause. "Yeah, but make it early. I'll APB the big dude, then notify the watch commander about tomorrow."

Hanging up, Wil turned to her. "I'm good for the couch, it's closer to the door."

Her eyes were on the gun. "I suppose that's necessary."

"You tell me."

"My father refused to have one in the house."

"Maybe he wasn't so afraid after all."

"What I meant was, they make me nervous."

Wil drank the last of his coffee, put the mug among the other dishes. "They should, they hurt people—or protect them. You, for instance."

"Is that the gun you shot that man with?"

The Innocents again: bullets in the tunnel, his return fire, a figure spread-eagled on the rocks. He nodded.

"And you can live with that?"

"Because of it, Holly. Not very noble, but it's why I'm still around."

She sighed. "Men and their him-or-me bullshit. No wonder things are so screwed up."

"Right," he said tiredly. Lisa hadn't expressed it in quite the same way, but the sentiment wasn't dissimilar. "At least I haven't been shot at by any women lately."

She watched him jam a chair under the knob. "Are we really safe here?"

"I think so. Delbaugh said he'd run a cruiser by later."

"Fucking FBI. You believe me now?"

"I believe somebody's trying to kill one of us," he said. "Any idea who?"

"*God*, you are naive," she said. "Doesn't it seem obvious, this happening right after you talk to that jerk agent?"

"Special agent."

She looked down at her sweatshirt. "Thank God I was

wearing this. What am I going to do? We can't let them get away with it."

"Lighten up. You're lucky to be alive."

"Forget you. They didn't burn *you* out. They didn't kill *your* father. These bastards think they can get away with anything."

Screw it. Wil stood, found Vega's envelope still in the shetland's inner pocket. Maybe it wasn't the right time, but he'd had a bellyful. He handed it to her.

"What's this?" She held the envelope as though fearful of what it might contain.

"See for yourself. I've had it for one day."

"Hardesty—?"

"Good night." He lay down on the couch, feet over the arm, conscious of aches and pains he hadn't noticed before. He closed his eyes.

"This mean you're still—?"

"We'll see."

Through half-sleep much later on, he thought he heard paper rustling and tight little crying sounds. But it could have been a dream.

TEN

Lincoln Stillman pulled on one bassett ear while he listened with the other, sounds from the hotel casino still whirring in his head. Fourteen K he'd let ride tonight before pulling back—just long enough to let the odds swing to the skinny Haitian with the gold chains who'd actually doubled down on treys. Bile rose in his throat, momentarily overwhelming the bourbon. *Gutless schmuck*—when was he going to learn.

He took a last pull from the whiskey glass and crunched ice. There was a click on the line, then the night manager: "Mr. Stillman? I have a call from your wife."

"Shit-oh-dear. What'd she say?"

"That you always visit Atlantic City when you're in Washington. That it was important."

"Life's a bitch and then you die, right, Claude? Put her through."

There was another click. "Lincoln?"

Stillman leaned across the bed until he could see into the bathroom where the call girl was showering, steam billowing through the crack in the door. He propped himself up against the headboard. "Monika," he said warmly. "You caught me working."

"Caught you at least is correct," she said.

That voice, he thought: Monika could make it colder and deader than any he'd ever heard. "Hey, what's a two-and-a-half-million-dollar windfall without celebrating?"

"I won't even ask how much you've lost this time. And take care what you say. Your tarts have ears."

"And *you* have a suspicious mind."

"Behr just told me about Tahoe. But then you know all about that, don't you?"

He said nothing as she went on; the line crackled as though swaying in an ice storm. "And don't blame him," she was saying now. "What in the world were you thinking of?"

Stillman reflexed the glass to his lips, realized it was empty, and hurled it toward a corner where it thumped against the baseboard. Nobody talked to him like that, nobody—except perhaps our lady of the roadkill tone and the body from God. Moments alone with that body, little eternities, flashed behind his vision like stripteasers enticing a randy adolescent. He put a lid on rising steam.

"Nothing I was trying to keep from you, sugar," he said, feeling stupid saying it. "Damn thing broke so fast, there wasn't time. I thought you'd be pleased I handled it."

There was a long pause. "And how *did* you handle it? Subtly and with a plan, or like panzers at a picnic? These are not the old days, Lincoln."

The old days, the world at their feet. Despite the windfall, today was all high risk and low return, an endless scramble for bodies. And caution: Stick your head out, jerk it back in.

"Why?" she asked into his silence.

Stillman began squeezing the rubber ball he kept handy for phone conversations, a holdover from his wrestling days. "My instructions were to strike when the time was right. Fast and clean." Three courtesy-bar bourbons speaking. If she wanted a fight, then Lincoln Stillman was ready.

"It failed, you know."

"Bullshit. What did he tell you?"

"There was a man, the girl escaped with him. Just when we had her back, Lincoln. Do you know how upset that makes me?"

Lincoln Stillman watched his knuckles turn white. "Where's Behr now?"

"Still at the lake. A difficult area to begin with, Lincoln, and you sent him up alone."

"And what would you have done, my strategist?" *Damn* Behr for screwing up. Monika's wrath would at least have been endurable if—

"You know full well, and thanks to you we've lost the element of surprise. We may yet have to kill her. That would be very sad."

Stillman groped for options; contrition seemed the best recourse. He swallowed hard. "Monika, I had only our best interests at heart. Don't fault decisive action."

"Decisions without intelligence can get an army killed," she said. "And the decision maker shot. Remember that."

Contempt? Ask those he'd chewed up in court over the years: Contempt was underestimation, fatal in his business. *Watch yourself, pet.*

"How could I forget with someone as beautiful as you pointing it out," he said finally.

"So you know, I've told Behr to find them and pick an appropriate time. We shall have to hope it's not too late."

He heard the shower water turn off. "Monika," he said to tweak her. "Haven't you always said that hope is the armor of fools?"

"Keep in mind who you are, Lincoln," she said, forcing him to strain to hear. "And who I am."

The line buzzed. For a moment he just sat, breathing and pulse winding down. "Hurry up in there," he shouted finally at the bathroom. He punched in a number on the phone. "Hello, room service? Stillman here in ten-eighteen. I want a bottle of Wild Turkey and a thing of ice in my room faster than I can finish pissing. You got that?"

Behr watched Monika hang up. Her talking to the old man that way excited him, made him want her again like the old days.

My God, she'd been like no one else.

He remembered when he'd first seen her: Berlin 1970, he

thirty-three, she not yet twenty-one and already widowed, her scarf worn peasant-style over the head like his mother on her way to church—his breath literally catching in his throat at hair the white-hot color of steel in the molds, at eyes the blue depth of lake water.

"I'm nobody," she answered, smiling, when he'd been able to ask. "And everybody," the beer and the smoke and the rest of them in the *kneipe* fading away to nothing.

He'd been there to watch a machine shop steward, Dolph Neiggemann, pass union secrets to management in return for morphine money, a score he'd settled later. But that night it was only Monika and that *way* she had. Even then, people looked to her. And *at* her.

Always *at* her.

It had been easy the first time. He'd simply asked, Monika sizing him up like a calculator totaling a column of numbers. They'd not even made it to the bed in her small flat; instead they knocked around the room, spilling sugar and coffee, books and her sketches, and afterward they lay back on Friedrich Engels and Karl Marx.

"Why me?" he asked her.

"You look like someone I can use," she said. That was it: Life was something you used every bit of, horns and hoofs included.

Through that winter and the next, he'd protected her. Challenges to her leadership he brushed aside, adversaries he crushed, rivals he convinced to support her. Her politics were nothing to him; she, however, was everything. She needed money, he got it for her; difficulties, such as when the bar owner tried to throw her out of the basement meeting room, he made go away. People, sometimes, he made go away.

But not Lincoln Stillman.

He looked down at himself, then at her, and in a manner that belied his size, drew her from the phone over to him. Entering her realm, he felt the day's failure drop like a discarded garment.

When he'd finished, she said, "You have work and I need

to get back. Now that we understand each other.''

He lit a cigarette. ''All too well, I'm afraid.''

''You get what you want.''

''Bits and pieces.'' He took a deep drag, blew smoke at the ceiling.

''I'm a married woman.''

''No jokes, please.''

She paused from brushing her hair. ''Poor Behr, after all this time.'' She took the cigarette, inhaled, and let the smoke out her nose. ''I'll say it once more. Try to let it in . . .''

He accepted the cigarette back, drew on it, thinking she had never looked so desirable. Even in those days; even before she said what he knew was coming next.

''It belongs to him.''

Behr crushed out the stub. Watching her dress slowly, stockings first and then undergarments, he was moved to empathy with the male spider, driven to risk everything—even being reduced to a lifeless shell—in the lair of the black widow.

Him

  Wolf Gerhard Hilke.

Monika Stillman looked out at the lights dropping away below the charter plane, stirred-up thoughts buzzing around her like bees defending a hive. She lit a cigarette, blew smoke as if to pacify them.

Beyond the glass, lumpy moonlit clouds reminded her of sheep.

She'd been Unseker then, Lilith Monika Unseker, herding the *Heidschnucken*, with their shaggy wool and curving horns, across the moors west of Lüneburg Heath, northwest Germany's contribution to national melancholy. Not to mention her father and mother—peasant stock worn as featureless as the land. Two sons dead in the war—and another, Willem, crippled by a tractor mishap—had taken their toll. If ever there *had* been love to give a daughter, it was long gone by then.

She pictured her mother, potato-shaped and sagging under all of it; her father, a stocky man smelling of lanolin, who thinly hid the bitterness of having only a daughter to help with the flocks. Willem carping from his wheelchair, scaring her with ghost stories as she left to face the wind-twisted junipers: *"Beware the dead whose hands reach up from the bog."*

Prickles came back, recalling his words—and the ancient, peat-preserved corpses found out there that had made her believe him. Hating it, she'd gone anyway, her schooling secondary to the needs of the *Heidschnucken*. One day her teacher sent her home with a sketch pad, pencils, and an encouraging note. Something at least—an outlet.

Sheep made good subjects, and trees, and the heather that turned purple, bringing with it the honey her mother sold. Then people. At her teacher's urging, she entered contests. But drawing was always a battle at home, Willem sometimes tearing up the sketches as fast as she drew them.

Until she drew an imaginary line and stepped over it.

Volunteering one day to take Willem out for air, she wheeled him through the long German twilight to a low bog she'd found while tending sheep. If she felt anything watching him go under, it was curiosity at how his invective turned to pleading, and at what point. From it she learned about men, what really lay beneath their bluster. Beyond that, she felt nothing in particular. She'd simply buried herself in art, her way out. An early admittance to the Staatliche Hochschule der Kuenste in Berlin, based on the work her teacher submitted for her.

The plane hit a rough spot, emerged from it; Monika relieved the pressure in her ears, crushed out her cigarette, and lit another as the drone of the engine turned her inward again.

In Bremen now, earning her Berlin bus fare: the sailor encountered on a trip to the museum to steel her resolve; the money counted in advance. As with watching Willem vanish, she felt nothing in particular.

Nothing exchanged for something.

Revelation.

She was seventeen. It was 1967.

Her first memories of Berlin: statues, bright lights and

chaos, stab-in-the-heart loneliness. Zoo Station and the Ku'damm, stopping there for coffee; sitting in the cafe until the owner told her she should work there if she liked the place so much. Three months later, after the botched abortion that would forever leave her free of such concerns, she met Wolf Hilke.

He'd come for dinner with friends, returning later to take her away: the worldly Free University student and the peasant girl barely free of sheep smell. He had brown hair and soft eyes and a flat in East Kreuzberg where he squatted with other students there to avoid national service and attend the university. Pooling their wages, they rented a one-room walk-up off the Dresdenerstrasse with a coal stove and a Turkish family next door.

Her life became *him*: museums, neighborhood street festivals, walks in the Tiergarten, shouting to be heard in the artists' taverns where she occasionally took her work to be critiqued. Standing in front of the Nazi execution hooks at Plötzensee. Rolling together in the autumn leaves.

He introduced her to fruit juice in her beer; *leberknödelsuppe*, the clear soup with liver dumplings; potato waffles. At their civil wedding service he said, "I christen thee Monika. Long live Monika, born in the year nineteen sixty-eight." She felt like a flower suddenly watered after years of neglect.

She felt.

And the politics—Wolf a leader in the protest for university reform, the Labor and anti-Vietnam movements. Introducing her to Hegel, to Engels and Marx, to Rosa Luxemburg and Karl Liebknecht. Bringing her to clandestine meetings in smoky basements to hear Horst Mahler and Andreas Baader. Encouraging revolutionary themes in her art, leading her into violent confrontations with the *Polizei* when afterward they'd dry off from the water cannons and make love in front of the stove.

And then life ended.

She'd been at the Dahlem to view the Flemish masters, home late to a street blockaded by fire trucks. What was left of the apartment still smoldered; Wolf Hilke she encountered on the stairs. From under the rubber sheet, a blackened hand stuck out, the left one with the cheap ring.

"*Ofenheizung,*" the policemen explained, shaking their heads. "Coal-fueled ovens will do that."

She'd known better. And bided her time.

"Ten minutes to L.A.," the pilot said.

Monika snapped out of her reverie, glad she'd responded to Behr's call by flying up there, getting it firsthand. *It*: as though the carnage at the bank wasn't bad enough. Lincoln: gone from drunken parody to clear and present danger. Behr: disappointing he hadn't come forward before embarking on this treachery—something to keep in mind. Cold water on her elation at hearing *she* was alive.

Men, she thought, and for a moment saw Wolf's eyes, brown hair swept back from a high forehead. Then wheels punched the tarmac, bounced, and settled.

ELEVEN

Wil snorted, coming awake from something nameless gaining on him. Early light filtered through the closed curtains; Holly Pfeiffer lay on her stomach, breathing deeply.

Some piece of work, Wil thought, rubbing his temples: more at home in an era she knew only through her father, a puzzle himself. He pictured her under fire and was impressed again.

Then his feet touched something cool—one of Vega's FBI photocopies. The others lay scattered. Thinking so much for *that*, he picked them up quietly, folded and stuffed them back in the shetland, headed for the bathroom.

Coming back, he heard, *"Shhh . . . what's that noise?"*

Wil cocked the .45 and pressed against the door frame, listening, motioning her off the bed. "Guests," he finally said. "Early risers."

"What now?"

"Get dressed, I'll order coffee. You want a roll or something?"

She nodded. "And then?"

"Check in with your neighbors. They're bound to be wondering after the fire."

"Who are you kidding."

"All right, explosion," he said. "Then I'll try to convince the rental people that bombs happen and it really is a good idea to loan me another car."

She sat on the bed as Wil called room service, her knees raised, the sweatshirt pulled down over them. "What about my house?" she said after he hung up.

"Notify your insurance company. Refer them to Delbaugh."

"Mr. Calm," she said. "Don't you ever feel anything?"

"Helps to put yourself beyond it, like an observer. You make better decisions. When that fails, drink decaf." He thought he saw a smile, but she turned away.

"I'll shower first, assuming you shower," she said. "Don't shoot the guy with my breakfast."

By eight-thirty they were dressed, Wil working on a second coffee, Holly running her hands through wet hair over the heater. Every few minutes, a sound would bring his hand up to the .45.

"What kind is it?" she asked. "The gun, I mean."

"You really want to know?"

She nodded.

He withdrew it, checked the safety, and handed it to her. "By the grip, that's right. It's a Colt Government Model .45 with modifications. Stop a moose, you have moose problems."

"What modifications?"

"Things to make it shoot more accurately. I actually hit things, much to the amazement of some of my friends in law enforcement."

She regarded it. "Have you killed other men with it?"

"Not since you woke up."

"Tell me," she persisted.

"All right. I've knocked some down, guys with knives, one with a crowbar. You'd like to think you kill only if you have to."

"I could never kill anybody," she said, handing him back the gun.

He reholstered it. "Sometimes it's dealt."

"No, that's wrong."

"Be nice if more people felt the same as you do. Like the guy yesterday."

"Could you identify him if you saw him again?"

"Height yes, face maybe." He picked up his Dopp kit, shoved it in his suitcase. "Which reminds me, we're due at Delbaugh's. Make your calls, then I'll see about a car."

Holly picked up the phone, paused. "Hardesty?"

Wil waited, half expecting some comment on the photocopies, but it never came. She just turned away and started dialing.

Not counting the cab ride, it took three hours: two with Delbaugh, another explaining it to the rental car company. As they left, the car's blackened hulk was being towed into the yard. Wil quickly started the Buick they'd given him and drove to a gas-station pay phone. Holly went across the street to buy basics with a couple of his twenties.

Wil reached Mo Epstein returning from lunch. "You call the lodge? I've been out trying to convince some people how reliable I usually am."

"Tough sledding, I'm sure. And yes, I did."

"Get something?"

"No. The databases struck out."

Wil ran a hand through his hair and rushed a breath.

"Hey, no obstacle for a hotshot like yourself."

"Damn. Just dead-on nothing?"

"Not that holds water. Might be a long shot or two I could run down, but—"

"Any idea how long?"

"Yeah, after I get back from Phoenix—couple, three days. If it's okay with you, of course."

Wil said nothing.

"My advice is don't get your hopes up," Mo said.

"No chance of that with things going so well."

Epstein misread it as attitude. "Hey, I need that like stale bagels. You realize what you're getting here? Kee-ryst."

"You know I do."

"I fucking doubt that." Epstein clicked off and the dial tone came on.

Terrific, he thought. No, just Mo, fed up and ready to cash it out, a recurring theme in their conversations. For as long as he'd known him—Nam included—Mo and authority were the proverbial oil and water. Which was why Mo bent rules sometimes, unauthorized access to database info now grounds for discipline. It fed his sense of justice, Mo was fond of saying—who cared, so long as it took down the bad guys?

Wil took a deep breath, gave some thought to their options. Holly could bunk in with a neighbor, a motel depending on what her insurance covered. But that took no account of the big man, and he had to assume she was still a target. Wil pictured him again, wondering who the hell he was—mob hitter, maybe, or ex-military misfit. But those guys generally had rap histories, scroll-screens a minute long. If Mo was right, this one was invisible.

A six-foot-eight invisible hitter.

He dialed Rose Pfeiffer's number in San Francisco, got put on hold after leaving his name. Baroque music played in the background, then the male oriental voice returned.

"Mrs. Pfeiffer says please you leave a message."

"It's about her granddaughter," Wil said. "Tell her I'll wait."

"Mrs. Pfeiffer is very busy. If matter concerns granddaughter, you should call her lawyer, she says. Mr. Rafael Canizares."

Wil interrupted. "Tell Mrs. Pfeiffer her granddaughter's home has been destroyed, that she needs help."

"You call Mr. Canizares." The voice gave him the number, then broke the connection.

Holly crossed back, put a package in the car.

"If you're through," she said, "I'll call our life insurance man."

"Hope your luck's better than mine." He left her looking up the number, went over to lean against the Buick. From the call at least, the girl had Rose Pfeiffer figured right—no love lost between them. He wondered when that happened and why. She was off the phone then, beside him and bracing herself against the car's roof.

"Uh-oh," Wil said.

A gust blew in off the lake, scattered papers around the phone booth; Holly drew her hands inside her sleeves. "The policy was cashed out, Bart said. How could he have done that?"

"Nobody owns a crystal ball. I'm sure your father had a reason."

"A reason? What am I supposed to do now?" She chewed her lip.

"I don't know. Why don't you hit the cafe there, get us some sandwiches. I'll be over soon and we'll figure it out. Okay?"

As she trudged off, Wil dialed again. The receptionist at Canizares and Laughton asked him to wait while she paged. Minutes passed.

"Rafael Canizares."

"My name's Hardesty, Mr. Canizares, private investigator working for Holly Pfeiffer. My call to her grandmother was referred to you. I hoped you could tell me why."

"How is Holly?"

"Bit stressed right now."

"I can imagine, with her father and all . . ."

"And all?"

There was a pause. "What was your name again?"

"Hardesty. You want my license number?"

"Mr. Hardesty, I represent the estate because of Max Pfeiffer. I both knew and liked him. I know how she must be hurting."

Wil explained his working for her.

"We heard Max jumped," Canizares said. "Is there something to contraindicate?"

"She suspects the FBI."

The chuckle in his voice was apparent. "Like father, like daughter."

"Had you heard from him since he moved to the lake?"

"Mr. Hardesty, not even his mother knew where he was."

Wil straightened, scanned the street activity as he talked: cars moving, tourists eyeing the shops, parents holding on to kids. "That might explain some things," he said. "Holly needs help, Mr. Canizares, but she's too proud to ask her grandmother. Yesterday her home burned; today she found out Max had no insurance. Right now it's pretty uncertain."

Silence, then, "I don't know what she's told you, but money's not a problem. I'll deposit some for her at the Tahoe City Wells Fargo."

"Then you did know where they were."

The voice cooled. "That is *not* what I said. Just have Holly open an account. I'll call my branch down here and have them transfer five thousand dollars. That her grandmother won't see her is not my province."

"Thanks for your time," Wil said.

Not even his mother knew where he was.

All she needs is her money.

Wil reached the lodge next, asked if the room was open for another night, heard it was booked but another was available. Then, "Mr. Hardesty, am I correct that you wished your visit held in confidence?"

"Good memory. Somebody ask for me?"

"Two people. A Lieutenant Epstein calling from Los Angeles and a tall heavyset guy who stopped in."

The tingle was more like a rush, blotting out the street noise. "What did you tell him?"

"That we had no one under that name."

"You're sure he knew it?"

"Yes, but I'm not sure he believed me. As he left, I saw him walking toward a white car."

"Notice what kind?"

"Sorry, I got busy."

Wil breathed deeply. "Okay—Michael, right? I won't need the room after all. If there's a way to do it, write yourself a twenty-dollar tip on the credit card receipt."

He hung up, did a hyper 360 of the street faces again but saw no big man. Blood racing, he entered the restaurant, spotted Holly sipping coffee, one for him cooling across from her. Reaching the table, he leaned over it.

"I've got it figured," he said. "Tell you in the car."

• • •

Hardesty. Behr pronounced the name he'd gotten off the car rental papers before torching the house; cross-referencing it then with the address at the library near his South Tahoe motel. An investigator—Behr's take on it neither worried nor unworried, merely something to sweep aside. Still, the man had tricked him, an amateur mistake on his part.

There would be no such mistake again.

Behr checked his watch, shifted on the car's uncomfortable bench seat. The lodge's alpinelike solidity and the lake beyond reminded him of places he and his father stayed after the war. His father had loved lake holidays. Even during the bombardments, Heinz Behr would tell his son about the lakes, swearing they'd return someday. Promise kept: Behr remembered the strings of lake trout and the soft postwar evenings. Sunset on the Alps, crystalline air.

Then the coal dust, Behr following his father into the mines at seventeen. He'd been large even then, a fact not lost on his union. By 1960, he was bashing strikebreakers, leading preemptive raids on management goons, too much force killing one in '64. The union scrambling, getting him to Berlin, fringe work where the pay was decent and the disavowal high if you were caught. He'd learned: explosives, weapons, techniques— sophisticated stuff he'd never have picked up in Essen. Especially the fat paychecks.

Through the unions, he acquired a reputation and was hired by others. He enjoyed it: ridding Berlin of its garbage. Then, in 1969, everything changed.

Behr looked again at his watch: 2:27. He opened the door and stepped out, strode toward the lodge. The same lobby clerk was on duty.

"Has Mr. Hardesty been in touch yet?"

The clerk looked up. "Sir, I believe I told you that we have no Mr. Hardesty."

Something about the way the man was shielding his writing: Behr's hand engulfed the clerk's, pulled it away from the credit card receipt. Under it lay one from which he was transferring information. Behr lifted the slip, saw the name imprinted there, handwritten on the other—a late charge of some kind.

"When?" he asked the clerk.

"Sir, I must ask you to leave or—"

Behr reached out, grabbed hair, and banged the clerk's head on the counter. *"When?"*

"Last night. It was supposed to be a surprise."

Behr winked. "He had a girl with him?"

"I really don't think—"

Behr's hand was a blur.

"They went to rent a car! Please . . . !"

In two strides, Behr was out the door, then gunning the white car out the drive, drumming the wheel, stuck in traffic backed up by the signal that split 89 off from Tahoe City—his savior, really. Just across the bridge, Behr saw them: two heads watching intently for the light to change. Maroon Buick.

He relaxed the drumming, turned on some music, stretched. As his car approached the left turn, he saw the Buick get the green and head north. Seconds later Behr turned left with the flow.

TWELVE

"I told you why," Wil said.

"And I'm telling *you,* I know places up here he'd never find me. Besides, you have a gun." Holly Pfeiffer bit a nail, rubbed the spot.

"Not like his, I don't. You have no idea why he might be after you?" They were past the summit now, Wil pressing the Buick over eighty on the downslope, cursing the time spent opening her checking account, simple as it was. He kept an eye on the mirror for road law and white cars. Only the most popular color—four he could see, at least keeping their distance.

"Isn't it obvious? He's one of their assassins." She bagged the remains of their sandwiches, tossed the sack over the seat.

"You look over that stuff I gave you?" Wil asked, knowing the answer.

Her focus left the car. "Those things are fake. All this time wanting to frame him and that's what they come up with. Despicable."

Wil swung around a tank truck, adjusted his sunglasses, took a deep breath. "Okay, let's assume you're right, the FBI wanting him dead. Why?"

Her voice rose. "Because he made them look like fools."

"Why you, then?"

"I don't know. Maybe because I tell the truth about them. Where are we going?"

"Your father ever mention a man named Rafael Caniza-res?"

She glanced at him. "No."

"Not even on the phone?"

"No," this time with emphasis. "Who is he?"

Wil spotted a black-and-white ahead and backed off the gas. For a few miles the CHP paced traffic, then cut off the free-way. Gradually the traffic resumed speed.

"Canizares is a lawyer, according to him a friend of your father's. We spoke earlier. A good place to start, I thought."

"Start what?"

"Our deal. Remember?"

Holly began rubbing her thumbnail against her middle fin-gernail. Then she began working it with her other thumbnail.

"You're welcome," Wil said. "But so we understand each other, an investigation finds the truth. Whether one party likes it or not."

"I'm aware of that, thank you very much."

He looked at her, then back at the road. "Canizares has an office in San Francisco. You can stay with your grandmother."

"Wonderful, but you just don't seem to get it. She doesn't want me."

"You don't know that."

"Then I don't want her." She crossed her arms over her chest.

"You want to know more about your father, don't you? What better place?"

"You're going to dump me, aren't you," she said with heat.

"No way. You work for me, remember?"

"Yeah right, all the checks I've cashed. Maybe I'll drop you with Vega."

"Goddamnit, I'm not some kid. I'm an adult."

"Then act like one. Better yet, think like one."

She threw back her head and exhaled loudly, then leveled off as though reaching a conclusion about something. "Look, this was a bad idea—let's forget the whole thing. You can let me out up there."

"Fine. Then what?"

"I'll manage, all right? Just do it."

"Sure. No problem."

"I'm telling you you're fired, Hardesty. That plain enough?"

"Sorry, already quit." He shrugged. "What's a girl to do?"

"Pull over."

"Ten-four—anytime now."

She swiveled one way, then the other, then behind. "Shit," she said. "Where's that highway patrol?"

"Never there when you need one, only when you don't. I've noticed that, too."

Holly looked away at the pines and oaks flashing past. When she did swing around to face him, her lips held a grim line but her eyes betrayed her.

"Is it painful?" he asked. "Looking like that."

The grin broke out fully, before she had a chance to recover.

"I saw that."

"Don't get any ideas."

"Only if I see a pattern develop. Like more than once in the same week."

She shook her head. "God, you're hopeless."

"Yeah." He extended a flat palm.

Looking exasperated, she abruptly fived the peace offering—humoring him, her expression said. A few miles later she said, "Seriously, even if my grandmother were inclined to take me, I'd be a thing to her, just like my father was. He used to tell me about it, the way she manipulated people. You can imagine what she thought of my mother, how she'll take to me wearing her sweatshirt."

Wil checked the rearview again; the white count was now down to three—two cars and a minivan. "You might be surprised. At least think about it."

"Don't expect much," she said.

He gave her an oblique smile. "Sorry, you've spoiled me."

They cruised awhile in silence: west through Sacramento, from freeway height a treed city punctuated by tall buildings downtown, then across the river, at this point wide and deep enough for ships. As the city retreated, they passed fields well into new growth. Here and there, late blossoms clung to fruit orchards; wild mustard still yellowed the rows between the trees. Off to the left, gulls and black-and-white magpies looking like tuxedoed waiters hustling up orders shadowed a tractor turning over dark earth.

"Pretty time of year," he said. "You ever see this before?"

"We kept to the lake, remember? To ourselves."

Wil let a moment pass. "Holly, did he ever explain why?"

"I told you, it was because of the FBI."

"Vega told me they knew where he was and that your father knew they knew. That seem strange to you?"

"Vega and the other guy killed him. Does that seem strange to *you?*"

"It does without more of a reason than your father made fools of them or blamed them for your mother. If they did kill him, why the wait?"

She faced away from him out her side window. "So they could pin this other thing on him," she said. "Look, whose side are you on?"

So much for logic, Wil thought. And yet her whole situation defied logic—father seemingly murdered, someone trying to kill her, everyone suddenly her enemy. The quiet, predictable life up in smoke.

Whose side are you on? Right . . .

"Yours," he said, thinking Lisa had a point. "Even though you might not know it yet. You want a soda or something?"

Behr figured he had three options: swing off the freeway and risk being spotted near the restaurant, pull over and wait for them to reenter, or chance going past and be waiting at the next on-ramp. He chose a gas station several miles up; after a pit stop, he found a pay phone with a view of the road. Henning answered, then Monika.

"They're heading west on Eighty," he said.

"San Francisco?"

Behr scanned; so far no maroon Buick. "Wasn't the mother from there?"

"Yes. Stay close. If you lose them, call me, but do *not* lose them."

"What about Mr. Stillman?" Respect was still best, he thought, the time not yet right for sides.

"It's settled, Behr, do you hear me? I'm informing my contacts. There'll be no failure this time." She hung up.

Behr slammed the receiver down so hard it bent the cradle. Who was she to question *him* that way? *I'm informing my contacts*—as if Berlin were yesterday. Gradually, he calmed himself with deep breathing, thoughts of the chi. And the memory, surfacing like a burp of oil from a long-sunken U-boat: the *Polizei* questioning her about *die Heuschrecke*, never suspecting the mother locust in a terrorist swarm taking her revenge against those she thought were Wolf's killers. Then just taking.

Suddenly he saw them and ran for the car. In seconds he was accelerating up the on-ramp, spotting the maroon Buick a safe lead in the thinned-down traffic. Keeping well back, using cars around him for cover, then edging closer as twilight deepened, Behr punched up headlights, Monika's warning hot in his head.

Wil followed a vaguely remembered grid of San Francisco to the Union Square parking garage; after a short walk, they located the building, checked the register, and took the elevator to nine. Rafael Canizares led them through a waiting area that smelled of leather chairs, past floor-to-ceiling books, to a sizable office that overlooked the city.

Holly went immediately to the window, the landscape of glowing shapes that rolled away like electrified carpet over the hills and hollows north to the Golden Gate. Her look was rapt, Wil thought—Disneyland for the first time.

"Something, isn't it?" Rafael Canizares said, smiling at her.

"Thanks for staying," Wil said.

"My pleasure—I'm glad you phoned." Canizares ran through what he had in the office to drink.

As Holly decided, Wil sized up the lawyer: Canizares was about his height, handsomely Latin with an athletic build and a forehead that reached well up into hair combed straight back. Pin-striped navy trousers, white shirt with rep tie loosened, patterned suspenders traversing wide shoulders, designer horn-rims softening a bent hawk nose. Easy to picture the man nailing a wide receiver on a crossing pattern.

"Ginger ale, please," he said.

Canizares left and came back with a tray, opened Holly's beer, then his own. "Our loss is mutual, Ms. Pfeiffer," he said after pleasantries. "I had great respect for your father."

"Thank you." She tried to smile.

"You knew him well?" Wil asked.

Canizares regarded him. "We were in law school together. Still, I'm not sure anyone knew Max Pfeiffer well."

"His mother, especially," Holly put in.

The lawyer drank from his beer. "Ms. Pfeiffer, the sixties were difficult years—everybody shouting, nobody listening. I'm not sure I'd have had the patience to be a parent then. I'm divorced, and it's tough. I particularly respect what your father did by taking you away, for being there as you grew up." He looked at Wil.

"At Berkeley, football players and campus radicals hadn't a lot to say to one another, but we did. Max was just back from the war. You could tell by listening to him the effect it had."

"This was . . ."

"Spring. Sixty-nine."

Holly looked at him intently. "What was he like then?"

Canizares focused on his beer. "Intense fits pretty well. I never knew he was aware of me until one day he requested I call his father about handling a matter. Maxwell Bennett Pfeiffer—hell, I was scared to death. But Max said he'd been watching me, that I'd be fine." He shook his head.

"Anyway, Max didn't smile much, never looked as if he

had money. Army field jacket, button undershirt—uniform of the day." He laughed. "Sometimes he'd come in just reeking of tear gas. But Max wasn't like the others. A lot of them just wanted to break things."

"What about after law school?" Wil asked, trying to draw together a timeline.

"Fall that would have been," Canizares said. "I was handling the trust for his father by then. Max did all the big ones: sit-ins, marches, People's Park. Berkeley Eleven with the cop getting it—the Max and Lincoln Stillman Show."

"My father hated him."

"As I remember, Stillman did about as much harm as good. Berkeley Eleven was really Max."

"One thing I don't understand," Wil said. "Why he went to work for Stillman if he didn't like him."

Holly moved forward on the couch.

"Stillman had a pack of young lawyers working the high-visibility stuff. Hell of an opportunity." Canizares's gaze drifted to the domino rows of lit high rises. "Holly, your father did it because he was good and he lived for the game, not because he liked him."

Wil finished his ginger ale, waved no thanks to another. "Whatever happened to Stillman?"

"Guy's still at it. Doesn't grab the headlines he once did, but you have to respect his drive—he must be pushing seventy." Canizares grinned, shook his head. "Still working the jury in those cheap suits and Birkenstocks."

He went to crack them second beers; Holly looked as though she was fixed on an old photograph. Wil smiled encouragingly, then Canizares was back, Holly asking him if he'd known her mother.

"Sure—not as well as Max, but enough to like her," he said, lowering his Heineken. "Paulette was knee-deep into antiwar and women's rights. I heard her speak once."

"And?" she said pointedly.

Wil recognized the tone, but it brought a look from Canizares. "Mexican boy with a Mexican father? I wasn't too big on feminism."

"What about now?"

"Some," he said carefully. "As I recall, she and Max were an item even before Max went overseas, sixty-six, I believe. You were born when?"

"Seventy-one."

"God, where does it go?" Canizares crossed his legs, fiddled with the gathering of material at his knee. "I've always wondered," he said. "Do you remember anything about the night she died?"

Wil half expected an outburst, but her expression softened.

"No, and my father didn't like to talk about it." She took a deep breath. "I was hoping *you* could tell me."

Rafael Canizares's fingers relaxed; he uncrossed his legs, smoothed the cloth. "How about over dinner," he said. "You like fresh fish?"

They went to a seafood grill, walking distance from Canizares and Laughton, a tang of bay in the air. Fog wisped over the buildings and glowed briefly in their light; a cable car clattered by, its bell scatting out conductor jazz. Holly Pfeiffer made Canizares explain how the cars worked, then they were seated in a dark wood booth, the white-coated waiter leaving with their order.

"You have your mother's eyes," he said.

Holly blushed, fumbled with the place setting.

Wil said, "What did your father tell you about that night?"

She looked up at him, then at Canizares. "That it was Christmas Eve. That she died and who killed her."

"Seventy-two, Mr. Canizares?"

The lawyer nodded. "All the antiwar groups had joined together for a vigil, the idea being stop the ammunition trains and you stop the war. In addition, it was supposed to counter the bad PR they'd gotten with the violent stuff. Max told me this later. He was working late on a brief when he got this call there'd been an accident."

Holly's grip tightened on her glass.

"Where?" Wil asked.

"Somewhere between the Naval Weapons Station and their place in Berkeley. Paulette had left early to go home."

The waiter set down their dinners and they ate for a while, the lawyer seeming to deliberate. "I don't know how else to put it," he said finally. "Both doors were blown off the squareback. Paramedics were working on Paulette when Max got there." He exchanged glances with Wil.

"You want me to keep going?"

When she nodded, he said, "Max got a search going, they found you in the bushes. Your clothes were smoking and you were deaf from the blast, but you weren't crying. I think your dad took a measure of pride in that."

"My right ear still rings from it."

"And then?" Wil asked.

Canizares swallowed a bite, cleared his throat. "Paulette lived long enough to recognize him. And to know Holly was all right."

Wil turned to her. "You okay?"

"*Yes.* Mr. Canizares . . . ?"

"Please, Rafael."

"Will you tell this man what the FBI told my father. It does no good when I tell him."

Something was loose in her voice, a wildness Wil recognized. "Holly—" he started, but Canizares waved it off.

"If it will help. Mr. Hardesty, they speculated—"

"*Said,* Mr. Canizares, *said.*" A couple at the next table glanced over, but she ignored them, her eyes now locked on Wil's. Rafael Canizares looked uncomfortable.

"They said Paulette intended to destroy government property. That she'd blown herself up instead."

"You hear that? My mother's heading home with her baby in the car, and they say she's going to set off a bomb—at a peace vigil she just left."

The couple were staring openly now; Wil looked them back to their dinners. "What happened after that?" he asked.

"Threats of violence, demands. The day of Paulette's funeral, a mob started down Telegraph, breaking windows and—"

"He stopped them," she interrupted. "With just a bullhorn. That's the kind of man my father was."

Her voice broke, and she brought a hand to her face; Wil let her out of the booth, watched her dart around a corner toward the rest rooms.

"That was dumb of me," Canizares said.

"No, it was due," Wil said. "Max did that?"

"Uh-huh. And for a while things were cool."

"What then?"

"The ARV. Robbing banks and stirring it up—meaner this time. People dying."

"The DeBray girl."

"No forgetting that one," Canizares said. "Can't say I shed any tears for that crew."

"What's your feeling on Max and them?"

"I think it's bullshit. He had nothing in common with those psychos."

Wil reached into his coat, pulled out Vega's copies. He sipped coffee while the lawyer read them, put them down.

"Makes no sense," Canizares said slowly. "Max was a father, for Christ's sake."

"You should know something else. That was no accident up there." He explained about the shooter, his tracking them to the lodge, about seeing Vega the same morning.

Canizares frowned. "You saying it's connected?"

"No. But I haven't been back in touch, either."

"Max always swore the FBI murdered Paulette, it was one of the reasons he left so abruptly. Day before he split, I brought some papers to his house. He had me slide them under the door, that's how bad it'd gotten. Next day when I went to bring him copies, the note was there."

"The note . . ."

"Right, Max's farewell. Rose and I each got one."

"Exactly when was this?"

Canizares rubbed his chin. "Seventy-four. May something—sixteenth."

"The day before the shoot-out in L.A. You're sure?"

"I talked to a neighbor who'd seen Max and Holly. Big hurry, like Max was running from bill collectors."

"Any clues in the note?"

"Not really. Don't try to find me, that kind of thing."

Wil glanced over his shoulder. "What about hers?"

"Worse—full of vitriol, as I remember. She was livid, even had me hire people to try and find him." He used his napkin to wipe his glasses. "You have to understand, Max was the apple of her eye: only child, incredibly smart, doted on by her friends. Then Vietnam." Canizares stirred his coffee. "Right off, she never understood why he went, let alone volunteered. Then not knowing him when he came back."

"Holly told me," Wil said. "What about the father?"

"He was better about it. But Maxwell died not long after Paulette. Which reminds me: Saying Rose Pfeiffer had no use for Paulette is to understate. Rose was convinced she'd turned Max against her."

"I'm hoping Rose Pfeiffer will see us tonight. Maybe take Holly in."

"Not sure I'd bet on it."

"Can you find out?"

A shrug. "Give it a shot."

As Canizares went to use the phone, Wil walked toward the back of the restaurant, around a lacquered divider panel to the women's room. He tapped. "Holly?"

Nothing. *"Holly . . ."*

Wil drew the .45, tried the door. Locked, no sound—just kitchen clinks and restaurant buzz. Putting his shoulder into it, he snapped the small latch and followed it inward.

She was on the floor beside the sink: knees tucked up, red eyes rising at the sound, her look disoriented. Wil scanned empty stalls, then knelt beside her.

"Hey, there."

She drew a breath and blinked, groggy but coming out of

it. "I was dreaming," she said. "About him cutting my hair—short, like he used to when I was little." She ran a hand through it. "What are you doing in here anyway?"

"You skipped dessert. Thought I'd better check."

Her eyes went to the gun.

He reholstered it. "Okay, I was worried—my job, worrying. You want some coffee to wake up?"

She shook her head, stood and stretched, then led him out. "Did Rafael tell you more?"

"Only good stuff," Wil said, sliding after her into the booth.

In a moment Canizares was back. "She's home," he said.

THIRTEEN

Wil stuck close to the Mercedes 300E, not wanting to lose Canizares's taillights. They kept to Geary Street, west into the Avenues, then turned right, dropping over and down into VistaMar. Even in the dark, the neighborhood lit by old-fashioned acorn streetlamps, Wil could sense the wealth: staunch homes, some set back, others hugging treed sidewalks; rock gardens, balconies, putting-green lawns.

"This sucks," Holly said as they drove.

"Maybe they earned it," Wil said.

"That's not what I mean and you know it."

"Give her time. That she's agreed to see me is something."

Up ahead taillights reddened as the 300E slowed.

"Assuming I care—which I don't—how would you feel if your own grandmother refused to see *you?*"

Wil let it go, swung in behind the Mercedes, thinking Wuthering Heights as he looked at the house. It was tall, three stories plus attic, reddish brick with light-colored stones at the corners, large leaded windows. Leading to the entrance were a curving drive and a mulberry-lined walk. A pair of rein rings topped chiseled stone supports.

"How many died to fashion this monument to excess?" she asked.

"Probably all retired now, with their kids in dental school."

Ahead, Rafael Canizares thunked his door, walked over to Holly's open window. "You're welcome to sit in my car—

the seat tilts and the locks are solid. I'm sorry about this. Maybe someday you'll appreciate what she's been through."

Wil touched her hand. "Anybody looks sideways at you, lay on the horn. All right?"

Holly said nothing; Canizares escorted her to the Mercedes as Wil cased the street. The chill air was mist-heavy and smelled of sea, the streetlamps haloed and glowing. Off to the right a portion of the Golden Gate Bridge showed amber lights. Foghorns sounded from the narrows. Canizares caught up at the rein rings.

"I tried, but Rose wouldn't bend. I can only hope it passes."

Wil nodded. At the door, Canizares pushed a lit button; low-toned chimes sounded inside. A graying oriental man in a black suit answered.

"Hello, Mr. Canizares," he said. His eyes switched to Wil.

"Kenneth, meet Mr. Hardesty. Mrs. Pfeiffer is expecting us."

"Missus very tired. Better you not stay long. Funeral is tomorrow." He led them down a paneled hall.

"You know Mr. Max?" Kenneth said over his shoulder.

"Indirectly," Wil said.

"Fine boy," said Kenneth. "We get him at Lake Tahoe. Very sad." He rapped on well-oiled doors, slid them apart on their runners, then closed them behind the two men.

She stood facing the hearth, arms clutched to her chest as she looked into the fire. Her silver hair was pinned, and she wore a fitted navy housecoat, floor-length and wide-collared, its brocade becoming distinct as they approached. Her ramrod posture fit the Tudor room like a suit of armor, Wil thought— the gray lady knight.

She turned then, showing aristocratic features, a serious mouth, nearly colorless eyes, and he was struck by the resemblance to Max. She said nothing, just looked him up and down.

Rafael Canizares said, "Mrs. Pfeiffer, this is the gentleman I spoke to you about. Mr. Hardesty was with Holly when her home was destroyed."

"Apologies for the hour," Wil offered. "I'll be brief."

"You will indeed. Where is she?" The voice was low and harsh; Wil figured her for a smoker.

Canizares answered, "Outside, Mrs. Pfeiffer. In my car."

Rose Pfeiffer swung cold eyes at him. "As close as she will get to this house, Mr. Canizares, is that clear? I hope you understand how distressed I am with the way you've handled this matter."

Rafael Canizares ran a hand over his scalp.

Wil said, "Mrs. Pfeiffer, your lawyer has been careful to make both myself and Holly aware of your feelings. I only thought you'd want—"

"How dare you speak to my feelings? My son was lost to me a long time ago, the worst kind of death. Every minute knowing he was alive, yet unable to reach out to him. Knowing that *she* had him."

"A young girl, ma'am. What could she possibly have had to do with his decision?"

"Mrs. Pfeiffer, please," Rafael Canizares said. "Can't we sit and—"

"You may sit all you wish, Mr. Canizares. But I must bury my son tomorrow." She stepped toward a side door between two couches.

"Perhaps I haven't been clear," Wil said. She stopped and turned to face him, housecoat sighing with the movement, her mouth framing a response, but he was faster. "Someone wants her dead, Mrs. Pfeiffer."

"Oh, please."

"I was there. The house was bombed, shots were fired."

"At you perhaps."

"Any one could have killed her."

"And now you'd visit that on me." She took a cigarette and lighter from a brass box, seconds later exhaled smoke upward.

"If there *is* trouble now, what my son once was is responsible. Time and again I begged him to express his dissatisfaction differently. But he was determined to chart his own course.'' If she'd been pale when they entered the room, she wasn't now. High color blotched her face and neck.

Wil controlled his tone with effort. "Are you saying you believe your son's death might be other than suicide?"

Rose Pfeiffer sank down in a high-backed chair. "How much is she paying you to hurt me?"

Wil looked at Canizares.

"Mr. Hardesty, my son was a genius who had misguided notions about the war, put there by that woman. Vietnam changed him as it did many fine men who fought at the whim of politicians without the spine to let them win. Who wouldn't be disillusioned by such treachery? But his father and I were making progress until he fell under that slut's influence again."

"Your granddaughter thinks the FBI had something to do with Max's death."

"I don't doubt it. That's her mother talking through my son."

"Had he made enemies you were aware of, Mrs. Pfeiffer?"

"In a few years, my son managed to alienate anyone with common sense, patriotism, or decency. He associated with scum, defended scum, worked for scum. His actions hastened his own father's death, leaving me with unspeakable loneliness. But for someone to want to kill him after all this time? Sheer fantasy."

"And the attempt on Holly's life?"

"She's your client. For all I know this is a scheme to extort money."

Rafael Canizares shifted positions on the couch. Wil said, "I think you know better than that. What you want is what we want—the truth."

"You're very glib. Max was like that. He could charm juries as though they were listening to a gifted nephew play the violin. Are you aware he would have been my husband's partner, the things they could have done together?" For a moment her look was distant. "No," she said abruptly. "I will say goodbye to my son once more and be done with it. Let the dead rest." She stood up stiffly.

"Do you know if Lincoln Stillman had anything to do with Max's leaving when he did?"

Her tone became ice. "My son despised that man, yet he took a job with him. Who knows what he was thinking?" She reached the door, looked back as she opened it. "Mr. Hardesty, I don't pretend I knew my son at the end, why he did the things he did. But I will tell you this—much as I loved him and know that he loved me, he wasn't the saint some would have you believe."

"Angela DeBray?"

She gave him a withering look. "I'll not dignify that with an answer. Call me tomorrow, Mr. Canizares—after one."

With a rush of brocade, Rose Pfeiffer was through the door and gone. Wil glanced at Rafael Canizares, the lawyer's bleak expression reminding him of a boy whose canoe has just been swamped by a retreating speedboat.

Monika heard only the one word: lost.

"Try to understand," Behr was saying now. "The electric bus jumped its cable. By the time I could get around it, they were gone."

For the moment she could think of nothing to say.

"No margin for error following at night. You know that, Monika."

"Mrs. Stillman," she lashed back at him. He was playing games with her, relishing the effect it had. Time to jerk the chain.

"Mrs. Stillman," he said in a more solicitous tone. "There are a number of Pfeiffers in the directory—"

"Verdammung!"

"Permit me a suggestion, something once learned from you: Dispassion accomplishes what emotion does not. As for myself, I seem to recall it was the name of a tree or something."

His drill triggered it, the name flashing in her mind like a road sign passed at speed. "The name is Rose. May I assume,

Behr, that you will be able to proceed from that?''

"There *is* an R here," he said. "Eight-four-four Camino del Playa."

"I hope for your sake it's where they have gone. Now, do your job."

"Certainly—*Mrs. Stillman*." There was a click and a buzzing.

Monika put down the phone, turned on the bathwater; in a moment the tub was full, mineral salts dissolved, the aroma of lavender reminding her of long soaks after tending sheep. She disrobed, stepped in, letting her ankles get used to the temperature. Despite herself, her eyes went to the bathroom's marbled mirror, the glance returned as if by a stranger.

She blinked free of it, busied herself tucking back wisps of blond hair that had loosened. Then she knelt, sat, lay back finally, her chin angled to the water's surface. Heat radiated through her bones like a tuning fork, momentary salvation against the chill concept of aging. So gradual the process had been, the erosion of her leverage, Lincoln's little ploy a good example, nothing he'd have tried in her prime. But the tiny tracks in her skin were becoming canyons now, places under eyes and elbows yielding to time and gravity. She'd noticed Behr's glances, heard it in his casual disrespect. Lately it was all she could do to look at herself.

A blast of urgency passed through her like a mistral.

He'd find them. Like the time he found the Berliner Bank president. For months the man had eluded them, altering times, driving different routes. And the security, the police escorts and armed bodyguards.

He'd done it anyway: Teutonic thoroughness, Behr its chief practitioner. He'd simply watched until he found the key, the banker's mistress, then persuaded her with electric wire to call the banker.

He'd come, all right.

Monika swirled hot water, remembering it as Behr described: window breaking, the banker twisting in midair, his screams dropping in volume with each level. Twelve floors.

Then glass and body hitting the street, body bass to glass treble—the music of the revolution.

Later that summer the fat industrialist, the assault on Tempelhof Airport; her knowing then the work was her life, the only time she ever experienced . . . what? Purpose—meaning? Meager expressions. More like being infused with one of the moor's secret springs, its raw heat bubbling up her spine and into her brain.

And Behr: the endless explanations to Lincoln, how he'd more than pay for himself. Making it conditional, finally. Now Lincoln was closer to Behr than she was, the girl a case in point. Lincoln feeling his oats, Behr anxious to be operative again—beyond just banks.

Two-and-a-half million dollars! Monika let her breasts break the surface—cool air on reddened skin—and thought of the calls she'd made, of Ammad Nassir's agreement in principle. The plan could still work. *If* . . .

Monika permitted herself a few exultant minutes contemplating the girl's place in history. And her own. She nodded, caught blue eyes looking back at her from the mirror, and this time she did not look away.

Yes—like a phoenix rising from the ashes. *Yes!*

Rafael Canizares stood at the window of his sparsely furnished flat, San Francisco's bright patchwork spreading out toward downtown. This late, traffic on the Mission and Market arteries was intermittent, headlights softened by the mist that had followed them home. He sipped his bourbon, walked toward Holly's closed door, listened a moment, then returned to face Wil.

"I don't know," he said. "Before seeing Max's handwriting and the prints, I wouldn't have thought. Now . . ." He shrugged.

Wil gulped from his can of Vernor's, the ginger ale fizzing on his tongue like a mouthful of sparklers. "You have any idea why he might have been involved?"

"None. Money was the last thing Max was hung up on. Christ, he had enough of it."

"Tell me about that."

"The old man left him fat—let alone what he stood to inherit from Rose. You have any idea what she's worth?" He drank some of the bourbon, shook his head. "Hell. Knowing Max, he'd have just given it away to causes she hated."

"How about Holly?"

Canizares straddled a wooden folding chair. "Doesn't matter what Rose does. As Max's kid, she'll inherit his trust fund."

Holly with money, the irony of it, brought a smile. Wil tapped his teeth on the Vernor's can. "How'd the money get to Max—through you?"

"Christ, no. Rose would have been all over me trying to find him. A Swiss bank handled it. Very solid, very close-mouthed."

"So you *didn't* know where he was."

"No—just that it was being disbursed. And then only because I knew somebody who isn't with the bank anymore."

"What about the money you put up for Holly?"

Canizares swirled his drink. "Call it a loan. Least I could do, seeing all he did for me." He thought a moment. "What was the house like?"

"Modest size, peeling paint, old furnishings. Never guess anyone with money lived there."

"Old Max. Still punishing his mom."

"If you say so."

"Just be glad you never met him in court, Hardesty."

"Yeah," Wil said. "Which reminds me—you have a State Bar Association directory in your office?"

"Sure. Why?"

"Lincoln Stillman."

Canizares looked at him, the surprise apparent. "You think he might know something?"

"Not necessarily, but worth a try, given his ties to Max. Hell, at this point, I'm wide open."

"I'll have Carol check it out. You might be in luck, though—I think he's coming here after some gig he's got with the Supreme Court. We'll check that too." He found a Post-it pad, wrote himself a note, and stuck it on his briefcase. "Mind like a sieve, you know?"

Wil nodded, and for a while they sat taking in the light show and not speaking, then the lawyer refilled his glass, got Wil another Vernor's from the fridge.

"Thanks. Mind an unrelated question?"

"Fire away."

"You mentioned you were divorced. Any kids?"

Canizares produced photographs: two boys and a girl. "Nineteen and seventeen," he said, pointing to the boys. "Nina's twelve—she and Robby live with their mom. Gabe's at Cal." He took a long sip. "That's my dad there. Shame he never got a chance to know them." He shook his head. "Cancer. Spent his whole career at Justice, died the year he retired."

Wil returned the picture. "Some group. This one has to be a player."

Canizares smiled. "Linebacker like his old man, all-city this year. Some pretty big names waving scholarships."

"Was it hard?" Wil asked at length. "Splitting up?"

The lawyer took his time with the words. "What's hard is coming home to this. Twin Peaks view, tile everywhere—I'd have killed for a pad like this once. Now it just says I failed. As for the divorce, it was mutual, no surprise really. You live in different spaces, see different people. After a while it becomes too much trouble to share. The questions stop, then the interest, then the love. Didn't help any that I was looking around—hell, I wouldn't have taken it from her, why should she take it from me?" He looked at the ice melting in his glass. "Not seeing the kids hurts worse than I'd have thought. Why the question?"

"My wife decided she wants a separation."

"I see. How do *you* feel about it?"

"Surprised, but in a way not surprised. We've had our problems lately. My fault."

"Nobody's fault, sometimes," Canizares said. "After all I've been through, you'd think I could muster up some great advice, but I can't. At least you got a warning."

"Hard for her too, I suppose."

Canizares looked at the lights, then at him. "Maybe I do have some advice: Respect is cool, but it don't keep you warm. It's not something you embrace with your mind." He finished his drink and stood up. "Speaking of which, she's pretty, isn't she?"

"Who?"

"Who do you think? Holly."

"You mean my client, don't you?"

"I've seen the way she looks at you," Canizares said. "But then maybe I've been a lawyer too long." He gestured at the couch. "That's it for me. You know how a hide-a-bed works?"

"Yeah."

"Good. Useful knowledge, you ever do split up."

FOURTEEN

The service was under way by the time they pulled up behind the other cars. Curving white headstones marched away in even rows; cypress trees, old and dark up close, graying farther out in the heavy mist, dripped uneven cadence on the grass. A burial detail stood by the flag-draped coffin. Fresh earth lined the open grave.

The three of them got out of Rafael Canizares's Mercedes. Wil could see Rose Pfeiffer, thin and straight under the umbrella Kenneth held up for her. Well-dressed people Rose's age formed a semicircle of dark statues.

They stopped short of the group.

Subdued all morning, Holly had finally asked Canizares about the funeral, found out that Rose pulled strings to get Lance Corporal Maxwell Pfeiffer, Jr., into the Presidio. She'd fumed then, deciding finally to go, Wil wondering about the wisdom of it. Last night he'd soft-pedaled the old lady's comments, but he knew Holly had seen through it, getting progressively quieter, finally shutting herself off behind Canizares's bedroom door.

He'd risen early, using the quiet to call Lisa. Waking her.

"I miss you," he said after stiff-sounding hellos and I'm-fines, the feeling of wagons already circled. He could hear her sitting up in bed, drinking something—water she kept in a green plastic glass by the bed—then clearing her throat.

"Wil, have you thought about what we discussed—the separation?"

"Separation," he said, giving it emphasis. "Like you've already made up your mind."

She sighed. "I'm glad you called. I wasn't sure how I was going to tell you . . ."

There was another feeling now, one too vividly recalled: the room-tilting impact of discount whiskey on a hangover. "Tell me what, Lisa? You out the door or something?"

"Will you just listen, please? Bev knows some people with a place in Santa Ynez. They're between tenants and—"

"Three days ago you were talking separation as a possibility. Today it's a place in the Valley?"

"Can we not make this harder than it is?" There was a pause, then she read him a phone number where he could reach her. "They understand it's probably temporary," she said. "And they're giving me a break on the rent. Wil, the house just seemed too empty."

"Or too full of something else."

She said nothing.

"Shit just happens, huh? How long?"

"Thinking about it? I don't know: days, weeks—who cares?" She paused again. "Look, I saw someone, no one you'd know. It was just dinner, but I wanted you to hear it from me."

Like a sucker punch driving the wind out of him; short breaths, hand over the receiver to keep it from her.

"Wil?"

"God. Where have *I* been?"

Her silence was her answer, then: "Maybe you should do the same. It's only fair. After all, I can't expect—"

"Thanks for the thought. You'll forgive me if I don't."

"Wil, this is something I'm doing for me, not against you. It's what now is *for*, if it's for anything."

"Listen," he said, trying to right the spinning compass. "I can be on a plane and down there in a couple of hours. At least let's talk this over. Walk on the beach or *something*."

"No, I really need the time alone. Can you understand that? Otherwise I'll never know."

"Sure," he said. "Do me a favor, though. Don't tell me any more about how hard it is." He drew in air. "Look, I'm on somebody's phone. There a time that's good later? I don't want to interrupt anything."

"Goodbye, Wil," she said. "Good luck on your case."

Hanging up, he saw Canizares making coffee. Regarding him.

"How it works is this," Canizares said slowly. "A day here, a day there, pretty soon you've got a week. Then a month, then six. Take 'em as they come, is all. Be no charge for that one either."

Holly nudged Wil back to what was going on, two soldiers folding the flag and presenting it to Rose Pfeiffer.

"He'd *hate* this," she said.

Wil said nothing.

"She knows how he felt about the Army. He belongs at the lake, anywhere but here. *Damn her.*"

Her voice prompted Rose Pfeiffer to look; she leaned over to Kenneth, who detached himself from the group and came over. Looking at the ground, he said, "Missus wants me to say you are not welcome here and please to leave. Okay Mr. Canizares to stay." Still looking down, he returned to where the detail was beginning to lower the coffin.

"*No . . .*"

It made the group turn to look. "This is just what you wanted, isn't it?" Holly shouted. "To have him for yourself. Well, he hated you. And this—obscenity—changes nothing."

Rose Pfeiffer motioned for the detail to continue. Then she strode over, her eyes locked on Holly's. "My dear," she said. "Do you think I don't understand why my son never came home, why he chose this way instead? He finally realized how big a mistake he had made. Mr. Canizares, please tell this *person* that if she is found anywhere near me or my house, I will have her arrested."

She turned and walked to the grave, picked up a handful of

dirt, and threw it in. On Kenneth's arm she then entered an older black Chrysler. Wil could see her facing straight ahead as the Chrysler moved off, turning past a white car he hadn't noticed before.

Hairs on his neck rose until he realized the car was empty. Still, his eyes scanned the cemetery grounds for the big man, returning to Holly after finding nothing out of the ordinary.

Her eyes were on the rend in the earth, abandoned now by the others after Rose Pfeiffer's departure. Holly stepped forward; Wil saw Canizares looking at him, and he shook his head. She halted graveside, said something he couldn't hear. Then she took off the faded Cal sweatshirt, held it out, and let it fall.

When she returned in her thin blouse, she was shivering.

Behr swept the field glasses, his father's good prewar German ones, back and forth across the group, targeting his players. Two hundred yards and it was as though he were standing next to them: the Pfeiffer woman, arriving early and greeting friends; the girl, all stiff and sullen body language; the Mercedes driver from the house on Twin Peaks—the lawyer.

And Hardesty, sportcoat bunching under the left arm when he stood a certain way. Shoulder rig.

For a moment he pinned on the tall form, watching the man's eyes scrutinize attendees, parked cars, headstones, the cypress grove from which Behr observed. Then beyond to other things—the undulating terrain, a car slowly navigating the paved lane, its occupants checking names on the stones; back again as some sort of spat developed between the Pfeiffer woman and the girl.

Behr adjusted the focus slightly and imagined crosshairs fixing on the blond head, just behind the ear. A difficult shot, but hardly impossible. The gentle squeeze then, a lover's touch on the trigger; the buck of the rifle, the bloom of red. The group stunned, then scattering in panic.

And Behr's moment of costly indecision erased.

His eyes swung to the girl. He'd take her too, her body

stiffened in fear an instant too long, eyes wide, mouth open; her protector blown apart in one shocking, savage act. Easy after Hardesty.

For a moment he was tempted. Certainly the old man would applaud his initiative and reward him financially. But Monika, of course, would kill him. No questions asked, no quarter given, their history together counting for nothing. Death itself when she wanted to be.

The proper time.

Sooner or later they'd separate.

For another moment he watched the ceremony conclude, guests drifting off, his targets preparing to leave the cemetery. Then he replaced the field glasses in his pebbled leather case with *Heinz Behr* embossed in gold and faded back to where he'd left the white rental car.

Rafael Canizares insisted on buying them lunch before they left, Holly Pfeiffer declining hers when it came. As Wil ate, he reprised the scene at the Presidio cemetery, wondering what didn't fit, not quite able to put his finger on it. Heading south now on Skyline Drive, Holly asking him more about their conversation with her grandmother, Wil held nothing back.

"I *hate* her," she said finally, thumbnail snapping at the nails of her other hand.

"Do you have to do that?"

"What?"

"That, with the fingers. Makes you seem about twelve."

She gave him a look, but stopped.

"Thank you," Wil said. "Not much love on either side, is there?" His eyes darted to the rearview mirror and back.

She glanced at him. "You think what I said was wrong."

"You think it did some good?"

"Buzz off!"

"Look, you didn't hire me to tell you how green your eyes are. You're first-rate at hurting people. In little kids that's annoying, at your age it's indefensible."

For a moment she said nothing. Then she snapped a fingernail and challenged him with a glare.

"Jee-zus," he said, shaking his head slowly.

"*What* . . . ?"

"You. Ever hear the expression 'what goes around comes around'?"

"Stop, I'm spinning."

"You get back what you put in. Simple as that."

"I know what it means."

"Good. Then try taking inventory sometime and see what shows up after a smart mouth. Shouldn't take long."

She reached over and turned on a rock station. He lowered the volume. She flipped it off suddenly, then slid the heater up all the way. He cracked the window an inch on his side.

"Close it, I'm cold," she said.

"No you're not, you're spoiled. Your father loved you to the point he made you his whole existence—that's hard when you're the one who's loved. Things get blurred."

Arms across her chest, ready for battle. "Oh? How?"

"Like seeing yourself everywhere you turn and thinking that's how it is. I'm not nominating Rose Pfeiffer for class act of the year, but she has feelings. How would you like being attacked like that? And don't say what you got back was unexpected."

She swung away from him, looking out at the scrub easing into coastal oak and pine. As they climbed higher up the ridge, the mist condensed into drizzle. Wil turned on the wipers, and for some miles their metronome sound tracked the time.

"Where are we going?" she asked.

"Santa Cruz."

"What's there?"

"I don't know," he answered.

"Some private eye. '*I don't know*,' " she mimicked.

Wil rubbed a headache that had started in at his left temple. " 'I don't know' is how it works, Holly. It leads to questions. Ask enough questions and you find out things. Pretty soon you're up to here in answers. Get it?"

A flash of white, well back. Imagined? For seconds his eyes held the rearview but saw nothing. He slowed, made the turn for Boulder Creek-Ben Lomond.

"Why aren't we taking the freeway?" she asked.

He was about to downplay it when he caught himself. "Easier to follow someone on the freeway and not be seen. Out here it's tougher."

"Somebody's behind us?" She swiveled around. "I don't see—"

"I don't either," he said. "Not yet, anyway." As he came out of a curve, Wil swung the car in behind a clump of young trees. For five minutes they waited, scanning the road. Two vehicles: a light-colored pickup driven by a man in a baseball cap and a station wagon full of family. Wil started the engine, headed south again, wipers sweeping tracks across the drizzle.

"No bad guys?"

"Guess not."

She cleared her throat. "Sorry if I was a punk back there."

He nodded. "As long as you're apologizing, you might think about including your grandmother."

"Don't push it."

"Be a start. Who knows what might happen."

"I know, all right. She'd just skewer me with that look or have me arrested or something." She looked out the window. "What are these trees?"

"Madrone," he answered, "and California bay." He stopped at a turnout to let her rub a leaf and smell the peppery aroma, told her about its use in cooking. Then he broke off a sprig, offered it to her. "It's good dried, too. Plunk one in your next pasta sauce and watch 'em jump up for seconds."

She took it. "This just grows wild?"

"Around creeks and canyons. Pretty neat, huh?"

"How do you know this stuff?"

"Just take an interest." He pointed at a grouping. "Those over there are redwoods. As I recall, there's a state park near here with some old growth."

"Can we go? Please?"

"Sure, why not."

They were in Big Basin in under an hour, losing the drizzle on the way. For a while they walked in silence, smelling the damp earth and looking the reddish girths upward into green lace.

She said, "You called your wife this morning. I heard you."

"Yeah."

"Didn't sound too good."

He brushed a low branch aside. "She's looking for something—what we had or what we didn't have. Some*one*, maybe."

"I'd be furious," she said. "Aren't you even going down there?"

"In time—what she needs right now. It beats arguing."

"Is it because of her miscarriage?"

"Holly . . ."

"Not being able to have more kids?"

Wil picked up a stone, tossed it in the stream running alongside, eyed the splash. Wild blackberry, its unripe fruit just starting to show, dipped and bobbed in the flow.

"That's it, isn't it?" she said.

"I don't know, things change. People change and get changed. You fill up what's empty the best you can."

"If you can."

"Not everybody does. It's harder than it sounds."

"You're thinking of my father, aren't you?"

"No," he said. "Let's drop it, okay?"

Farther along, they stopped at a large spiderweb across an opening in the undergrowth, drops of moisture silver-beading the strands. "Look," she said, "I'm sorry about your wife and all."

"Yeah, well, you can't force someone to love you." What a jerk, he thought after saying it; at least she's being honest. On the way back to the car he kicked savagely at a rock, sent it crashing into the underbrush.

"Mr. Calm," she said. "You feel better now?"

He growled, took a mock swipe at her as she ducked away grinning.

As Holly browsed through magazines, Wil found what he was looking for just before the library closed.

He'd started with the phone book: no luck on the pilot's wife's sister, Paula Anspeth from his notes—any other Anspeth, for that matter. He checked the city directory for 8757 North Sorrel, Vega's address on Paula. No listing, not surprising after seventeen years. He made a mental note to cruise North Sorrel if need be, the houses perhaps renumbered.

Next he scrolled through old editions of the Santa Cruz *Sentinel*. Within an hour he'd found the obit: ex-resident Lacey Louise Jones, bus accident, living in Los Angeles at the time of death. Survived by her mother, Karla Anspeth of Atlantic City, New Jersey, and one sister, still of Santa Cruz, Paula Anspeth Rocker—the second Rocker he called, listed under David J.

She was not happy to hear from him. Her husband was due home at any minute, there had been reference to her in the paper when they ran the article on Clayton's being found, and she hated having it all dredged up again—David especially hated it. Wil told her about Holly, about her trying to understand what happened; promising to keep any meeting to a minimum and anywhere she'd like. One-thirty tomorrow at her house, the woman finally agreed, her only time between hair-styling appointments.

He managed one more call, first checking the Post-it Canizares had handed him at the restaurant—Lincoln Stillman's L.A. address and phone number, stuck to the ABA mailer announcing Stillman's appearance in San Francisco. The voice that answered had that quality about it: one beep shy of a recording.

"Let me guess," he said. "You're the answering service."

"That's right, sir."

"One of those mailbox places attorneys retain for the address?'' He read her the Wilshire Boulevard suite number off Canizares's note.

"Correct. Do you wish to leave a message?"

"How often does he check them?"

"I'm sure I don't know, sir."

"Is Mr. Stillman in town, do you know?"

"No, I do not." So you can go rob his house, I suppose, her tone having none of that.

"Any idea if he even lives in L.A.?"

"Sir, I'm quite busy. If there's no message . . ."

Wil thought a moment, recalled what Canizares had said about Stillman being involved with the Supreme Court—out of town and bigger fish to fry, likely. Regardless, he left his name and La Conchita number, his machine checkable for calls left. With that, he and Holly walked outside into dusk. He told her about the Anspeth lead, such as it was, agreeing that it was a long shot, then he opened the car door for her.

"Not again," she said.

"Client privilege, part of the service."

"And if I were a man?"

Wil expelled a breath. "Is this going to be one of those 'Sisters Are Doing it for Themselves' conversations?"

"Answer my question," she said, her voice rising.

"Nice mood. If I do, will you drop it a notch?"

"It's not just a mood, and I might."

"Okay—no, I wouldn't. I did it because it's something I enjoy doing. You don't want it, fine. Simple as that." He eased into traffic.

"Not quite," she said. "It's degrading to women."

He could feel his own juices heating up—ridiculous, but there it was. "I happen to know some who appreciate having doors opened. How about letting them decide?"

"Because nothing will change that way."

Wil stopped for a red light and faced her. "Change to benefit whom? You're big on seeing tyranny everywhere—how about the tyranny of your own ideas?"

"God, I wish my father were here."

"Amen." The light changed and Wil kicked the Buick, burning rubber, then backed off.

"Very male," she said. "Where to now?"

"Someplace I used to go." After a few minutes he pulled off into a parking lot overlooking the ocean. "Come on," he said. In a bit they were at the edge of a rough cliff, thirty or so feet above where regular swells lapped.

"Point break," he said. "Steamer Lane, it's called. The waves angle in that way—not much now, but in winter they are. I won a contest here once." A wave tossed spray upward. "Then I quit."

"Quit surfing?"

"Surfing contests. Just when the money was getting decent. I had a sponsor who had it all figured out—prize money, endorsements, the whole deal."

"I'll bite," she said. "Why?"

"Because sometimes there's more possibility in saying no to somebody's idea of how you and it ought to be. I decided the reason I surfed was me and the water. Nothing else."

"And that relates to me?"

"You're sharp, you decide," he said. The drizzle had begun again, glazing the cliff and bleeding the lights of the pier and the boardwalk in the distance. Wil could smell the iodine odor of kelp as they walked back to the empty parking lot. He opened his door and got in.

After her door thunked shut and he'd started the car, he said, "What do you say to dinner and a place to stay?" But her head was already turned away, her eyes fixed on something he couldn't see.

They found a motel near the Rocker address with what he was looking for, two rooms with adjoining door. The pizza they ate had made him thirsty and restless, and after a terse goodnight, he sat in the dark, looking out at the lighted boardwalk a couple of streets over.

What was it about the funeral, about Rose Pfeiffer's hard edge? He'd met cold parents before, people driven beyond

reason, especially in custody cases—messy affairs whose res-
olution seemed possible only by cutting the child in half, Sol-
omon style. But Rose so far took the prize. Could someone
really be that bitter? More the question: Why?

Holly Rose Pfeiffer. Rose Lorraine Pfeiffer.

Something in what she said about Max: her parting shot
about his not being the saint some would make him out to be.
Candor was usually beyond such people, objectivity long since
drowned in hate and self-interest. Unless it was an act, Rose
had both. Wil made a mental note to talk to her again, wondering if Canizares had survived *"Call me tomorrow, Mr.
Canizares."* Hoping he had.

Angela Justine DeBray.

What had Rose's look said? Anger a given, but something
else as well, nothing he could pinpoint. Wil could only imagine the pain she'd felt: her only child dead, Max implicated
in the worst of the worst.

He sat up, what was missing suddenly present: no outraged
press conference, no incendiary remarks, Rose more than capable of such. No lawsuits threatened, no challenging of the
evidence, no demands for independent investigation. Only
hostility toward what *he* might represent to her. Another
chance to find out the truth.

I can only think it came back to haunt him. Her son, her
phrasing.

Wil tossed it around a bit longer, then called his house to
check the machine, hoping something from Stillman might
have come in. Nothing. There was, however, a message from
Mrs. Stillman, along with an L.A.-area-code number. There
was also one from Mo Epstein.

Wil checked his watch—almost eleven-thirty—too late to
call Mrs. Stillman. Regarding Mo, he debated, then tried him
at home.

"Wonderful," Epstein said after hearing who it was. "The
end of a perfect day."

"Always there for you, Mo. You call, I answer."

"How'd I get this lucky?"

"Let me guess. The big lug walked into your office and gave himself up—just had enough. Am I right so far?"

"Thought you were done with tequila shooters, Pedro."

"Since you're socially challenged, I'll ignore that. What's up?"

"The FBI was in today asking Freiman about you. Wanted to chat, if you had a spare moment." He paused. "Sounded serious."

"Nah, just fans. Happens all the time."

"Your party."

"Nothing more on the big man?"

"Not really," Epstein said. "Somebody I know ran it through Interpol, keying on the height and the weapon—best he could do. What he got is old, though. Hang on a sec."

Epstein put down the phone. There was silence, then rustling paper. "Six-foot-seven, ex-union enforcer and sometime blaster—guy's still wanted for questioning in a couple of old Berlin bombings, one a fouled-up bank job. Some terrorist group—*Hoysh*-something. *Reckuh. Hoysh-reckuh.* Means 'locusts,' apparently. This was . . ." The paper rustled again. "Sixty-nine. Zip since then."

"Pretty ancient."

"Don't say I didn't warn you."

Wil rubbed tired eyes, the burn starting in behind them. "Tax money well spent, I'm sure."

"See if I stick my *tuchis* out next time. You want this guy's name, or what?"

"Sure, what the hell." Wil flipped open his notebook.

"Ernst Jürgen Behr," Mo Epstein said. "Born Essen, 1937, aka Arne Harmer, Fritz Harmer, Leo Buckmann, Udo Reutner—you name it. Better than nothing, sport."

"Thanks, Mo, it's on my tab." Wil finished writing, rang off, and for a minute contemplated the FBI's checking on him—Vega, doubtless, wanting to know about the bombing, their fast exit from Tahoe. Where they were now.

Damn.

But not unexpected.

Other thoughts began to etch themselves in his mind, battery acid on metal. After a time, he rummaged for the Santa Ynez number Lisa had given him, fidgeted for another long moment. Then he dialed, two rings before the shortness of breath hit him and he had to hang up.

FIFTEEN

Monika was in her studio, blocking out a still life—sunflowers in a blue Delft vase—when the call came in. To keep her brush hydrated, she dropped it in with some others in a glass of water, then picked up the phone.

"Yes?" She stole a glance back at her composition—morning light on Van Gogh green and yellow. Purity itself.

"Mrs. Stillman?"

"Who is this?"

"Wil Hardesty. You returned my call to your husband."

Instantly Monika shifted gears; she began to pace. "Oh, of course. I called to explain why Lincoln won't be getting back to you. I felt you ought to know."

"I see. Thanks for taking the trouble." The voice was like so many in California, devoid of accent, something she'd learned to emulate. Forties, she guessed, trying to visualize him—telling her now that he'd heard her husband was in Washington, that perhaps she knew how he could be reached.

She smiled: The man had no idea how little time he had left—ironic, since without him Lincoln would have had his way with the girl. Curious her speaking to him in this manner; innocuous, but it made her uneasy. After all, he had escaped from Behr. "If my husband has one rule, Mr. Hardesty, it's that he's not to be disturbed when arguing a case. Particularly in front of the Supreme Court."

"It won't take long, Mrs. Stillman. A few questions—"

"Monika, please." Her cue for warm and inviting.

"Monika, then. And it is important."

"But distracting nonetheless. He demands complete isolation." At the thought, she almost smiled: Lincoln without his whores.

"Any way you could leave a message for him to call me?"

"I guarantee you, it would do no good."

"What about if you gave me the number?"

"That would be a serious breach of faith on my part."

"Do you know when he's coming back?"

"He had no idea when he left. I know it sounds odd." Monika timed a pause, then cast her lure. "Mr. Hardesty, Lincoln and I have been married a long time. Perhaps I can help."

Silence: the man thinking it over. "Did you know Max Pfeiffer?"

Bait taken. "Of course—he worked for Lincoln once. A very unique man. Sad to read about his death."

"Unique in what way, please?"

Monika feigned reflection. "Max was very passionate about life, very much for the underdog and against the state. He and Lincoln held much the same beliefs."

"They got along, then?"

"For the most part. They'd argue occasionally in pressure situations. Nothing serious, differences of opinions."

"Would you recall what about?"

"No. Not after all this time."

"Then you wouldn't know why Max stopped working for him?"

"I wouldn't, but I'm sure Lincoln would. Are you aware he has some speaking engagements after the Supreme Court?" She hesitated. "Perhaps you could intercept him, save time. Where are you now?"

"Northern California, but moving around."

"Really? Where?" Trying to keep her impatience under control—bad enough not hearing from Behr since San Francisco. But it was taking too long, the man obviously wondering at her persistence. "The reason I ask is that Lincoln's in San Francisco for a speech May twenty-seventh. At the Saint Regis.''

"That might work, Mrs. Stillman—Monika. Thank you.''

"Mr. Hardesty, may I assume this has to do with Max's daughter?''

There was a pause. "It's a factor, yes.''

Maddening. "I read about what happened. Poor thing, I feel so sorry for her.''

Doing fine, he told her.

"Then she's not in danger after all?''

His hesitation was all she needed: "Something just occurred to me, I don't know why I didn't think of it before. You must bring her here.''

"I don't—''

"Nonsense, she'd be most welcome. Lincoln would never forgive me for not insisting.'' Monika held her breath in his silence, then eased in with "It's just us and this big house.'' Setting up trump—surprising what a name, Behr its source, and a little research will do. "You see,'' she said with emotion, "we lost a daughter. Years ago, but the pain is always there.''

I know you, Sean Wilson Hardesty, know about your boy.

Finally, he spoke. "I'm very sorry. Believe me—''

"I can't expect you to understand, but isn't there a way? Surely her safety must be a concern.'' *Do it, you son of a bitch.*

"Your offer is very generous. I'll keep it in mind, I promise.''

Close, so very close, she thought—too bloody much to hope for, the dream simply coming to her. After he'd hung up and the dial tone returned, Monika hit the off switch on the portable phone. Then she hurled the goddamn thing with all her strength at the sunflowers.

Lincoln Stillman lifted his feet one by one off the squat bar table and pushed up to welcome the visitor: Harry Wellington Carper, "Bucky the Beater,'' named for his protruding teeth, long since shoved back, and his absentminded habit of jerking off during boring lectures.

Frat brother, class of '46; professor emeritus; district court judge.

Functioning imbecile.

Hard to believe they went all the way back to Moses Lake, the days when Bucky's father owned the land on which Aaron Stillman raised his blighted little potatoes. Binding them then: a mutual hatred of both fathers, Bucky's well-off and Scrooge-like, Lincoln's stubborn and dirt-poor. They'd parted when Lincoln's mother finally had enough and packed up her youngest son, first for Ritzville, then on to pay dirt with the King of the Meatpackers in Spokane. Ironically, Aaron's first good crop had coincided with his son's polio.

Stillman eyed the overstuffed bald man with the florid face. Had he really palled around with this moron after they'd met up again, first at Washington State, then Gonzaga; called him brother; helped him study for the bar exam? Bucky the Beater, who'd made a career out of misprosecuting gangsters, finally hitting one because the jerk confessed—at least he hadn't fucked that one up.

Showed you what a sorry circus the law had become.

Stillman waved to the waitress, and in a few minutes Bucky's Tanqueray was sliding down the inside of his chins. Stillman took in bourbon and branch, mentioned an incident from the Moses Lake days. There he went, right on cue: Just give Bucky the lead and you never had to say another word. Feigning interest, he imagined sparring with the Beater on Bucky's best day. Shit, he could beat this dildo wearing a blindfold, he decided for the umpteenth time. Then what was it that made him call whenever he was in D.C. waiting for a flight?

Who else? At least Bucky'd *have* a drink with him.

Stillman knocked back his glass and caught the waitress's eye, having primed her to be on alert. As she left him a new whiskey, he watched her rear—not as good as Monika's.

While Bucky droned, he thought of the first time: featured

speaker, Democratic Peoples Front convention, Bonn, November '69. The group hadn't been worth spit, just another loud bunch gathering to embarrass Willy Brandt's government. It was toward the end of the convention that he'd looked up from breakfast to see her coming toward him across the dining room.

Bucky cracked up at one of his own stories and started on his second martini. Lincoln eyed him, saw Monika.

She was the most exquisite thing he'd ever seen. Oddly, the crutches and the age difference hadn't seemed to matter to her; he'd poured on what charm he could muster, still shy in those days around women other than hookers. He wondered about that, but by then she was mounting him again, no time to wonder, approaching him then with her proposal. Like a dream, it was. Then her secret: laying it before him, a death sentence if he turned her in. But she hadn't had to worry.

Only back home did he begin to realize the full extent of her talents, her power. Ol' Max never had a chance.

He felt a tingle at the thought of her, love and lust inadequate distinctions for what they had going. Whatever he'd let loose by bringing her here, whatever he would face with Behr's screwup, he and Monika were bonded by fire and time. And he'd been away too long.

Little images began to flare, matches on tinder, followed by a strange longing just to hold her—nothing more. As though he could silence for a while the whining dynamo that drove her, watch her face sleep-soften into Lilith-who-walked-the-moors. His fantasy of her.

He shook himself from the reverie.

Bucky the Beater began giggling in his third gin, spilling it down his front as Lincoln Stillman heard the boarding call. Making a mental note to be sure to wash after shaking Bucky's damp hand, he drained his fourth bourbon, tossed a fifty on the table, and gratefully made for the gate.

Wil took the car even though the Rocker house was within walking distance, a small neighborhood down where the river met the bay.

Holly's reaction to Monika Stillman's offer of shelter had been predictable—all you're-kiddings and how-can-you-even-bring-it-ups. Less so had been Mrs. Stillman's curiosity about their whereabouts. Probably nothing, he concluded, a by-product of the media hype, her call an act of kindness. He'd been close to accepting, too; not a bad solution, the girl safe with someone who cared about her until things cooled off. Ace in the hole for now. As far as Stillman's whereabouts went, Wil made a mental note to call the Supreme Court, try having the lawyer paged, Monika's explanation of his quirks to the contrary. Not that he held much hope.

Holly's debut in the Gap store where they went to get her jeans and a top was similarly productive. Still peckish from last night's confrontation, she groused about the racks and displays, finding fault with everything, most of all the idea of such opulence when half the world was hungry and oppressed. America, he told her finally, after she'd challenged the clerk ringing up her purchases. At least you got to choose your half.

Humor hadn't helped—up and down with her the norm, it seemed.

A sullen peace between them now, he looked the Rocker place over: peeling mustard paint, forest trim, potted plants concealing most of the steps and the small porch. One yellow rose bloomed under the floral-curtained bay window. They parked the rental, stepped around the plants, and rang the bell. She answered without speaking, a tall willowy woman in a pink smock. He introduced them, handed her his card.

She moved back for them to enter, led them past a couch and TV, the floral drapes Wil figured as sheets pressed into service. Down a hallway and into one of the bedrooms: no bed; two beauty salon chairs, one reclining against a sink with a neck-size lip; trays and cases of hair and nail products.

She left the room, came back with folding chairs, motioned them to sit, then took one of the parlor chairs. "You don't look like your voice," she said. "I usually judge these things pretty good."

Holly stifled a grin.

"Mrs. Rocker," Wil began. "We—"

"That's Paula." She smoothed hair tinted pink. "Used to be Anspeth, but then you know that."

"Is your husband—"

"David's a millworker. You being here is something that would only trouble him, and you don't want no trouble with David Rocker."

Wil nodded. "Right. How well did you know Lacey's husband?"

She made a face. "Clayton? Not much to know, just a small time weed grower and hauler. Had customers at the university, that's where he met Lacey. She married him for the free dope. Great luck we Anspeths have with men."

"Lacey ever say anything to you about Clayton's last charter?"

She began arranging bottles. "Maybe," she said. "I never said nothin' about it back then. Why should I talk to you now?"

Wil drew out two twenties. "All I have," he said.

She eyed the bills, went to the window and angled a look out past chintz curtains, then sat again. "Clayton never said much about his business. But he did tell Lacey about this big score he'd lined up. Naturally she told me. She thought it was just Clayton bragging—man never gave a rat's ass for the truth. But he described this guy."

Vega's comment flashed: *Jones never told her what he looked like.* Holly straightened on her folding chair.

"Some black dude, Clayton told her. Turned out it was the guy that got burned up later, that Z character."

"Cleon Chapman."

"That's him. Around here we get our share—including some like that—but this guy carried a gun. Lacey didn't ask beyond that. She hated guns. Our dad was shot in a bar."

"How big a score?" Wil asked.

Paula Rocker reached for the money; Wil gave her one of the bills and she tucked it into a pocket.

"Lacey didn't know. What's this for anyway? Thing's almost twenty years done, at least for Clayton."

"What about Lacey?"

She checked her watch, glanced again at the money. "Look," she said, "I don't have much—you're looking at most of it. But I got my health. Maybe you should leave."

Holly spoke. "Please, it's important."

"Not to be rude, honey, but ain't it all."

Wil looked around. "Nice business, lots of chemicals. You have a license, of course."

She glared at him.

"Just asking," he said, feeling like a prick.

Paula Rocker found a cigarette and lit it. She waved the match out, blew smoke from the side of her mouth. "Lacey called one night—this was before she left. Some guy'd been to see her."

Wil perked up, saw Holly do the same.

"Anyway, she sounded bad on the phone, so I went over there. She's crying, her face is all swollen, got the ice out— pretty beat to hell. Well, damn, I'm ready to call the cops, nobody pulls that shit with *my* sister. '*No*,' she says. Like I don't mean no, I mean *NO!*"

"This guy," Wil said. "She say what he looked like?"

"Big, every which way—taller'n Clayton and he was six-one. She was really shook, figured it had to do with Clayton's game."

"Why was that?" Holly asked.

"The guy wanted money—where was the damn money, he keeps askin' her. Lacey figured maybe Clayton'd scammed the cash and was gonna send for her. By then she'd reported him missing."

Wil said, "She told the man that?"

Paula nodded and looked pained, tamped ash into a glass tray filled with lipsticked butts. "Like a fool, I agreed not to tell anybody about it. She liked Clayton and didn't want anything to happen if he was still alive. Well, forget that. The guy was back a couple of months later, beat on her again. This time when she called, it was from L.A.''

"She bolted."

"What would you do?" Paula ran a hand over her eyes; when she spoke, her voice was shaky. "Fifteen years she's been dead, and I still wish I'd played it different."

They waited as it passed; finally she blew into a tissue. "Lacey sure didn't deserve to get pushed under no bus. What'd she ever do except pick the wrong guy?"

"You're saying she was pushed?"

She wiped her eyes. "Damn right it's what I'm saying. She was being watched, thought she'd seen the big guy again. She was scared."

"You tell anyone that?" Wil asked.

Emphatic nod. "After somebody murders my sister? Goddamn right. Fat lotta good it did."

Wil handed her the second twenty.

"Something else," she said. "I just now remembered it. There was this other guy."

He watched Holly's color fade. "Somebody else watching her?"

"No," Paula said. "Clayton phoned her just before takeoff. Said this other guy'd showed up in a real sweat and changed things around, offered more money—funny I didn't think of it before. Last she ever heard from him."

Holly leaned forward, her face taut. "Did your sister tell you if he described this other man?"

"Honey, it's been a long time." Paula Rocker looked expectantly at Wil; smiled as he rummaged, found another ten, and passed it to her.

"Bonus round, Paula. What did he look like?"

"As I recall, blondish, about Clayton's size. Eyes like water, he told her. Empty-like."

Wil said, "Why didn't you or Lacey tell this to the police?"

She sighed. "We both were heavy into weed then and that was Clayton's business, so none of us talked to cops. Besides, we expected him back any day."

Wil looked at Holly, who was ashen-faced, staring at nothing. "Thanks," he said. "One more thing. Did Lacey ever tell you where Clayton had his runway?"

By three o'clock they were passing UC Santa Cruz, somewhere off in the mist to the right, according to the signs. Forty minutes later they started watching for the turn, then left the two-lane for an overgrown road, winding first up a treed ridge and then down into a small valley. This high up, the sun had bored through and touched the valley floor with color: white Queen Anne's lace, yellow sunflowers, scarlet bugler, blue flax, greens ranging from pale through verdant. As the road became increasingly cracked and weedy, saplings poked through. Small rabbits darted in front of the car.

Wil stopped and stood on the trunk, looked around.

"Anything?" she said from inside.

"Over there," he said.

They found rutted tracks, and in minutes were standing by an old camper shell, barely visible through tall plants. Wil walked over.

"Cannabis," he said. "Clayton's heirs." He stepped through them to the pole-supported shell—faded, dented, its door much rusted at the hinges. With a groan it gave, and he was inside finding nothing much: moldy blankets, empty cans, torn charts spewing silverfish, rubber wrappers, a split in the roof admitting shafts of light. Wil prowled a few minutes longer, then backed out, figuring the shell had been well picked over since Lacey reported Clayton missing.

Holly called him from a clump of trees.

The frame and a few shreds of rotted material were all that was left of the shelter, but it had been big enough at one time to hold a small plane. Wil examined a flap of the material: camouflage canvas. Clayton Lee Jones, if not elegant, had been thorough.

He stepped inside the frame: dirt floor weeded over except where oil had leaked, some shelves on cinder blocks. He paced the perimeter, found old tools, coffee cans with nuts and bolts and springs rusted together in clumps. He tossed one aside, walked to where she was standing.

"He was here, wasn't he?" she said.

He nodded. "Wind through that draw would have favored takeoffs."

"I didn't mean the pilot. I meant my father."

Wil shoved his hands into his pockets. "It checks out, yeah."

Sunlight glistened on tears forming. "Then it was all lies, wasn't it—all the things I believed. He *was* a thief. He *was* a murderer. No wonder we had to live the way we did." The tears were coursing now; she made no effort to stop or wipe them away.

"Holly—"

"You must think I'm unbelievably stupid, because that's how I feel. All those years. *Damn* him!" She stormed off, the sound of her anguish diminishing with distance.

Wil let her go, walked back to the car. He broke off a foxtail stem and chewed it, trying to imagine who stood where, what was said and by whom—Max Pfeiffer changing the game. He moved off after her then, found her sitting in a clear patch, looking into middle distance. Her face was tracked and puffy, her eyes red.

"However it looks, he had a reason," he said, squatting beside her. "I told you I'd help you find it, and I will. Meantime, how about having some faith."

"In what? You were right, the FBI was right." Her voice was flat and dead-sounding. "I don't even know who I am anymore. Daughter of a criminal."

"He never mentioned any of this? Angela DeBray?"

"Oh, he mentioned it. I remember him once saying the people who did it deserved to die, that he couldn't understand how anyone could do that to a child." She touched a sleeve to her eyes. "Now I know what he must have been like in the courtroom."

"Holly, do you recall him talking about the ARV?"

She thought. "I don't know. Does it matter?"

"I guess not."

"He must have had a good laugh all those years. Dumb little Holly, do anything for him, never suspecting—"

"The last thing he said to anyone was, 'Trust me.' You remember?"

"I can think of things that ranks with," she said. "Now I wonder how many lies he told my mother, whether she knew the kind of man he was." Her face contorted. *"God."*

Wil looked up at the fog starting to close in again and thought about the ripple effect of Max Pfeiffer's actions; about sins in particular, sins in general. Living things they almost seemed, complete with life spans—some that cast shadows across generations. Sly ones committed in the name of virtue, paper-cut sins verging on the acceptable, big ones that cut like scythes. Who bled the most were always those without guile or guilt.

"Come on," he said. "Let's get out of here."

Beyond the yip of tires on curves, the ride back was silent. By six they were in the motel, Holly soaking in her tub, Wil at his window regarding the roller coasters two blocks down on the boardwalk. He felt nothing like eating; his thoughts were with the girl—pedestal under her father's memory shattering, him dead to her all over again. The debilitating pain of betrayal.

His thoughts shifted to Max's changing the game. What change, exactly, and why? Had the road been too full of law to risk driving the money to L.A.? No—Field Marshal Z set it up before going there, Paula made him from pictures she'd seen in the paper. Which meant flying had been the plan all along and the change must have involved people *not* going. What people?

Why?

Burning out on it, he tried his home answering machine: still nothing from Lincoln Stillman, not that he expected anything now. No other phone messages. He was considering a call to Vega when he heard Holly's voice, muffled by the dividing door.

"Hardesty?"

Wil did a final scan outside, closed the curtain, and tapped on the door. Nothing. He called her name, got silence. He unholstered the gun, held it against his thigh, and entered the room. Breathed again.

She stood in a shaft of light coming from the bathroom. Her long blue T-shirt had "Lake Tahoe" written in script under a sailboat. She was barefoot, her hair wet and slicked back; across her nose, the freckles stood out from the afternoon of sun. Her arms were crossed under her breasts and the nipples looked like willow buds pressed against the cotton. Her skin seemed to glow.

Hard not to see her for what she was, but he fought it. "You okay?" He was surprised at how husky his voice sounded.

"You were right," she said. "The photocopies didn't lie."

"I'd just as soon have been wrong," he said. "I'm sorry."

"It's me who's sorry."

Breathless? *Come on.* "Can I get you anything, food or something?"

"I'm ashamed. All you were doing was trying to help."

"We're all misunderstood sometimes. You're looking at an expert." He hoped it relieved the—what—static electricity that threatened to raise the hair on his arms? *Bullshit.* "I'll be next door if you need me."

He was nearly there when he heard the rustle.

"Hardesty . . ."

He turned, the feeling in his gut jarring and aftershocking through him like an L.A. five-point-seven. Her breasts were high and firm and pulled his eyes down from hers; more freckles danced across them. Her belly was tan and taut-smooth, punctuated by navel. Auburn down led under the shirt she was wringing now in her hands. Hiding. Revealing.

Uncertain seconds, her eyes pinning his: "Well?" Her whisper held an underlay of something else—an echo of who and what she'd been to him, plus some new thing, an essence.

Where a hard-shell chrysalis had been, there stood a butterfly, its wings drying, colors pulsing to vivid life.

"Don't you want me?" she said finally.

Sweet Jesus, God Almighty.

"You have no idea," he breathed finally. He realized then he was still holding the gun, stuck it back in the shoulder rig, shook his head—no graceful exit possible.

"Absolutely no idea."

SIXTEEN

Just after nine, nothing else to do but watch TV, they went out. After a short stroll, they hit Beach Street and across it the boardwalk, well-peopled even in the mist. Wil adjusted the shoulder rig to seat the .45 more comfortably under his coat, then took in the scene from streetside.

The boardwalk was several blocks long, all turrets and flags and facades, anchored at one end by a fanciful-looking domed building, at the other by the third of three roller coasters, lights racing around the rims. The coasters called him: windup clicks on the upgrades, hesitation at the top, the dopplered sound of roars and screams.

Holly Pfeiffer stood rooted, staring.

"Bet you've never been on one," he said. "Come on."

He pulled her up the ramp to the first one, where he bought tickets, enjoying her skeptical look—which turned wide-eyed as the line surged forward and they were strapped in by the attendant.

"No way. Lemme off this thing."

"It's okay," he said. "Everybody wants off about now," the coaster moving then, straight up by the pitch of her voice.

"Damnit, Hardesty."

"Hang on," he said, then they were into the first dip, yelling and clutching the bar as the colored lights of the boardwalk blew past in the soft night.

"Try this," he said, raising his arms as they approached

another drop. "It's an old trick. Now close your eyes."

The coaster plummeted, turned sharply, nearly barrel-rolled, then cycled again; this time her screams were louder. She grabbed at him as the car stopped.

"Again?" Her voice was a gasp.

"With two more to try? Let's go."

Afterward they bought corndogs and cotton candy, cruised the walkway to the smell of saltwater taffy and popcorn, the sound of pipe-organ music. They hit the computer-chip concessions—fortune-tellers, guess-the-weight, love charts— things that made him realize how long it had been since he and Lisa had done this. Simple, dumb pleasures.

Holly's enthusiasm was infectious, pleasurable to him, her laugh a kid's, laced with discovery. He showed her how to shoot: video games, bazookas, snappy rifles aimed at playing cards. He won her a stuffed bear, and after it they posed on a plaster surfboard under a breaking plaster wave, the ridiculousness of it cracking them up.

"Ohmygod," she said, pulling his arm.

They had to try it: a double-hammer ride, the hammers opposite, arcs increasing—cresting finally in a giant three-sixty amid much shrieking. After it, laughing at each other getting their legs back. Easing up, they took the sky tram that ran above the crowd, the rides, the beach darkening out to black water.

"What's that?" she asked, pointing.

"Pier lights," he answered, aware of her closeness, the smell of her hair. "You having fun?"

"You kidding me?"

"Good. I'm glad."

"Hardesty . . ."

"Yeah," he said, figuring by her tone what was coming.

"Earlier. Why didn't you—you know . . ."

He cherry-picked the words. "Because once upon a time I promised I wouldn't. Besides, I didn't think it was what you wanted. Not really."

"Oh? And what did I want?"

"Your father back where he used to be, things in order again. I was there, that's all."

She clutched her stuffed bear.

"Believe me," he said, feeling strange. "I wanted to."

She looked at him and a little smile started. "Really?"

"Damn right," he said too gruffly. *Jesus, where's the chapter on this one?* He kissed her forehead. "Look, we have a ways to go yet, so watch it. I'm not sure I could be that noble twice."

They made a loop walking: boardwalk to pier, then across the street and back, past motels, shops closed now, older apartments. All the fun seemed to be on the opposite side, glitz and people milling around.

He felt a touch on his hand and then hers was in it.

"Okay if we hold hands?"

"You'd be the first client," he said, not letting go. Her hand felt cold. Small but strong.

"Thanks," she said.

"For what?"

"Two things. Warming my hand for one."

"Don't mention it. And the other?"

"For being different than I thought. You are, you know."

On the street, cars passed in waves generated by the traffic signals. Bass lines boomed out from rolling sound systems; guys in pickups eyed girls in VW convertibles and were eyed back; kids up late gawked and pointed at things. "You're welcome," he said. "I think."

"You know what I mean."

He squeezed her hand, feeling it tense suddenly.

"Ohmygod. What is that?" She timed a break, releasing his hand, angling her sprint for the lights and collision sounds.

He was about to follow when a horn and another wave of cars drove him back. Across the street, he could see her leaning to catch the action in the bumper car rink, turning once to wave and grin at him, Wil shaking his head at her wide-eyed wonder.

Two cherried-out Harley-Davidsons eased past him in the stop and go—newer versions of his old SuperGlide, twisted junk in his driveway now, a rusting reminder. He scoped them out, nodded at the riders who noticed him looking. One gave the throttle a tweak for his benefit, smiling with him at the roar it made. Then they were past, throbbing up the street, making him want another bike bad, either one of those just fine.

From that point, it got insane: honking from the far lane, traffic stacking up behind a white car; whirl of movement, a tall figure in a dark raincoat, the coat flapping as he strode around to raise the trunk lid. Heading for—

Shit!

Wil drew the .45, thumbed the hammer back and the safety off, and stepped into the street to a chorus of horns. Dancing with the cars then, the drivers disinclined to give ground until he flashed the weapon.

"Hardesty—" Her scream was diluted by noise. He saw her lifted up, one huge hand around her waist, the other over her mouth as her free arm flailed at the attacker.

Wil caught a movement of the big man's wrist, saw Holly go limp, and then she was in the trunk, the man lifting something out before slamming the lid shut. Raising the something to his shoulder.

Wil threw himself down as the red Explorer blocking him took several hits. Glass exploded into the street. He caught a glimpse of the driver bouncing off the headrest and down as the automatic transmission, freed of a foot on the brake, surged the Explorer into the car ahead.

More flashes came: asphalt ripped up, sparks flying off sheet metal. Screams sounded from the pickup behind the Explorer, a student-type and his date piling out and running. Wil saw the big man searching the pavement for him. He got up, angled ahead of the scramblers, hoping for a shot that didn't include the white car's trunk in the line of fire.

An arc tore into the pin-striped van in the next lane: three kids, two parents racing for safety, just ahead of the whoosh of flame erupting from the van's gas tank. Wil edged toward the front of the white car as the big man swung around suddenly at two security guards shouting and fumbling at holsters. Wil yelled a warning, but too late; the big man triggered a burst and the guards were jerked back like strung puppets. He saw the big man look back, wide-apart eyes sweeping the scene, not finding him, lowering the submachine gun, turning to open the car door.

Wil's angle still was no good, disabled vehicles blocking all lanes, even though the distance was better. Suddenly a thought, desperation and Interpol-inspired.

"Behhhhhhrrrr!"

The man stiffened, turned as though shot. Wil yelled the name again and there was a long burst as he flattened himself behind an abandoned sedan, ricochets sounding and more screams.

Door slam, tire squeal.

Wil rose up to fire, ID'd the white car as a late-model Olds, saw kids panicked alongside. He caught a flash of big head, big hands gripping the wheel, and knew there was no way. Cursing, lowering the .45, he tried instead for a crack at the license number, missing both his make on the plate and the two cops closing in from disparate angles.

"Freeze, fucker! Move and die!"

Wil froze, his eyes fixed on the white car accelerating down clear pavement, swinging left, and then gone.

As it turned out, holding fire was what got him off the hook. Even then it took until one the next afternoon to finish up— three civilians wounded, a security man dead, the other diagnosed as out of immediate danger after a touch-and-go night. Miraculous, considering the firepower and the crowded street.

He could still smell damp asphalt, feel his face flattened against it, the cop's gun pressed to his head. Then the cuffs and the sorting it out as he lay there, circulation leaving his hands, shouted commands and radio communications flying above him. Thinking about Ernst Jürgen Behr; trying to recall Mo's friend's hit on the big man, match it up with what they had going. Old Berlin bombings—*Holly Pfeiffer's house*. Fouled-up bank job, some terrorist group—*Holly abducted*. Professional yet showy—*standard terrorist procedure*.

The big question: why Holly—something she knew, entrusted by her father? Some new ARV thing, Max's DeBray connection the catalyst? Not the ransom money, certainly— they'd recovered that, all but Clayton's share. Pittance for this kind of effort.

Then the cops yanking him to his feet and into the patrol car, spilling him out minutes later into a too-small room with too many people asking questions. They'd been semisatisfied with his answers, righteous-pissed in general, particularly about him exposing their turf to this kind of L.A. bullshit. Now, fifteen-and-a-half hours later, they were letting him go.

He caught bright lights—a TV interview in progress—and was not envious of the interviewee. Outside, he caught a whiff of body begging for a shower, caught afternoon brightness in sleep-starved eyes, station-house coffee the only thing still holding them open.

One of the plainclothes gave him a lift to the motel. Key turning, his eyes adjusting to the curtained dimness—

"Tough night."

Wil froze, saw Albert Vega looking back at him from the lone chair. "Special Agent Vega," he said, letting the adrenaline rush subside, if not his annoyance. "What timing."

He went to the sink, filled and drank two glasses of water, his heart still pounding. From the mirror, someone's face looked back at him, pale with red-rimmed eyes.

"Manager let me in," Vega said. "I watched for a while behind the two-way. All things considered, I'd say you were lucky."

Wil said nothing.

"Guy knew how to block pursuit, didn't he?" Vega drank a Styrofoam cup empty. "Santa Cruz notified us when it came out who was involved. We're dovetailing it into the father, although I'm not sure quite how yet. You have any ideas?"

"No," Wil answered. "Mind if I shower?"

"I was going to suggest it. You want some coffee?"

"No, thanks, just sleep."

Wil stripped, stood a long time under the hot water, thinking how to play it with Vega, concluding that by ear was best. At least the drill distracted him from what lay beneath the surface, stuck there like shrapnel festering—his letting Behr separate them. Just long enough.

He heard her scream again.

Shut it off.

Play it by ear.

Vega had the TV on as Wil emerged, finger-combing damp hair. "You just missed a segment on it," he said. "They don't see much of that stuff here." He remoted the set off. "Tell me again why you're in this thing?"

"A promise I made the girl."

"Something more concrete would be nice."

Wil sat on the edge of the bed. "Holly Pfeiffer contacted me. She was convinced you guys murdered her father and were tying him in to Angela DeBray via the money in the lake." He shrugged. "What the hell, Vega, a weakness I have for women and children in distress—she being both, sort of."

"And?"

"We'd gotten to accepting her father's involvement. That was it."

"What makes me think it wasn't our talk that changed her mind?"

"We saw some people, her grandmother. Beyond that I'd rather not say."

"No surprise," he said. "You cowboys are right there when you need our help, aren't you? But lose the heat and it's all fuck you."

"Things are tough all around, Vega."

"You like that little business of yours?"

Wil leaned back and sighed. "Quit flexing. I'll tell you what you want to know. Enough anyway."

Vega no-expressioned him, then nodded. "How'd you know about this Behr character?"

"Interpol. Behr was the long shot of the week."

"I won't even ask how a private dick gets access to Interpol. How come no call when the bombing went down? Not very sociable."

Wil rubbed eyes that felt as if they were marinating in brine. "My client was unimpressed that it happened right after I'd been to see you—for that matter, I'd been there at all. Anyway, I figured you'd get wind of it through Delbaugh."

Vega smoothed his mustache. "And what were you going to do next?"

"I'd asked myself the same question."

"No games, please."

"No games. How about I ask you one?"

Vega raised his palm.

"How does Behr tie in to Max Pfeiffer?"

"No idea yet," Vega said. "This German terrorist cell he's linked to was a real pain in the ass late sixties, early seventies. Robbed banks, bombed police stations, kidnapped prominent people. Shot some to make their point."

"Which was?"

"Death to the fascist state and its lackeys, some such shit. They're all dead now or doing time."

"Behr wasn't a member?"

"Nope—hired muscle. The Germans verified it years ago by cross-interrogation. They were real surprised he turned up." Vega lifted the flap on the briefcase alongside him and handed Wil a sheet of paper. "This your guy?"

Wil took it and saw big head, dark pompadour, wide-apart eyes—a distant, hooded look he'd seen before in pictures of SS storm troopers. The photo was snapshot contrasty, the face much younger, but a make when you pictured him with a brush cut. What didn't come through was the man's sheer size.

He nodded. "Anything yet on the car?"

Vega shook no. "The plate was taped, according to a witness. We're checking rental registrations, but it won't matter. Krauts told us not to underestimate him."

Wil raised himself off the bed, slipped on a cotton sweater

and jeans. He walked to the window, looked down at the boardwalk where the coaster cars were climbing and dipping: moving fast, getting nowhere.

"What did you and the girl talk about?" Vega asked.

"Her father and mother mostly. Who they were, what they were like. Nothing startling."

"What about the grandmother?"

"Some tough cookie. Wasn't sure yet about having a dead son and a grown-up granddaughter."

"Why do you figure she *got* snatched?"

"Hell, I'm still trying to figure out why they tried to kill her."

Vega stood up and stretched. He reached down for the brief-case, rested it on the bed. "You can forget about it now. You're out."

Wil turned away from the window.

"I researched you, the stunts you pulled on that child murder case. Depending on how smart you are, this is either a request or an order to desist."

August Freiman, Captain, L.A. County Sheriff's—Epstein's boss. Bad blood, the man vowing to fuck him over, given the opportunity; old debts come due and payable.

"And if I don't?"

Vega smiled. "You will—it's good business, remember?" He picked up the case, started to leave. "No, that's a cheap shot. You will because you know this is what we're good at and what's best for the girl." He opened the door. "But in case I'm wrong, here's how it plays. Muck around, screw things up and get us ticked off, you'll wish you hadn't been born." Vega dropped two cards on the floor. "That's in case you lost the first one and something else comes to mind. The second is out there in the unmarked. Name's Doty, got a personality like distemper." With a soft click of the latch, he was gone.

From the window, Wil watched them drive away, thinking that was all he needed now, government muscle rolling him up. And then it all came back in spades: sheets of flame consuming the A-frame, tires squealing in the street, wild struggles and her going limp.

Thanks for being different than I expected.

Apart from why, it was as if two groups were at work, one wanting her dead, one intact. A thought came: Behr working for both sides, a double scam going—conceivable given Vega's assessment of Behr as a hired gun.

Maybe. Maybe not.

He dialed a San Francisco number and caught Rafael Canizares in—anxious, questioning, saying he'd seen it on the news, had tried to reach Wil but found no one able to say where he was. Wil told him the basics, his fears for the girl.

"How's Ma Pfeiffer taking it?" he added.

There was a pause. "Let's just say concerned, but unchanged."

"Not exactly the auto-defrost model, is she?"

"If you're asking me why she's the way she is, don't bother."

Wil shook his head to clear it of cobwebs. "An FBI guy just warned me off; they'll probably show up there soon. You might alert Rose to be thinking about ransom."

"I'll tell her."

"In the meantime, I'm going after some of Max's old haunts. Anybody still at Boalt who'd have known him?" He heard music playing, early Joni Mitchell.

"Never say die, huh?"

"You think I'd just let it go?"

"Sorry, didn't mean it that way. There's this criminal-civil guy, Sol Polluck," Canizares said. "He might still be there. Beyond that, I don't know, but I'll ask around."

Wil thanked him, then hung up, one last mission before he crashed. After a couple of tries, he caught someone in at the clerk's office, U.S. Supreme Court, who informed him that Lincoln Stillman had finished and was not scheduled for another appearance, no idea where he could be reached.

Idly, he clicked on the television set, looking for news coverage. Finding none, he killed the sound, marveling at how

fast things could turn to shit. *Don't you want me?* Wil pressed
fingers into his temples, stretched tight neck muscles, hoping
that the thought now twisting in his gut was right. That the
way to find Holly, even beyond duplicating efforts and thun-
dering off after the Feds—Vega right about that at least—was
first to find Max Pfeiffer. It was there, he'd felt it all along.
Something *not right*. His problem now: years to sift through
and uncover, settled layers on a lost city. *Time*.

Wil sighed deeply and closed his eyes, let it all spin down
through the floor. *You have no idea* . . . Without getting up to
close the curtains, he went dead asleep in the chair as a news-
break came on and scenes from the previous night flickered
silently across his face.

SEVENTEEN

Behr eased the stolen coupe—notable for the size of its trunk and nothing else—through the gate, up the drive, into the far garage bay. The fourth since dumping the rental, parts fodder within the hour, it had been lifted outside a beaner bar near Maricopa, Behr figuring the baked-on mud and the source his guarantee of CHP overlook. Getting out, he pressed a button that rolled the bay door shut.

He opened the trunk lid, crowbar-sprung to provide the girl with air, and looked into her face. There was dried blood from where he'd hit her a little hard, but otherwise she appeared all right. He locked on her eyes, signaled silence with an index finger, then lifted her onto the concrete, where she stood wobbling and holding her head. Behr stepped forward, but she brushed his arm away, straightened, and glared at him.

He brought water, which she drank greedily; afterward, he spoke into a phone on the wall. Feisty, he thought, looking at her now, more angry than fearful. Bad sign: Hard to think that what Monika had in mind was going to work unless she could break her down totally. And yet he'd seen her in action with the newspaper reporter: Six days of sensory deprivation and the man simply caved, begged to fight her enemies. He had, too—been a far better minister of information than the woman lost in the Tempelhof raid. They'd been lucky then—long enough for Monika to realize Germany was too hot and to strike her deal. He wondered if Stillman was back yet.

"Stay there," he told the girl.

Reaching into a metal cabinet, he found a clean polishing cloth and tore off a strip. As he approached with it, she flinched; with one hand he took her by the throat, lifting her off the floor until her eyes rolled. He let her down then, easy this time to put on the blindfold and plastic wrist restraints.

He'd just finished when Monika entered, the old man trailing behind. Lincoln Stillman flashed him a half-smile that Behr ignored. Stay neutral, he warned himself; instead he watched Monika.

Silently Monika circled the girl, scrutinizing the jeans, pink shirt with blood on it, the reddish hair, thrust-out jaw. She examined the wound, ran a finger along the girl's cheek with a look Behr had never seen before: fascination, curiosity, recognition—a mother reunited with the now-grown child she'd given up for adoption. Immediately Behr discounted the observation—Monika had never possessed a motherly instinct in her life, at least that he knew about.

Behr looked at Stillman and saw disapproval, wheels turning on black thoughts—jealousy perhaps in a youngster, not that he was any kind of expert. But Monika noticed, too, and whispered something to her husband, watched him flush then turn, go the way he'd come, his crutches leaving marks on the concrete. She gestured for Behr to join her out of earshot.

"There's precious little time," Monika told him. "After I finish here, take her upstairs." She regarded the girl cocking her head deftly for sounds. "It's been all over the news. You couldn't have picked a quieter spot?"

"One chance. I had to wait till they were apart, separate her from my line of fire. Knowing how you'd react, I wasn't about to get her killed."

She just looked at him.

"She's here, Monika. *Alive*. Take a look."

"She's also very hot. Already they're saying it's because of the grandmother's money."

"It will force caution on the police. And heat dies, you know that."

"On the phone, you said this man used your name. Could you be mistaken?"

"No," Behr said.

"And how is that possible?"

"I have no idea, none. But I'll take care of it."

"As before, Behr?"

He said nothing. Anyone else, he'd have broken her back.

Monika tapped fingers on her cheek. "Right now the risk is too great, thanks to you. In a while she'll be gone. Then, perhaps. Meantime, we have more pressing matters." She swept past him and toward the girl.

The Wild Turkey bottle smashed the mirror; glass and liquor hit the floor. Lincoln Stillman opened another fifth, was pouring a double when Henning entered.

"I heard, sir. Are you all right?"

"Hell, no," Stillman said. "If I'd had any balls, I'd have aimed for the Van Gogh, or whatever it is."

"Vermeer, sir. And it would not have pleased the Madam."

"General idea, Henning. You ever been castrated?"

"No, sir. And if I may say so, I am uncomfortable with this conversation."

Stillman sighed, downed a gulp of bourbon. "Right," he said. "Not your fault I can't handle my reins. Have somebody help you with the cleanup—and watch out for glass."

"I will, sir."

Feeling like an ass, he entered the study, slammed the door, turned to face green lawn. He was about to wing his drink at it when he stopped, counted slowly to ten, envying Behr his t'ai whatever-it-was. Behr was always calm—centered, as he put it. Cold logic and spite, that was the ticket. No letting your adversary know how you felt.

Pussy-whipped. Tang-tied.

The more he showed it, the more he sensed their ridicule: Monika, Behr, Henning—he was tempted to pull the door open, catch Henning smirking with one of the kitchen staff, and fire them both. Instead he took a long pull on the whiskey,

felt it start to fuzz things over—one more in a burgeoning
body of fuzzed-over slights that refused to retreat, standing
just beyond his focus like an army of battle-torn ghosts. Out
past something starved and twisted and hard at bay.

Love? Hell, who knew anymore?

Stillman drew the drapes and eased down at his desk, a
Louis the Fuckteenth or some such. He had no illusions about
his weaknesses, but this had to stop. He was turning into men
he knew: shrew-gnawed souls who sat passively, clutching
their drinks like life preservers to keep from drowning in
bullshit—no, cowshit.

Yet even without Behr, Monika was nobody to cross. She'd
not told him half of what she'd done, but Behr had let things
slip, and he'd done some reading. Then there was this obses-
sion of hers: *Jesus*, never mind the risk she was exposing *him*
to by bringing the girl here.

He refilled his drink, hoisted sandaled feet up on the Louis.
The way Monika had looked at her—made him want to gag.
She's mine, Lincoln. Lay a hand on her and I'll kill you myself.
And what was Monika without him? Another gulp, the heat
descending, spreading. Enough! He knew what to do—wait
for the chance to take her down a notch, then *do* it. Make her
respect him again. Want him.

All he needed were the stones.

Behr, of course, was a problem, but Behr would go with
the power, and right now the big man thought Monika had it.
He sipped the whiskey, savoring its fire and the reassuring
thought that Lincoln Stillman had made a career out of being
underestimated.

Monika scissored through the plastic restraint and watched the
girl rub feeling back into her hands. "I say this once," she
said. "If you remove the blindfold, you will die. If you dis-
obey or attempt escape, you will die. For now you'll listen. Is
that clear?"

When the girl had nodded, Monika passed Behr the scissors,
leaned forward in the hard chair across from hers. "Whatever

you may be thinking, this is not it. You've not been kid-napped—there will be no ransom and no rescue. Instead you've been given a new life. The sooner you grasp this, the faster true freedom will come. Do you understand me?''

There was a shaking of head, then a grimace, pain from her wound. *Scheiss*—she'd warned Behr about being too rough.

''Who are you?''

"Friends. Your blindfold is a blessing. It allows you to not be tricked by what you see. Listen now to another voice. Hear the words and the thoughts as though your life depends on them.''

Monika reached down, levered on the cassette recorder. The voice was thin and distorted by the bullhorn through which it was filtered, overpowered here by cheering, there by shouts. It was a man's voice:

You want answers? Listen to your heart. It knows the killing is wrong, that this government is wrong. *(Cheering)* This president. *(Wild cheering; the speaker pausing for it)*

You and I will be heard. And if not, we must take control before it's too late for your children and mine. We must free this university—and we will! *(Crowd roar)*

Free Berkeley—and we will! *(Sound building)*

Free America. *(Crescendo)* And we will!

The old ways favor those who cling to power and privilege, terrified of their passing. But pass they shall, replaced by equality and brotherhood. *(Bullhorn squeal and shouting, the voice louder now)*

You want honest-to-God change? *(''Yesss . . .'' roll-ing, rising)* Then stand up for what you believe.

You want peace, FIGHT for it.

You want better, then GET better.

The dream is yours, TAKE it. *(The crowd chanting a name, hard to decipher)* WHAT ARE YOU WAITING FOR?

Monika pressed OFF. Holly sat rigid, her hands like clenched bone; wet streaks tracked down from under the blindfold. Monika motioned to Behr, who stepped forward, bound her wrists again. The girl did not resist.

"You will now be left alone to think, to contemplate the words. Tomorrow we'll play the voice again, then talk about what was said, what could be. Do you understand?"

There was a faint nod.

"Need I ask you whose voice it is?"

Nearly inaudible: *"Daddy,"* she said before the sobs hit.

EIGHTEEN

Wil wheeled a hard left and parked. After walking several blocks, he wondered what year it was, Telegraph Avenue a living time warp.

On both sides, plywood was nailed up over Berkeley store-fronts, the result of some new confrontation spilling out of People's Park, cops and protesters still at it twenty-two years later. Slogans were spray-painted on the plywood: FREE SPEECH and FIGHT POLICE BRUTALITY. Boom boxes competed with coffeehouse riffs and street musicians, car horns, strident talk. Vendors clogged the sidewalks, tie-dyed shirts and peace jewelry back with a vengeance.

He wondered what Max Pfeiffer would think.

Entering the University of California, he asked an older student for directions to Boalt Hall, having to shout over the conga rhythms throbbing up from lower Sproul Plaza. "Group's been here forever," the man said, voice raised. "One drops from brain damage, another jumps right in. Boalt's up the street a couple blocks, with the inscription on it you can't understand. Lawyers, right?"

Wil nodded thanks and swung a loop through the campus, across a wooded creek to a blocky building, shallow-U'd around a long courtyard. He checked the directory, found Sol Polluck's office on the third floor. Two raps and "Come in" had him inside a cramped space with two old desks, one of which fronted a thin balding man, one hand over the mouth-piece of a Princess phone.

"Sit . . ." The man gestured toward an armless chair. "Be just a sec."

Sixties, Wil guessed, not feeling much younger. He took in framed diplomas, stacks of blue books, Polluck's nameplate, three desktop snapshots: homely kids with braces. Angled away from Wil, Sol Polluck was saying something about plea bargains and delays. He finished abruptly and hung up.

"You here for the blue books?"

Wil passed him his card. "Rafael Canizares mentioned you might be able to help me."

Polluck looked blank. "Canizares—somebody I'm supposed to know?"

"Boalt graduate," Wil said. "Class of sixty-nine. He has a firm in the city, said you might know Max Pfeiffer. I'm looking into Max's death."

"Max Pfeiffer I know. Wasn't that his daughter somebody grabbed the other day?"

Wil nodded.

"Some can of worms."

"Rafael said you had Max in a class once."

Sol Polluck slid open a window behind him. "That's right. Berkeley was a trip then, everybody pissed at everybody over some flaming issue. Hell, these days, everybody's just pissed. Max was hell on wheels—gone a lot, but consistently in the top percentiles. Dynamite in the mock trials."

Wil shifted on the hard chair. "Did you know him outside of class?"

A shrug. "Who didn't know him—not personally, though. The guy was something of a loner."

"He have any friends that you knew of?"

Sol Polluck considered. "Nobody I'd remember. If you like, I'll ask the old farts today at lunch." He wrote a number down. "Call around two-ish. No guarantees, though."

"Appreciate it," Wil said.

Polluck rose with him. "Terrible business, that stuff with

the DeBray girl," he said. "Living with that, I'm surprised Max didn't jump sooner."

"Thanks for the time," Wil said. "You familiar with a lawyer named Lincoln Stillman?"

"That's like asking if I ever heard of Clarence Darrow. Now you mention it, I think Max used to work for Stillman."

"Anything about that?"

"Nothing beyond the fact. Sorry."

Back on the street, Wil checked his watch: time enough for what he had in mind. He asked directions to the public library, then reparked the car on a side street. Here the homes were handsomely brownshingle and Victorian, picture windows fronting formal rooms with bird's nest ferns. Elm trees reached for each other across the pavement; college students lugged backpacks and books, chattering to each other or looking intent. He felt an ache for simpler places, simpler times—things not his anymore.

Working his way toward Shattuck, he stopped for a sandwich and a scan of the *Tribune*. So far the FBI had located three cars stolen and ditched—all figured as Behr's—plus a possible match, Behr as the tall shooter in a recent L.A. bank job. Blood in the white Tahoe rental but in none of the others led them to venture that Holly Pfeiffer's wound was nonfatal. The trail ended near Maricopa.

Damn . . .

Just past noon he entered an umber-colored deco building, asked the library archivist for old *Berkeley Gazette* microfilms and a viewing machine. Settling into April 1967, when the indexes first flagged Cleon Lamar Chapman/Field Marshal Z, Wil tracked him toward the fires of May 17, 1974.

EAST BAY MAN SOUGHT IN AREA HOLDUPS

COPS SUBDUE SUSPECT IN MOTHER'S HOME

HUNG JURY: ACQUITTAL FOR CHAPMAN

Released when the witness refused to testify. Wil made notes, scrolled into October '68, found Chapman and two others, Bobby Eugene Hightower and Freeman Fredrick Lyles:

ONE DEAD IN WILD STORE SHOOT-OUT

Two-time losers Hightower and Lyles, along with Chapman, hitting an electronics store: the owner waiting, shotgun ready—alerted by Lyles's boast to a friend. Hightower catching a load of double-aught buck full on; Chapman and Lyles returning the owner's fire, wounding him; surrendering then to three off-duty cops on their way home from a bowling tournament.

STILLMAN TO HANDLE

CHAPMAN/LYLES DEFENSE

CIVIL RIGHTS VIOLATION,

LAWYER CONTENDS

D.A. first-timers prosecuted and ran into a Stillman buzz saw:

CHAPMAN/LYLES CLEARED—S'S BIG WIN

Sure enough, the store owner was brought up on civil rights charges, Hightower's death bringing an additional manslaughter rap. Chapman and Lyles pulled ten months apiece: B&E/parole violation.

Next came the Mamba Negra. Wil scrolled through a feature on the Black Panther Party spin-off group's functionaries: Chapman joining the Mambas in '69, working his way up to assistant minister of finance, then minister of defense and East Bay chapter president. Quitting to found the Army of Revolutionary Vigilance in '72, he renounced the Mamba Negra Party as a weak-sister verbal revolutionary.

Three months later:

ARV SUSPECTED IN BANK HEIST
MORE BANKS—Z'S WAR ON AMERICA

Chapman's words to a radical journalist: "You will call me Field Marshal Z exclusively" and "Armageddon is here." So much crap until:

DEBRAY GIRL IS OURS—
FIELD MARSHAL Z

The end of the beginning. Hoping for something new, Wil went through the rest; nothing surfaced and he rewound the spools. Checking his notes, he found the Oakland white pages and scanned for the mother—no Arnella Chapman listed, though he did find an A. Chapman, street and number both different than in the article. His chances: slim unless she'd had Cleon in her teens. From the pictures, she'd be at least seventy by now.

He checked the time. Too early yet to call Polluck.

At one of the bookstores on Telegraph, he bought a street map, then walked to the rental car. Twenty minutes later he was in an older part of Oakland, craning at addresses, cursing whoever had numbered them, parking finally near a squat bungalow alongside a storefront-conversion church. Iron bars secured the bungalow's windows; Cyclone fencing ringed the yard. Wil raised the latch, swung the gate inward, and mounted the porch, worn planks creaking under his weight. His knock was answered by a large black woman in a nurse's uniform.

"Arnella Chapman?" he asked. Too young to be her.

"Who wants her?"

Wil gave her his card.

"Lurene?" asked another voice, thin and screechy.

The big woman looked over her shoulder. "Don't you fret now, hon. Just soak your feet like I showed you." Turning back to Wil: "She's old, got health problems. What you want?"

"To ask her some questions. About her son."

The screechy voice: "What son? Mine all dead."

Lurene said, "You a reporter? Had quite enough of those, thank you."

Wil realized she couldn't read the card, so he told her who he was, her look saying maybe that was worse.

"Let him in," came the voice. "Maybe Jesus sent him."

Lurene pulled back the door, let him into a yellowish room with religious art everywhere: Jesus at the well, Jesus in the temple, Jesus praying under an olive tree. The air was hot and humid and smelled of menthol wafting from a vaporizer on a table marked with cigarette burns and water rings.

She sat in a dingy recliner raised to upright. Near eighty, or looked it, Wil thought, more gray than black, her fingers permanently stained by nicotine, puffed feet in a small tub that hummed and vibrated. She had on a blue terry robe, a scarf over matted white hair. She still looked cold.

"Look at me," she said. "Gettin' it from both ends. I'm not complaining, mind. Where'd I be without Lurene and the gospel next door? *Did* Jesus send you?"

Wil glanced at Lurene, then back at Arnella Chapman. "Nice to think so. Would you mind some questions?"

Lurene frowned. "Just a few, Arnella. You know how tired you get."

The old woman leaned toward the vaporizor and gulped in steam. "Sit on that stool there while Lurene gets my tea, praise the Lord."

Lurene walked out, shaking her head.

Arnella Chapman regarded him. "With them draggin' up that plane and all on TV, I bet you're here about my boy got burned up."

"Yes, ma'am."

"Lamar's what I always called him, Cleon was the father.

Name Lamar come from my side.'' She made a rumbling noise in her throat.

"God sure gimme my share—emphysema, gout, high blood pressure—not to mention my husbands and children. Tell me your name again, Satan's put stuff in my ears.''

"It's Wil, Mrs. Chapman. And I'm sorry about your son.''

"Not many were. Lamar needed a strong hand to show him the Lord's ways—heaven knows he never listened to me. Course, I don't stand much on what I had to say in them days, me ridin' the high horse and all. Closest Lamar ever came was that lawyer, God's gift to the race. When *he* talked, Lamar listened.'' She coughed into a handkerchief and checked the spot. "Course, by then it was too late.''

"You mean Lincoln Stillman?''

"Sat right up to that table like this was the Ritz, poor soul, that curse in his legs. Was him got Lamar out on bail, told him how to act at the trial. All the good it did.'' She sighed. "God's will be truly hard to fathom.''

Lurene returned, set a cup and saucer down in front of Arnella Chapman, asked her if the tea was hot enough; Arnella dipped a knuckle in it and nodded. "You want some?''

"No, thanks.'' He watched Lurene retreat to the kitchen. "How did Lincoln Stillman come to represent your son, Mrs. Chapman?''

She took tea, set her cup down with a rattle. "He just showed up. Freeing the innocent's what he does, he says, generous in Lamar's case. From that point on, it was kind of like he seen some'n in Lamar.''

"He stayed in touch after the trial?''

"Praise Jesus. Helped me to get free of the heroin and Lamar to get in with that Mamba group. Never saw much in them, the stuff they wore.''

Wil recalled pictures: camouflage pants and sunglasses, Stillman representing the group in a number of cases, public record. "What about after?''

Arnella Chapman looked toward the kitchen. "He still come around—even after that Z craziness. Used to leave messages for me to give Lamar, sometimes with the law parked right outside." Her eyes locked in a stare.

"After that bad thing with the baby though, the messages stopped, even the ones for me. Can't blame him, I s'pose."

"Do you recall any of the messages?"

The eyes focused, took him in. "Messages is private."

Wil leaned forward on the stool. "Mrs. Chapman, a few days ago a young woman was kidnapped—knocked unconscious and dumped into the trunk of a car, then driven off to God knows what. The people who have her may kill her, they tried once already. What you know about the things Lamar did, long ago as that was, might help me find her."

She stared at him.

"This girl never hurt anyone in her life."

"Maybe I don't remember too good."

"It's better than nothing."

Arnella Chapman called for Lurene; this time the nurse appeared with an old teapot. "Just hot water," she said. "You know what the doctor said's well as I do." She left, shaking her head again.

Arnella took some and made a face. "It was right when the baby was taken from those rich people. A man died, worked for 'em."

Wil nodded. "Thomas Littlefield. The kidnappers shot him."

"Mr. Stillman made me say the messages back. This one I remember 'cause I knew Tommy."

Wil felt a prickle start in his scalp. "You knew Littlefield?"

Her nod became a cough, building until Lurene came and put a shawl around her. Gradually the cough subsided and Lurene withdrew, giving Wil a warning look.

"My daughter, Marguerite—she died after that from the cocaine, curse its name forever. She was seeing Tommy. That was the message, not to say we knew Tommy in case Lamar made it to court."

"Mr. Stillman say why?"

"Never said nothin'. Wasn't till that day I learned Tommy had a wife and children. Figured it was that."

Lurene loomed at the doorway, drew a finger slowly across her throat. Wil nodded and stood.

"Mrs. Chapman, did Lamar ever mention a man named Max Pfeiffer?"

"Hard sayin'," she said. "Long time ago and mosta his friends not worth remem—" Her words dissolved in coughing.

"You, out," Lurene said. "I mean now."

NINETEEN

Stopping for gas, Wil reached Sol Polluck from an open pay phone. As he spoke he held one ear against the rush of traffic.

"Where are you?" asked the lawyer. "The freeway?"

"Close. Any luck?"

"Could be. A name came up, somebody this other prof thought was tight with Pfeiffer. Hang on a second."

Wil opened his notebook. Behind him a horn blared, then Polluck was back on the line.

"Okay, the name is Shirmir. S-h-i-r-m-i-r, Henry—my guy remembered him and Max from Torts. Radical type, good student, in Max's shadow academically, but capable. Phil said he thought the two of them planned to open a practice."

Wil finished writing. "Anything else?"

"Shirmir bounced around Berkeley, then left, all disillusioned. Phil remembered him because he came around the other day, looking for work. He hired him."

"Phil say where he'd been?"

"No, just that he seemed gun-shy—not untypical of sixties burnouts. Guy's living at one-twenty-seven E, Peoples Way. Real Berkeley name for you. I think that's the flatlands, but you'd better check a map."

Wil flipped back a page the wind had advanced and wrote it down. "Did he say what he looked like?"

"Medium height, hair in a ponytail. Somewhat wounded looking."

"You ever consider this line of work?"

Polluck chuckled. "How goes it?"

"Inch by inch," Wil said, "the job in a nutshell. Thanks for the help."

Hanging up, he took stock: rush-hour traffic forming, five o'clock in another ten, a possibility that Shirmir might be home. From the gas station, he drove north through business districts and tired minimalls, okay neighborhoods and those just hanging on. Pulling over to recheck the map, he noticed a stop sign. Below STOP, someone had stenciled in RACISM. A couple of blocks later, one said WAR; at the next corner, DOING THAT. Wil figured he had to be close and was, Peoples Way a seedy, comma-shaped appendage ending in a cul-de-sac, 127E the end unit in a grouping of older cottages. A garage sat next to it. Faded laundry hung limp on a next-door line, paper-doll clothes against the overcast. Somewhere, someone was frying something.

One-twenty-seven E's front door had a square of windows similar to the garage's: Wil knocked, peeked in at bare walls, brick hearth, unlit floor lamp, two armchairs, a bicycle. Light spilled from a door cracked open across the living room. He waited. The door was pulled wider and a man passed through, shut it behind him, then glanced out through the square of windows. He opened the front door.

Five-ten maybe; behind thick glasses, guarded eyes lurked in a face that had seen hard use. His graying hair was long and ponied in back. From there down it was gray sweatshirt, worn Levi's, running shoes.

"Yeah?"

"Name's Hardesty. I'm looking for Henry Shirmir—Max Pfeiffer's friend."

"Any particular reason?"

Wil told him: Max, Holly, Tahoe, Santa Cruz. "Ask you a few questions?"

Curiosity and resignation in equal parts. "Yeah, I guess. Half expected somebody to show up, what with all the stuff about Max. Just making some java, if you want some."

"That'd be great. Thanks."

Wil leaned against the kitchen door frame as Shirmir spooned instant coffee into heavy mugs, adding hot water from a dark-stained kettle. "I'd offer to spike it, but I'm AA these days," he said, stirring them in turn. He rinsed the spoon, chucked it into a drying rack. "How'd you find me?"

Back in the living room, Wil told him.

Shirmir blew on his coffee. "Phil Ackerman's good people. Not easy to find a job here after you've been blacklisted. Hell, at one time it was a badge of honor."

"He told Sol Polluck you and Max went back a ways. Mind talking about it?"

"If there's a point."

"Holly's the point."

Henry Shirmir sipped. "Christ, what is she now—nineteen, twenty?" He spread a palm. "I used to hold her like this in one hand. She still have red hair?"

Wil said yes and waited; Shirmir shook his head.

"Max dead—shit, who'd believe it? Did Phil mention we were going to start a practice?" He drifted, came back. "He was real different when he got back from Nam, but then so was I, active in Free Speech and all that. We were going to change the world, save it. What do you think so far?"

"Maybe you quit too soon."

"Thanks, but when the deck's stacked, the wise man folds. Even before Paulette died, we were starting to see it, but that took the heart right out of us. I still carry her picture in my wallet."

"You think like Max did—the FBI killed her?"

He shrugged. "Maybe. Who cares anymore? Fucking tilting at windmills."

"You ever see any proof, Henry?"

Shirmir downed a slug of coffee. "No," he said. "But Max did."

From a built-in box beside the hearth, Henry Shirmir gathered two-by-four pieces and kindling that Wil pegged as construction scraps. He arranged them with paper on the grate, fired them with a match. For a minute they watched the wood crackle and flare.

"Heat and light," Shirmir said. "No way for us to screw *them* up. Not that we wouldn't if we could." He stared at the flames. "Least Max took himself out, some consolation in that. Sometimes I wish I had the guts."

"You said Max had proof the FBI killed Paulette."

A nod. "So he told me, some FBI memo he saw. Made sense if you were them: take out two birds, Paulette by bomb, Max with grief. The Feds knew how out of control things were getting—like a grass fire they couldn't stamp out."

"You remember how Max came by this memo?"

Shirmir clunked down his mug. "You know Lincoln Stillman?"

"I know who he is." Stillman again, the name reminding him to check messages, just in case—something he hadn't done yet today.

"SOB represented us a few years earlier at the Berkeley Eleven trial."

"Us?"

"I was one of them—it's where I met the gentleman."

The trial: multiple defendants charged in the U of Cal cop's death, no convictions—a thought occurred with his surprise and Wil went with it. "Tell me if I'm out of line, but now that it's history, I'm curious," he said. "You happen to see who beat that cop?"

Shirmir's face came alive suddenly. "What do you think?"

"I think you were there."

He smiled. "Put it this way. The guy was going after Max, broke his arm, for Christ sake. What would you have done?"

Wil shrugged. *Stand up for it, maybe?*

Shirmir's look became inward, as though still weighing it. "Hey, man, those days it was all for one, one for all. Not like today, everybody out to fuck you over."

Wil gave it a moment. "You were talking about the memo."

Henry Shirmir blinked. "Right. Max said Stillman acquired it through another case he was working on. Thing nailed the Feds but good."

"Yet they never took it public."

"They couldn't—never stand up in court, Stillman said, because of how it was acquired. Besides, it'd compromise his other case. Max was convinced, anyway, the state of mind he was in."

"What about you?"

"Never thought much of old Linc myself. Conniving son of a bitch, and I hated the way he used to ogle Paulette. But the memo seemed to bring Max out of it, galvanize him. Right after, he went to work for Stillman."

"The end of Shirmir and Pfeiffer."

Henry Shirmir's face set hard; his eyes held the fire. "Wasn't to be, I guess. Still, you have to wonder if Max coming to work for him wasn't what he had in mind all along."

"What's your opinion?"

"No love for the FBI, no love for Stillman. I don't worry about it anymore."

Wil waited while Shirmir added more wood to the fire. "You see the stories about Max's link to the ARV?"

Shirmir leaned back in the worn armchair and nodded. "Max knew Stillman was a sore spot, so he and I kept some distance after Paulette. Whenever I'd see him he was always, '*the fucking FBI*.' Not that he didn't have his reasons. I'd sympathize, ask what I could do. Said he was working on it."

"Meaning what—ARV?"

"Possibly. I had this feeling he was helping train them, giving shit back to the assholes. Max's sense of justice worked like that." Shirmir stretched his legs at the fire. "He was pretty intense there for a while. Late seventy-three he began to mellow out. Never said it in so many words because he knew how I felt about Paulette, but I think he got involved with someone."

"You ever find out who?"

"Didn't want to. Besides, I don't think it lasted. The following spring, he began to tighten up again—Holly had him worried. I'd baby-sit and notice how her ears still bothered her. Max had her to a doc and in for tests a couple times."

The burning wood collapsed on itself, sending up a chuff of sparks. Despite the fading light, Shirmir made no move to turn on the lamp.

Wil said, "This doctor . . ."

"Joel Beck, Max knew him from Nam. Worked at Good Shepherd, King, one of those. God-awful places, hospitals—I should know."

Wil drained the last of his coffee, cold now, like the room. "Ackerman implied you'd had a hard time."

"Yeah, well, the sixties took down a lot of us Don Quixotes. See, they gave us this anthem—no more war, equality under the law, freedom. Then you realize you're singing to yourself, there's nobody behind you on the barricade, it's just you and the drugs. After Max, I floated out of here, joined a commune up in Oregon—woke up one day and figured out I'd lost ten years. Five more in and out of hospitals, I remembered why I'd left. As for the sixties, all they did was make the ruling class stronger, like the antibodies after a vaccination." He seemed to notice the fire. "Sorry, last of the wood."

"You mentioned Max's sense of justice. Could he have killed Angela DeBray?"

"No. *Fuck no.*"

"I saw the note, Henry, Max's fingerprints."

Shirmir sat forward, hands twisting as though a drama only he could see was looping inside his head. "I knew him, goddamnit."

"Just before Max split, what was he like?"

Shirmir refocused. "Jumpy as a cat. Wouldn't answer his phone. Next thing, he was gone without a word, him and Holly, except for this note—*Fuck you all* or some such. I gave it a Viking funeral in the bay."

The note again . . . Another thought flashed: "Max lived near here, didn't he?"

Shirmir grinned wryly. "You *don't* know, do you?" he said. "First place I looked up when I got back. Half expected Max to answer when I knocked, instead of some chick ready to bail out. The landlord let me have it because even after all this time he remembered me and Max and Paulette. Sometimes I wake up and think they're standing there watching me." He shook his head.

Wil wondered if Shirmir was serious, decided he was. For a moment he looked around, picturing Holly here, wondering what nicks on the doors were hers, which scars on the furniture; the fires that drove Max and Paulette; them planning, making love; Max in the final days, distraught. He saw the coroner's picture of Max, Holly naked again, Lisa's smile, and felt like smashing his watch.

Instead he drew out a card. By firelight he wrote down Rafael Canizares's number, told Shirmir that Canizares would pass on messages.

"*Rafael* Canizares?"

Wil nodded. "He referred me to Polluck."

"Funny Rafe didn't mention me, he must have forgotten. I can see why, me just back and all."

"Canizares knew you were here?"

"Hell yeah," Shirmir said. "Couple weeks ago, I talked his ear off outside Ackerman's office. We agreed there weren't many of us left." He paused. "How about another coffee? Got some good stuff in the fridge."

"I'll take a rain check, thanks."

"It's no trouble. Wouldn't take a minute."

Wil eased out of the chair. "Sorry."

"Way it goes these days."

"Don't get up," he said, shaking hands. He retrieved the shetland from the back of his chair, started for the door and opened it, stopping there to say goodbye to Henry Shirmir staring into the dying fire. There was no response. Just a faraway shine in Henry Shirmir's eyes.

•   •   •

Mist swirling, enough to bloom neon signs and wet the streets; fragrance of damp Berkeley neighborhood and browning garlic. Wil left the Thai place, walked to his car, and headed for the Bay Bridge. Driving the Eastshore Freeway, he could make out the arc of lights disappearing west, then he was half-masting the window, handing a buck to the woman at the kiosk, accelerating past her to the sound of wipers set on pulse.

He left the window down. Whiffs of bay reached him, chewable almost—kelp and salt flat, then city air steeped with the smell of coffee roasting.

Where are you, Holly? Buy me time.

Tires hissed on the upper-deck pavement; spray from cars around him fogged the windshield, then vanished, swept away. Ahead and to the right, San Francisco reminded him of a reclining Mae West, old and spangled, photographed kindly through gauze. Come-hither lights, hills thrusting up—a town that still had it, whatever it was. Something to keep the travel writers panting.

Who are you, Max? Help me find her.

Having tried Canizares's office number from the restaurant, getting no answer, Wil exited the freeway and took Market Street toward Twin Peaks—9:37 as he parked up the street from the house with the balcony.

He knocked, tried again, looked in and saw a single lamp lit, familiar furniture, no movement. Beside an open newspaper, a bowl and spoon rested on the table by the couch. Wil raised his collar, settled in on the porch, forced himself to think about what he had so far.

Cleon Chapman/Field Marshal Z plugged into the DeBray household seventeen years ago via Tommy Littlefield, possible coconspirator via Z's sister Marguerite. Why then was Littlefield killed during the raid—a question mark.

More concrete: Chapman/Z's ties to Lincoln Stillman—well beyond Stillman's defense of Chapman/Lyles for the electronics store shooting in '68. Stillman helped establish Cleon in the Mambas, then supported his involvement with the ARV, even to mouthpiecing ARV motives. Not that Stillman didn't do similar things for radical groups from Black Panthers to Weathermen, even representing several of them. No surprise there.

But why his interest to begin with? Chapman was a street hood, thief, and bank robber—kidnapper too, although even Stillman had shied from Angela DeBray if Arnella Chapman was right, disavowing it despite his role as ARV legal counsel. So why Cleon? Wil made a mental note: additional research on Lincoln Stillman.

Then there was Max: saint, crusader, fallen angel, enigma—wisp-difficult to get a handle on. Was he Holly's Max, Rose Pfeiffer's Max, or Henry Shirmir's—Max of the new woman friend and the early link to Chapman/Z via Stillman? Canizares's Max, perhaps, though his not mentioning Shirmir still stuck to Wil's thoughts like a burr.

Headlights shone and the garage door opened; Rafael Canizares waved from the Mercedes, parked it, came up the steps. "Hey there—I screw up or you not phone?"

Wil shook the offered hand. "Last-minute decision," he said. "I missed you at the office, decided to try here."

"Anything new on Holly?" Canizares unlocked the front door and preceded Wil inside.

"Just what made the papers. Today was Max day for me." He accepted a can of Vernor's from the lawyer, who poured himself a bourbon.

"Sol Polluck get you anywhere?"

"Nope. But then I think you knew that." Wil gulped ginger ale and waited.

"Not sure I follow," Canizares said. "Didn't he talk to you?"

"Uh-huh—verified he'd had Max in a class, knew him by reputation, all that. But he didn't stop where you figured he would, he put the word out among some associates. One recommended I talk with a close friend of Max's, Henry Shirmir. Lucky thing, that." He touched the rim of the can to his teeth. "You knew about Shirmir, counselor. Why the holdout?"

Canizares made a gesture of dismissal with his free hand.

"Henry's kind of a sad case. I didn't want to burden you with him."

Wil said nothing, just looked at him.

Canizares sighed, stood, and walked to the window. "All right," he said. "You tell me, I tell you."

Nothing like legwork, Wil thought. He went through Shirmir's comments as Canizares faced the city.

"And that proves that Max may have known this Z character?"

"*May* have?" Wil said.

"You fishing or speculating?"

"Fingerprints, counselor. Max's handwriting on the note."

"Evidence without motives, Hardesty. Tangential association with the money and its disposition, putting Max Pfeiffer neither in bed with a sociopath nor in on the worst of murders."

Wil fired the ginger ale can at the kitchen sink, the noise spinning Canizares around to face him. "What the hell is it with Max Pfeiffer? Even if I bought in, which I don't, I'm convinced Holly's gone, maybe dead, because of this guy's 'tangential associations.' Now, do you open up or do I call the Feds?" Hoping the bluff worked.

Canizares's look was the response he wanted; the lawyer walked to the bottle, refilled his glass. "He was my friend, you understand that? I owe him. It stops here or gets used only if absolutely necessary—your word."

"This Rose Pfeiffer's money talking?"

"*Fuck you*, her paying me doesn't mean she owns me. What's more, I never took a penny from Max."

"Sorry, it's been a long day. And you have my word."

Canizares drifted back to the window. "From here it all looks so clean, doesn't it?" He sighed, squared his shoulders. "Max knew Cleon Chapman through the Mamba Negras. He did pro-bono work for the group, even before he went to work for Stillman. Minor stuff."

"This was?"

"Seventy, seventy-one, somewhere in there. Wasn't that he

liked Cleon—hell, nobody did. But Max gave him the benefit: druggy mother, no father, raised in the streets. Stillman, of course, he knew through Berkeley Eleven.'' He paused.

''After Paulette died, it began to unravel for Max—you know that from Shirmir. He and I were concerned he could even take care of Holly. For six months or so, he was extremely vulnerable.''

''To what?'' Wil asked.

Canizares sipped his drink. ''His rage. Revenge.''

''The memo Stillman showed him.''

At the window, a nod.

''You think it was real?''

The lawyer shrugged.

''What reason would Stillman have to make it up?''

''None that I know of, unless he was duped,'' he said. ''At any rate, it made Max crazy to get back at the FBI.''

''Which explains what?'' Wil asked.

''Shirmir's theory. Max began teaching Chapman's people military tactics, anything he could do to give the FBI problems. I'd argue with him, but . . .''

''What?''

''*Damn*. Max helped with the first couple of bank jobs, actually went along on one.''

''And you knew about this?''

Canizares hesitated. ''I told you I owed him. Max kept insisting it was the new American revolution—fix the inequities, redistribute power, rebuild Vietnam after the war. Atone is how he put it.''

The ginger ale tasted flat and tinny now, and Wil put it aside. ''Henry Shirmir said something about him mellowing later on—a woman, he thought.''

Canizares nodded. ''There was someone, yes. Look, there's a letter in my office, Max's own words.''

''The note?''

''No. This is something he wanted opened in case anybody got to him. The way things have gone, maybe it'll help his girl.'' He looked back at Wil, then out the window again.

"How long have you had it?"

"I don't know—since the beginning."

"And you didn't wonder what was in it? Even before she was taken?"

A snort. "Wondered yes, opened no. The FBI said he killed *himself*, remember?" Canizares looked at his watch. "That's it for me. You cutting out or bunking in?"

TWENTY

Seven-fifteen showed no signs of the fog lifting, just socked-in mist. Rafael Canizares emerged from the bakery carrying a white bag and a cardboard holder with covered foam cups. He got in the Mercedes, handed Wil the stuff, then eased away from the curb.

They bucked the downtown traffic in silence, sipping coffee and eating warm croissants, then they were parking, taking the elevator, stopping at mahogany double doors, CANIZARES AND LAUGHTON, ATTORNEYS AT LAW across them in burnished metal letters.

They were the first ones in the office.

Still holding his cup, Canizares made for the window. He looked down at the street, up at the TransAmerica pyramid, cater-corner at the bridges as cable-car rumbles and dings floated upward. Already they'd checked the *Chronicle* for news of Holly and seen nothing new.

"You want to get to it?" Wil said. Last night's finding no message again from Stillman had left him in a foul mood.

"What the hell." Canizares stepped over to a framed diploma and flipped it back. Opening the wall safe, he withdrew a sealed envelope.

"Be my guest," he said.

Wil examined it, saw nothing unusual, and slit the envelope with a desk knife, then withdrew and unfolded the eight-and-a-half-by-eleven bond inside. Clearly Max's writing—the same hasty scrawl he'd seen on the money note.

May 16, 1974
Rafael—She's at 1871 Cedarcreek, Lakebridge (Tahoe).
Whatever she needs, whatever it costs.
Just keep RLP out of it.
I'm trusting you,
Max

Wil reread, then dropped it on the desk. " 'In case anybody got to him.' You think he expected it?''

Canizares rubbed his forehead. "Paranoid as he was then? Why not?''

"And all that time you never knew where he was.''

"You want me to say it again? No—N-O. That clear enough?''

"What about the woman he was seeing?''

The lawyer looked toward the window, fixed his eyes on the view. "I saw them once—obviously they were fond of each other. Wasn't until afterward that I recognized her. It was the woman they shot at the airport, the one in prison now.''

"Deborah Ann Werneke.''

"That's right.''

Wil tossed his empty cup in the trash. "I see. You still thinking 'tangential association,' counselor?''

Canizares knew no doctor named Joel Beck who'd served with Max Pfeiffer in Vietnam and who might have cared for Holly at one time. From another office, Wil tried the East Bay directories, turned up some Becks, called without luck until the office occupant arrived for work.

Wil split for Berkeley.

Eastbound on the Bay Bridge, overcast giving way to sunshine the farther he got from San Francisco, he tried reading something into the letter and got nowhere, its brevity a wall. Harder yet was not jumping to conclusions: Max and Deborah

Ann Werneke, Rose, Henry Shirmir, Holly. His burning impulse was to head south, follow the stolen-car trail, and to hell with Vega. Little enough there, he knew, nothing the FBI couldn't put more manpower toward.

Keep plugging.

He took a calming breath, then Ashby toward the hills, the rush-hour traffic now a steady midmorning pulse. Just this side of Oakland he found Good Shepherd Hospital. From streetside, it was all granite facade and smoked windows; from inside, all plants and pastels. They had never heard of Joel Beck.

He left, drove north.

Martin Luther King was in the Westbrae, just above San Pablo, with a peek at the horse track that jutted out into the bay. King at least looked like a hospital: brick wings enclosing a parking lot, glass entrance with porte cochere, entry ramp on which several patients were being wheeled. Greeting him inside: grooved paneling and dated prints, numb-looking people waiting, his own memories of recouping after Nam—different hospital, same feel. At the courtesy desk, he was told that what he wanted was downstairs in records.

The Asian receptionist there reminded him painfully of Lisa; she led him through an open area to a room that said DICTATING. Minutes later a youngish-looking black woman entered.

"Mr. Hardesty? I'm Lea McDevitt."

Wil told her who he was trying to locate, no idea of specialty, associated with the hospital around 1973. He also spelled Holly's name for her.

"Has she been a patient since then?"

"Not to my knowledge," Wil said.

Lea McDevitt leaned against the table. "We keep inactive records seven years, not that I'm authorized to show you even if we had them. The name Beck sounds familiar, though." She moved toward the door. "One moment, please."

Wil found a magazine, sat flipping alternately through rich-looking desserts and pages devoted to blowing off unwanted pounds. Finally a slim girl with dark eyes opened the door. She held a computer printout.

"You were interested in Dr. Joel Beck?" Her speech held a trace of Spanish; *Carla* her name tag read.

"If he treated a Holly Pfeiffer in the early seventies."

Her eyes went to the paper. "I haven't checked that yet."

"Then he did work at this hospital?"

"Treated his patients here, yes."

"Which means he would have had an outside practice."

She nodded and flipped through the printout, located the patient entries under *Beck, Joel*—fourteen of them in approximately three years, ending February 7, 1974, with the last of six entries for Holly Pfeiffer that began Christmas Day, 1972. He pointed to the dates.

"Any way of knowing what these were for?"

"Not without the medical records."

"And Dr. Beck would have them?"

She paused. "That would be impossible for two reasons. One, they belong to us—doctors can request copies, but the records may not be taken from the hospital. Since no records exist for the Pfeiffer girl, I'm assuming they were destroyed."

"And the second reason?"

"Dr. Beck is dead."

"I see. May I ask how?"

"He was killed in 1974. Hit-and-run."

Lacey Louise Jones, dead under a bus in L.A. "Would you happen to know the circumstances?"

Her expression hardened. "That would depend on your interest."

Playing off something in her tone, he thumbnailed it for her, noticing the black eyes never left his. Three white-coated men asked for the room then; outside, Carla agreed to continue over coffee. She checked out with Lea McDevitt, then led him up a flight of stairs through double doors. At long tables and smaller ones, people talked in groups or brooded over books or nothing at all.

Wil pushed a tray through the line: coffees, a sandwich for

him, cinnamon roll for her. They took one of the smaller tables.

"You knew Dr. Beck?" he asked, starting on the sandwich.

"Joel was married to my cousin. I took Elizabeth's job after she left to have her baby."

"Hit-and-run?"

"Yes, around Halloween. He'd come here to see a patient and parked on the street. It was raining. The car never stopped."

Wil waited while she took a sip of coffee.

"Liz was all broken up but got over it eventually. She moved, got herself a new husband."

"Let me guess—Liz doubted it was an accident, but there wasn't enough to warrant an investigation."

Carla looked up from her cinnamon roll.

"I'd like very much to talk to her," he said. "Can you tell me where she is?"

"I don't think so."

"How about letting her decide? Tell her it might mean life or death to one of Joel's old patients." Wil dug out two dimes, held them up.

"All right," Carla said reluctantly. "But it's gonna take more than that. She lives in Vallejo."

Wil found the address in a part of town that smelled like low tide and diesel fuel. Stenciled on the door was NORTH BAY FREE CLINIC; inside streaked windows, mini-blinds were drawn tight.

He entered to bedlam: kids bouncing off the walls, crying infants, hollow-eyed mothers groping robotlike for small hands. Electric fans stirred up humid air and ruffled the public-service posters. Wil approached a harried woman at the front desk.

"Would you be Elizabeth?"

She turned and shouted down the hall. "Liz. Somebody here."

Two kids chasing each other thumped into him and spun

off. "Clifford, Arthur, come here," one of the mothers said, mostly for Wil's benefit. Before returning to her infant, she followed up with *"Boys!"*

Walking toward him was a tall Spanish-looking woman: skin café-con-leche with freckles, the face strong but attractive. Dark hair curled around her neck and touched the crew collar of a white T-shirt with the clinic's name screened in red. The faded black denims looked good on her.

"I'm Elizabeth."

He smiled. "Carla called about me—Wil Hardesty. Is there somewhere we can talk?"

She wiped her forehead on her sleeve. "Outside's cooler. Believe it or not, things are actually under control. You should see it some days."

She got her bag and preceded him through the door, then fished out a cigarette and offered him one. He refused, she lit up. As they walked, Wil told her what he'd told Carla, what she told him.

"Carla tell you I'd married again?"

He nodded; they crossed the street to a sunny area, sat on a bench overlooking a greenish strip of water. Gulls squealed and banked over them, drifting away when no food was thrown.

She gestured across the estuary. "That's where my husband works, Mare Island. I don't even have to work now. So what do I do? Volunteer, bust my butt for no pay." She exhaled cigarette smoke, watched it break up. "Joel's why I'm there. That was his dream, start a free clinic like the one in Berkeley. He was going to work like hell, put money away." She shrugged, reached again into her bag. The photo she handed him was old and cracked, but it showed a well-muscled black man in glasses, no shirt, baby in one arm. His pants were army fatigues.

Wil gave her back the print.

"We were happy," she said. "Despite all the crap from our families. I met him when I was at King—the Mexican virgin and the witch doctor. Back then we got it from all sides."

Wil showed her a photo of him and Lisa; Elizabeth looked at him with new interest.

"You're still together?"

"For the time being," he said, feeling the hurt. "What can you tell me about Joel and Max Pfeiffer?"

She crushed out her cigarette. "They were in the same outfit. Joel was a medic, told me he empathized with Max because of how Max was treated. After Joel was discharged, Max loaned him money to finish medical school. He was Joel's first patient. He'd eat with us sometimes—this was after his wife died, when he was really stressed out. I liked him, all but his politics."

They watched a ship making way, seabirds circling its wake. Wil asked her about Joel treating Holly.

"Poor little thing, we worried about her. Joel did tests—I don't remember what for, but they related to the bombing. She seemed all right the times she came over with Max."

"He have her on medication?"

She frowned. "Don't ask me what, but I think so."

"Joel ever show you her medical records?"

Her lips tightened; something there.

"Elizabeth, did Joel's death have something to do with the records?"

She lit another cigarette, watched the smoke float toward the water.

"It's important or I wouldn't ask."

"I know that. It's just . . ." She drew hard, sucked it deep, then exhaled in a rush. "After Max took off, Joel got a note asking if he could hold on to the records for him. Max figured Holly might need them someday, the X-rays and everything, and he knew the hospital kept them only so long." She fixed her eyes on Mare Island. "Since I worked records, it was easy for me to take them. Right before Joel was killed, he thought he was being followed. Then his office was broken into and they were stolen. Two days later he was dead—run down like a dog."

"You tell the police this?"

"Everything but the records part, the hospital would have had me jailed. Worse, it would have killed my family and any hopes with them, me a widow with a mulatto baby. Cops were polite, but nothing ever came of it." She sighed, flipped the cigarette butt in the water; a gull dove for it and veered off. "It wouldn't have brought him back anyway. Such a sweet guy."

They said nothing for a while, then Elizabeth checked her watch.

"It's late, I have to go."

They crossed a small patch of lawn to the boulevard. New clouds, low wads of cotton, were piling up, and the breeze was fresh with hints of salt and mud and seaweed. From across the estuary, an air horn sounded. They walked quietly back to the clinic. She pulled open the door, looked back at him.

"Goodbye," she said. "I hope you find her. For Joel's sake." She slipped inside.

Wil watched as the door eased shut behind her, diminishing the cacophony of children and mothers, and suddenly he felt a deep need for double bar bourbons and dim quiet corners.

TWENTY-ONE

Behr watched Monika put headphones on the girl, watched the girl clutch her knees tightly as the words came through.

The tapes: one more example of Monika's genius. Four days now, six hours a day—not just Max anymore—interspersed with six hours of interaction with Monika, so far just a voice to the girl. She still wore the blindfold, but this time Monika had indicated no more restraints; she was pleased with her progress.

For her part, the girl seemed acquiescent.

Just like the reporter after Tempelhof.

Behr yawned, lit a cigarette, got a harsh look of dismissal from Monika. He stepped outside into mauve twilight and tried to imagine what the passage of time must be like for someone blindfolded—free of distractions, to quote Monika, her blindfold meant to disorient as well.

He checked his watch calendar: three days left, the girl Nassir's problem then—Ammad Nassir, Scourge of Jerusalem, number-two man in the Revolutionary Command Council, overlord of camps from Benghazi to Baghdad. Waiting for him: $2.5 million. Seed money to plant Monika's protégé in his desert garden, the succulent among the thorns.

Behr spent a moment appreciating his observation, then shifted thoughts to Lincoln Stillman. Something about him of late, his manner deferential, attitude unreservedly cooperative, as if he had reached some silent pact with himself, no longer

at odds with Monika. Either that or the calm before the storm.
So far, Monika had said nothing, although Behr knew her
guard was up. Monika's guard was always up.

Tomorrow Stillman was off to an engagement in San Francisco, bodyguard duty for Behr normally. But Behr was
needed here, Monika had insisted. And there was his unfor-
tunate celebrity status. Not only had he been ID'd by this
meddler, they'd dredged up his old union photo in the papers.

He wasn't particularly worried—layers of assumed names
lay between him and them, everything well documented at the
crucial German end, right down to new fingerprints. They'd
even staged the demise of his U.S. entry persona in 1977, no
way to trace him from that. All he needed now was to lie low.
But it would mean he'd have to be careful, an inconvenience
he would certainly repay in kind.

Behr crushed out the cigarette, a French kind that always
made him spit afterward. He spit, went back inside, closed the
door after him and heard Monika, still at it:

"You know the kind of world your father wished for you."

Her voice was reasoned and the girl responded with a nod.

"The freedom there? The promise of the revolution?"

Nod again.

"And you appreciate fully the impediments to it—even
though you have not seen these things with your eyes?"

Nod.

"Then you're ready to become the someone you've been
all along. From this point forward, you are reborn into the
revolution." To Behr's amazement Monika's voice nearly betrayed her, so thick was it with emotion.

"The name you will take is Eve," Monika continued after
a long breath. "Wear it as the first woman wore it. Imagine
its power entering you, its strength. Say it now."

"Eve . . ."

"Say it again."

"Eve."

"Again."

"*Eve!*"

"Very good. I leave you now to be with Eve—to love her as you would your mother, your child, yourself. And from this love will emanate a power beyond limits." Monika nodded, a gesture that left her eyes in shadow.

Behr helped the girl to her feet and upstairs to her room. As he came out and secured the dead bolt, he looked for Monika, to confirm this uncharacteristic new thing about her, this thing he'd not seen before, but she was already gone.

Lincoln Stillman split a lamb chop with his knife, then toyed with the couscous, the pickled lemon, the bstila: la-di-dah grub Monika had the cook attempt before serving it up two nights hence to the Scourge of Jerusalem. The guinea pigs: himself, Behr, and Monika. And there she went again, more incidents from her Locust days when she'd been a visitor to one of Ammad's camps. Chatting up his rise through the ranks, his work with C-4 and miniaturized electronic detonators.

Jesus Goat. Enough already.

Still, it was a kick to watch her: the gestures, the flush of enthusiasm that had his juices racing around like midget cars on a short track. Behr's too, he could see. What the hell—in her white dress and gold jewelry, Monika reminded him of a crack actress sharpening an opening-night performance.

Candlelight reflecting off the mirrored walls and crystal stemware only added to the effect. Rare that they used the formal dining room now; when they did, it was for show. But a fucking rehearsal dinner for a killer of women and children in airports? Few pictures of Ammad Nassir existed, but one he had seen revealed a cleft chin, eyes-on-the-horizon gaze, desert B-movie looks. Stillman chased a bite with Wild Turkey and wondered how the prick would look with a pair of Canadian crutches. Then he half-listened to Monika's run-on.

"Pity the West," she was saying. "Socialism seemingly dead, its countries ripe for consolidation. Yet at the moment of triumph, Western nations are either financially strapped, obese, or paralyzed by indecision. Their victory is an illusion. Do nothing and they risk civil war. Intervene to keep these

countries afloat—so many at once—they go broke. The irony
is they've been granted their exact wish.''

Behr forked in lamb and nodded politely.

''What's clear is there's an even greater opportunity than
before,'' she said, glancing pointedly at her husband. ''You
remember, Lincoln.''

Stillman felt her needle enter, his eros deflate. He waved
for more bourbon, realized Henning was gone, and got it himself. After a long pull, fortification for the fray, he interrupted
Monika's diatribe. Something about ethnocentrism and vacu-
ums of leadership—masturbating, from the look on her face.

''Behr, would you excuse us. Mrs. Stillman and I have
something we need to chew on. Wouldn't want you to get hit
by the gristle.''

Behr's sidelong glance at Monika spiked his blood pressure
momentarily, but then he excused himself with a nod, Stillman
thinking better of a Nazi salute, but tempted. The door closed
behind Behr.

''Now what, Lincoln?'' As though she'd pulled each word
from the freezer and laid them out on the table.

''I just thought being alone with my wife'd be nice. And if
I haven't said it, you look ravishing.''

''Romance ill becomes you. I suggest you get to the point.''

''Such a lovely skeptic.''

''I know you, Lincoln.''

Put up or shut up, he thought. God, she looked good. ''All
right. I've been thinking about the windfall.''

''*My* windfall. Remember?''

''Not this time, pet. I've decided the money should go for
something else, an investment. Land I've had my eye on for
years.''

He watched for reaction. Beyond a brief flare of nostrils,
none came, just a long sigh as though she were dealing with
a retard.

''I see,'' she said carefully. ''And if I object?''

He drew in a breath: crunch time. ''I sincerely hope it won't
come to that.''

"This is absurd."

"Not to me. And I'm still part of it."

"All right then, insane."

"What can I say? Call the cops. Sue me."

"And my plans—what of them?"

"Try credit. If that fails . . ." He shrugged, then drank slowly, alcohol fueling his momentum, definitely on a roll now. "I suppose you could try fucking Ammad Nassir. After all, look how well it worked with me."

Her index finger slowly circled the rim of her wineglass and she smiled, something he did not anticipate.

"The difference is, I never mix pleasure with business," she said. The crystal emitted a low hum. "What about the girl?"

He watched her finger, shook himself from its spell. "Easy come, easy go. Nothing new there."

"Oh, but there is, Lincoln. She's like no other, everything I'd hoped for. Her progress is astonishing." A cold light came into her eyes and her finger left the glass. "But why are we even discussing this? It's out of the question."

"Sorry, I've contacted an attorney. He's holding the money."

"You're not a fool, Lincoln, but you are a bad liar. Things will be clearer in the morning. You have your speech, I have Eve. Now pour yourself another drink and go to bed."

"Not without you, sugar . . ." *Too facile, damnit. Get a grip.*

"Be serious," she said with heat. "Have you forgotten that inexcusable attempt on her life?"

"Monika, did it ever occur to you that was for *us*?" He took a last gulp of bourbon, tasted nothing. "How do you think I feel, sharing you this way, reduced to a fucking ring bearer in my own marriage? I want what's mine—now."

"Stop acting like a child."

The early confidence was eroding like soft rock in a sandstorm. Words flitted beyond his grasp. Like magic, then, fate conjured up trump: "What would you know about that, Monika? Look in the mirror—anybody you see there getting any younger?''

As intended, she recoiled as though slapped. Then a light came into her eyes and she smiled as though experiencing a change of heart. She rose, reached behind her, and unzipped the white dress. Stepping out of it freed full breasts—Venus rising. She paused, kicked off high heels, slipped out of white lace panties. Candlelight gave her skin the appearance of burnished ivory, the patch of gold a life of its own.

Following her movements, Stillman felt as if his veins were overheating, 110 wires on a 220 source. Sweat beaded his forehead and there was a roaring in his ears. The chandelier seemed to pulse with light.

With a deliberate motion, eyes locked on his, Monika took a corner of the tablecloth and pulled slowly. Silver, crystal, dishes, centerpiece, and food approached the edge like a flotilla of doomed ships being sucked over Niagara. They hit the floor with a sound like little collisions.

She lifted herself onto the table then, leaned back on cocked elbows, her legs spread apart, sex beckoning. When she spoke, the room, the shattered mess on the floor, the supine position of her body—all seemed to mock him.

''Well, Lincoln . . . ?''

His chest constricted; the room's oxygen had vanished, burned up. With fingers that felt like balloons, he unzipped and freed himself, moved toward her in a daze.

The door opened.

''The noise,'' Behr said. ''Are you—''

For seconds they were an absurd still life, three subjects in an obscene living painting. Then her laughter began, low at first, then soaring and diving like some bird of prey tearing the heart from his resolve. Lurching past Behr and down the hall toward his study and whole cabinet full of Wild Turkey, Lincoln Stillman felt as though his head would explode.

Cigarette smoke drifted upward; morning sun coming through the blinds sliced it into undulating bands of light and shadow.

Outside the window, birds sang in the crape myrtles.

"Quite a show last night," Behr said, exhaling.

Monika shifted her weight away from him, raised the sheet above her breasts. "Henning will be back from the airport shortly," she said. "I have a plan."

"As does the old man, it seems."

"You know as well as I do he's obsolete. Worse, a liability."

Behr sat up. "You think it's true about the money?"

"The money's in his personal safe. He thinks I don't know the combination."

"But you do."

"Give me *some* credit."

"Always." He was quiet a moment. "Killing him is not without risk, Monika. You want me to reason with him when he gets back from San Francisco?"

She drew in smoke. "No, Behr, I want you to listen."

TWENTY-TWO

Federal crime, federal time; Wil put in a call to the Western Regional Office, Bureau of Prisons, Department of Justice.

In a few minutes he had her: Werneke, Deborah Ann, one of eight hundred women at the Federal Correctional Institution in Dublin—judging from the map, about an hour away. He phoned the facility, explained who he wanted to see and why, waited for a call back while they checked. Forty minutes later it came. Deborah Ann Werneke would see him.

Wil pulled the shetland on over his shoulder rig, tossed off black coffee that had lost its heat, and closed Canizares's front door behind him. He didn't like imposing, but it saved expense money, something in that. His contribution: croissants and groceries, dinner last night. He'd been in the shower when Canizares left for work, six-something.

Three-thirty now: Wil started the rental, eased it down twisted streets, then onto Market toward the freeway. In a few minutes he was merging lanes for the Bay Bridge and thinking that not far back of him, Deborah Ann Werneke had picked up a metal case full of money seventeen years ago. Right before getting herself shot.

Werneke had been twenty-four when her life as a revolutionary ceased at SFO. The library microfilm articles showed a mousy girl in big glasses, hard-pretty underneath a smirk and a pudding-bowl haircut. He tried to project the look forward to age forty-one, freezing the frame in his mind for comparison later.

Scrolling: Twenty-one months Deborah Ann served for firebombing a UC research lab. Back on the streets in '69, she'd fallen in with the Mambas, then Cleon Chapman, left them when he did, quit prison-sponsored employment to become ARV full-time. Angela DeBray's kidnapping and a bank job traced to her gun set her up with twenty-five years to life after she'd recovered from her gunshot wounds. Like a roman candle sputtering, the trial had been brief and showy, then quickly forgotten by a public up to here with all of it.

Wil drove through Yerba Buena Island and beyond, late-afternoon traffic bumper-to-bumper on the bridge, sun slanting through the lower deck girders. He'd found surprisingly little of a personal nature on Lincoln Stillman, mostly newspaper stories on the famous cases, things he already knew. There was one, however—Stillman overcoming poverty and polio in rural Washington state: debating team at WSU, Gonzaga University Law School, Spokane. Long odds, Stillman on crutches even then. The article in *Time* noted the paradox: dead-last law graduate going on to become top gun among defense attorneys—Stillman paying back the doubters by flashing his every accomplishment, his "List" spurring him like a pony express rider's whip.

As a green public defender, he'd inherited the dregs—lost causes turned around with pit-bull tenacity and unconventional tactics, things that made his reputation in private practice. More than a standard-bearer, the writer saw Stillman as a chip-on-the-shoulder scrapper. Most dangerous when cornered.

Avoiding the earthquake-damaged Nimitz, Wil headed south on the MacArthur, then bent east to Dublin. After exiting the freeway he found it, in among the decaying barracks of an old military reservation, the prison sprawling and campus-like inside fences crowned with coils of razor wire. Out front, pines and bare-trunked eucalyptus moved in wind funneled up through the Diablo Range.

Wil followed the signs and parked. Four forty-five: visiting hours in fifteen minutes. He checked his .45 with security, then was escorted to where a smallish woman in jeans and a light blue pullover waited at a table. During introductions, they sized each other up. Deborah Ann Werneke's short dark hair was touched with gray now, the face attractive, features even but set hard. Cautious eyes searched his face from behind round wire glasses. She reminded Wil of a schoolteacher too long on the job—in all, he hadn't been far off. Then he noticed the snake tattoo on her right forearm.

She noticed him noticing. "Souvenir," she said. "Mamba Negra symbol. Ever hear of them?"

Wil nodded. "You were a Mamba before the ARV. I read about it."

"Why bother?"

"You read the newspapers—watch TV?"

"Look, mister, I got a lousy cold and a thesis to finish. You have something to say, say it."

"Okay," Wil said. "Max Pfeiffer. I'm looking for his daughter."

She blinked; curiosity flashed, then was gone.

"I think the key is Max. It's a hunch, but it's why I came. Will you help me?"

"Makes you think I even knew him?"

"Let's not play games, Ms. Werneke, this thing's on the clock. The man who kidnapped Holly has already tried to kill her."

"What's in it for me?"

"Maybe you remember her—pretty little girl with freckles and red hair?"

"You ever been shot?"

"Yeah. Look, I don't know what your life is like now, but at least you have a life."

"Tell it to the parole board." Deborah Ann Werneke massaged around her sinuses. "How old is she now?"

"Twenty."

"I was twenty once—about a hundred years ago." Her eyes drifted, refocused. "What the hell, I always wished him well."

Wil drew a breath, nodded. "Okay if we start there?"

"I suppose. Max used to talk to us about military tactics. He was in Vietnam, knew all that stuff. He knew Z."

"Through the Mambas."

"I don't know. Anyway, Max had this quality about him, sort of hurt like. I was fucking Z, but the other sisters were too, so I figured why not Max. At first he shined me. Then . . ." She shrugged.

"That why you never mentioned him at the trial?"

A nod. "Hoping he made it out."

"What about Holly?"

"What about her? I wasn't at the house but a few times—Z didn't like us going around, especially after we did a few bank jobs. That pretty well took care of Max and me." She shrugged. "He never said, but I think I reminded him of his wife."

"When was that?"

"Just before Christmas—seventy-three."

"And after?"

Deborah Ann Werneke took a tissue from her pocket and blew her nose. "Funny," she said absently. "After all this time, still feel him, even in here. He nearly strangled me one time. Discipline he called it. Guy was cold."

"Max?"

"No, not Max—Z." Her hands were clasped now, thumbs rubbing together as she talked. "I still see him in the shadows, think he's coming for me because I lived. Z was big on dying together." She hesitated. "My point is that during DeBray even Max was a victim."

"I don't understand."

Her eyes took in the room, slowly filling with visitors. "I'll get there, okay? Z wanted to pull off something big, a real step up from banks. Dude was crazy, taking Angela, but I never figured him for the idea. Z was mean but he was never smart."

"What made you think the idea wasn't his?"

"The language was too high-tone. I remember thinking

somebody's fed him this shit, not that it wasn't sound. More diabolical, where Z liked to hurt people.'' She paused, rubbed her face again.

''Rotten headache . . . The plan was to take some rich person, hold him for ransom, then release him when the money came in. If one of us ever wound up in jail, the guy'd be a bargaining chip.''

''Sounds familiar,'' Wil said.

''Ahead of its time is what it was, not like Z at all. Z was a product of his time, but never ahead of it.''

''You always this perceptive?''

She flushed. ''I've had lots of time to think. Anyway, Max raided for prisoners once in Nam, so he helped with the tactics. That was until Z showed us this floor plan he'd gotten hold of, told us who our target was.''

''Angela DeBray—age three.''

Deborah Ann Werneke's lips tightened. ''Nobody said a word until Max did. 'Forget it,' he goes. 'No way in hell.' ''

Wil leaned forward.

''Max splits then. Right away Z asks if anybody else feels the same, and if they do he's gonna start blowing heads off. And don't worry, *he'll* be back. Sure enough: an hour or so later, Max comes barging in, this wild look on his face. He charges Z, picks him up, and slams him into the wall. Then he slams him again.''

''And Z?''

She shook her head. ''Nobody fuckin' believed it, you didn't do that to Z. But he just smiles and goes, 'What'd I tell you, what'd I say?' And Max stands there not saying anything, just that look. So Z reaches into this bag he has, pulls out something, and I look and it's this doll I've seen before—one of Holly's. Z throws it at Max's feet. 'Welcome back,' he says.''

While Deborah Ann Werneke went for aspirin, Wil tried to imagine what he'd have done in Max's place. Or if the gun

were at Devin's head. Same, probably—enough leverage and
you'd do damn near anything.

He looked around for distraction: The visiting area was alive
now with little scenes, talk and tears, movement as people
came and left. Chair legs bumped together, babies cried. Then
she was back, looking sick and drained despite the break.

Wil picked up where she'd left off. "Z took Holly so Max
would cooperate. Did you know where?"

"No. I felt sorry for Max, but what could I do? I was too
scared of Z—all of us were."

"So Max led the raid."

She nodded. "From outside. He had to—Z'd have aced his
kid. But Z kept saying nobody was going to get hurt, this was
for the money. Filthy lucre, he called it."

"Filthy lucre—he said that?"

"All this time I remembered. You see what I mean by the
language?"

"Yeah. You ever tell anybody?"

Deborah Ann Werneke sneezed into a tissue, wiped her face
with it. "Who was in a mood to listen? The Feds got what
they wanted, everybody fried. Now Max is dead and it doesn't
matter anyway."

"It does to Holly. What happened with Thomas Littlefield?"

She leaned back. "One of the guys, Danny, got overheated
and pulled the trigger. We about done here? I feel like crap."

"Was Littlefield in on it?"

"The butler? Come on."

"What about the day of the drop?"

"We'd mapped the whole thing out, gone over it for weeks.
I was in this garage we'd rented in Daly City."

"Z was in L.A.?"

"He had some bank action lined up down there—figured
nobody'd expect it so soon. Rest of them went down in stages,
found us a place. Z left the night before."

"Everyone was gone but you and Max."

She snorted and swallowed hard. "Deal was, I'd pick up

the money, give it to Max at the airport, then get lost. Z'd tell Max where Angela was, Max would fly her and the money south and get his girl in exchange. No idea how they missed him. First I knew about the plane going down was when they fished it out of that lake.''

"Deborah, at the trial, you claimed no knowledge of Angela's death. That still how you remember it?"

He could see in her eyes the way it was taken.

"I never even saw *Max's* kid then. Jesus Christ."

"Maybe so. But Z got close to Holly somehow."

She was standing now, flushed and sputtering. "You implying it was me? Well, fuck you, it wasn't—I'm no Benedict Arnold. You go to hell."

Thoughts: dots connecting, parting, connecting.

Forming what?

Eight-ten, by now the darkness nearly solid in Berkeley; Wil hauled, making California stops through FASCISM, NUKES, and BIGOTRY. Braking then in front of the bungalow court. Killing the headlights.

In contrast with the other units, 127E showed only the yellow porch light, the way it had been when he left Henry Shirmir sitting in the dark two nights before. Wil knocked, looked in the door glass, shielding the bulb's reflection with his hand. Yellow highlights gleamed dully from the mantel, the mug on the chair arm, the bicycle. Something about the way the bike leaned, something familiar, a feeling that it hadn't moved. He tried the door, found it locked.

Wil looked around the quad: nothing but curtained glow in the windows of the other units. He reached up and with his handkerchief unscrewed the porch bulb. With a credit card, he released the old-style lock, was easing the front door open when it snagged on a security chain. Fumbling with the chain was no good, not here—pushing his luck as it was.

He closed the front door, then eased around the side of the house, shadows from the garage lending cover. The back door was under a small overhang and sandwiched between hibiscus bushes. It also was secured with a chain.

With his pocketknife, he cut a branch from the nearest bush, trimmed it down to a stem, used that to jiggle off the chain. He entered the kitchen. For a minute he stood listening to nothing, then he flicked on his penlight to dishes in the single sink, ant streams crawling over them; refrigerator, stained kettle on the stove, wall calendar above the wainscoting. By the phone, Shirmir's answering machine was lit with four messages. Wil pressed the button, heard three expressions of concern from Boalt Hall—two by a female voice, one from Phil Ackerman wondering where he was, that other people were beginning to question his judgment and he was sure Henry didn't want that. The fourth was a voice that didn't identify itself, but didn't have to.

Behind him the refrigerator clicked on, began to creak and hum.

Wil withdrew the .45, held it ready, followed the penlight into the living room, to the door from which Henry Shirmir had emerged. He pushed it open, saw unmade bed, a pile of laundry in the corner beside the dresser. On the wall an early Doors poster hung in a metal frame; Wil looked close and caught Morrison's autograph. A prized possession.

Beyond it was a closed door.

The knob worked, but it wasn't until Wil put his shoulder to it that the door moved. There was a tearing sound as some kind of tape around the edges gave way and his head was snapped back by the smell. He pulled out the handkerchief, held it to his nose, and directed the penlight—into the whites of half-closed eyes.

Henry Shirmir was on the toilet, his body wedged stiffly between the sink and shower. His fist was still clenched, as though he'd intended taking it with him that way in death. A syringe protruded from his tied-off arm.

On the floor, by the hand that hung down, was a snapshot, its corners dog-eared. Wil tightened the handkerchief, turned over the photo, played light on it. Mugging up at him: three people, their arms around each other. Max and Paulette Pfeiffer with Henry Shirmir.

Benedict Arnold.

Eyes watering, Wil stuck the photo in his shirt pocket, stripped the tape off the door, seeing masking tape and a hot spike Shirmir's way of sealing himself off from the world. He wadded it up, stuck it in his jacket pocket. Then he shut the door behind him.

For several minutes, he gulped air, then used the handkerchief on surfaces touched. After a last scan of the interior, he let himself out and dumped the tape near a phone booth where he called Berkeley PD, requesting that the cops look into the no-show of Henry Shirmir, 127E Peoples Way. When they asked his name, Wil just said he was a friend who was concerned.

Rafael Canizares was hunched over documents spread out beneath a gooseneck lamp. He looked up when Wil entered. Light from the lamp reflected off his glasses, obscuring his eyes.

"You eaten yet?" he asked, leaning back. "There's pasta left."

Wil shook his head, walked to the table.

"Jesus Christ," said Canizares, grimacing. "What is that smell?"

"Henry Shirmir," Wil said, not moving. "Thought you'd want to know why he didn't get back to you. I've got a theory, but I wanted to hear if it matched yours."

"The hell you mean by that?" Canizares stood up, fists clenched.

Wil straightened. "See if you can follow me, counselor. You sandbag me on Shirmir, I luck out and find him. Something I say, maybe just my showing up, triggers something, enough to make him OD. Except guess who happens to be trying to reach Henry about the same time he's checking out? Funny how you seem to be in the middle of all this."

The swing came directly out of the light. Wil reacted, but

not fast enough for it to miss the side of his neck with enough force to send him over the couch. Rafael Canizares scrambled after him, reaching down to yank him up by the shirt with the hand that wasn't cocked back in a fist.

Wil let himself be pulled up, then stepped inside the punch, driving one of his own into Canizares's middle. As the lawyer sagged, Wil hit him again in the gut and stepped back. Canizares dropped to hands and knees, gasping.

Wil went to the refrigerator, wrapped ice in a kitchen towel, and held it to his neck, throbbing now as the feeling came back. Canizares made it to his feet, staggered to the bathroom, and threw up. After a bit he came out.

"Time was," he said, still getting his breath, "you'd have stayed down."

"I don't doubt it. You all right?"

"You think I had something to do with Shirmir?"

"I don't know. Did you?"

"No."

"That's reassuring. Why'd you call him?"

Canizares smoothed his hair, placed the hand back on his stomach. "I wanted to find out what else he'd told you. Henry always had this flair for drama. I didn't want you getting side-tracked from Holly."

Wil handed Canizares the photograph, then put the shetland out on the porch to air. As he sat down again, Canizares looked up from the photo. "What a goddamn waste," he said.

Wil nodded, told Canizares what he'd learned from Deborah Ann Werneke. "Shirmir's moving into Max's old house closed the circle," he said. "The other night you used the word atone—I think he was planning this all along. Square it up with Max for looking the other way when they came for Holly."

"You think Z paid him?"

"Henry had a habit. He was already pissed at Max because he'd abandoned their partnership, and Z would have promised him the girl wouldn't be harmed. I can see it."

Canizares got a container from the fridge, began eating from it. "For some reason I'm hungry," he said. "Sure you don't want some?"

"Not where I've been, counselor." Wil watched him eat. "Something still bugs me—Rose Pfeiffer's bitterness toward the girl. Doesn't seem natural."

Canizares gave him a wry look. "You should be in my business, you want nice, natural human motives. I've seen families go at each other in the courtroom with everything but kitchen knives. Don't fool yourself about maternal love."

"You know something I don't?"

"She's my client, Hardesty."

"He was your friend."

Canizares tossed the bowl in the sink, poured himself a bourbon, and nipped a finger off it. "Public record, I suppose. It was right after the old man died—he'd never have stood for it. Rose saw in Max a grieving, distracted father, one who hated everything she embraced, Holly growing up with that. First she offered, then she pleaded. Then she intervened."

"That's usually a polite word for something else."

Canizares finished the rest of the whiskey in one gulp. His breath caught, then he said, "Rose Pfeiffer sued Max for custody. At first she asked me to handle it, but I was able to beg off. Not my kind of work."

"And if it had been?" Immediately he was sorry for having said it; blood rose in Canizares's face.

"You want to try again?"

"Mea culpa," Wil said, raising a hand. "What happened?"

"She hired Jerome Lizardi. Heard of him?"

Wil nodded: Jerry Lizardi was custody cases, high-profile divorces, palimonies. Birth-mother suits against contract parents.

"Max defended himself," Canizares said. "By the time it was over, he'd aged twenty years, but he won. To my knowledge, Rose never saw Holly again."

Wil thought about the woman losing first her husband then her son and granddaughter, seventeen years of no word, no love, just a hardening. Being reminded of all that by someone she'd come to hate.

"You think she blames Holly for being the wedge?"

"In some dark part of her, yes," Canizares said. He got up slowly, stretched painfully, and yawned. "I've had enough depressing shit for one day." He moved toward the bedroom. *"Mañana."*

"Yeah," Wil said, feeling his own aches spreading. He looked at his watch; Lisa'd be home about now—unwinding with a glass of the chardonnay he used to pour her after a long day. Wanting him to rub the kinks out, to nibble her ear.

He picked up the phone and dialed, first checking her new number from the card he'd written it on. Hearing one ring . . . two . . . three. A male voice answering.

Wil cradled the receiver, felt the shock move through him like a bowling ball, the rumble hot-loud in his ears. After a while he went over and spun the top off Canizares's bottle, poured a large whiskey and stood staring at it, arms braced against the drainboard, muscles tight-trembling and his breath coming in rasps. Sweat poured off him. The amber smell of the bourbon was gasoline-sharp.

Ready for the flames.

Wil turned on the faucet in the sink and dumped in the bourbon. He watched it lighten and clear, then he let the cold water run for a long time on his face and neck. Still damp after toweling off, he stood numbly at the window, looking out at bright lights converging into blur.

TWENTY-THREE

Wil was up at seven-thirty, Canizares long gone. By eight, he'd showered out dark thoughts of confronting Lisa, demanding explanations, burning bridges. Instead he had flowers sent to her office, a white crysanthemum he knew she liked— all he could do until something broke with Holly. At eight-thirty he was staring at the black stream filling the automatic dripper, the sight and sound and smell of the coffee hypnotic. After a bit it stopped and he poured some, added milk, honey from a plastic bear.

He sipped it slowly, frustrated at being stuck there and the uncertainty of what to do next. Philosophical then, mulling questions of time and mortality: Henry Shirmir, for whom time no longer had meaning; Deborah Ann Werneke, with little else but time; Holly Pfeiffer, running out of time if she hadn't already. Wil Hardesty, on a fast track to nothing and nowhere. *Damn it, Max.*

The phone snapped him out of it.

"You see the paper?"

Wil checked the table, the floor, came up blank.

"I meant to set it out for you," Canizares said. "Check the bedroom." Pause. "Sorry about last night in more ways than one. I'm sore as hell. Not very lawyerly."

"My fault," Wil said. "I'll find a place today. You've been more than decent about putting me up."

"Bullshit, I'm glad for the company. Meantime check A3,

then the Business Briefs. Tonight's the Stillman thing—remember the flyer?''

"I remember. You going?"

"Nope," Canizares said. "But have a ball."

About to hang up, Wil said, "You remember what happened to the DeBrays?"

"Makes you ask?"

"I'm running out of people to talk to."

"You're out of luck, with him at least. He drank himself to death—late seventies or thereabouts. There is a DeBray Foundation."

"And her?"

"*Nada.* That I know of, anyway."

"Thanks, Rafael." Hanging up, Wil found the *Chronicle* in sections on Canizares's unmade bed. Page A3 first:

PFEIFFER KIDNAP CAR FOUND

Los Angeles. FBI agents have determined that a car found in the unincorporated city of Valinda by Los Angeles County Sheriff's deputies was used to transport Holly Rose Pfeiffer. The car, a 1986 Mercury reported missing near Maricopa, was discovered nearly dismantled during an LASD raid on a stolen-car chop shop. Deputies became suspicious when they found the initials HRP scrawled in blood in the car's trunk. FBI Special Agent Albert Vega said several suspects were being questioned and search efforts were now being concentrated in and around Los Angeles. The discovery proves, as had been speculated, that she was alive to that point, Vega said.

The story concluded with the FBI hot-line number.

Wil clipped the article, put it with the others he'd saved. Then he checked the Business Briefs, found: *World-famous*

defense attorney, Lincoln Stillman, St. Regis Hotel, 7 P.M.
Topic: A Time for Outrage. The public is invited.

Thinking about Holly's bloody HRP and what it must have taken, Wil tossed yesterday's Shirmir-rank clothes into Canizares's washing machine with a liberal amount of soap. The shetland he dropped off at a one-hour dry cleaner, returning to the house and three cold croissants with peanut butter. After drying the clothes, he found a San Francisco number for the DeBray Foundation, got a smooth-sounding female voice, and told it he was inquiring into the status of Collette Debray.

"Unfortunately, Mrs. DeBray is not in the best of health," the voice said. "She suffered a stroke some years ago. Who is this, please?"

"Small paper near Santa Barbara. We want to run a feature on Mrs. DeBray."

"If seeing Mrs. DeBray was what you had in mind, I must disappoint you. She's convalescing."

"May I ask where?" Wil said.

"I'm sorry."

"Is there someone else I could speak to about this?"

From her tone, hell would freeze before he bothered Collete DeBray; the man to whom the voice referred him was even less optimistic—after saying no, he hung up.

Wil checked the phone book, began calling convalescent hospitals: a new, confused lab manager wondering to whom should he send Mrs. DeBray's test results. Nothing. Two hours later, he gave up, added striped tie to blue shirt and cords, left the house, and swung by the cleaners, sniffing the shetland before putting it on. Even the aroma of cleaning fluid was an improvement.

Curbside in the rental, he confirmed Atherton—no address given—from his microfilm notes: the DeBray home in '74. He checked his map; Atherton was just north of Stanford University, roughly an hour from San Francisco. Eight hours before Stillman.

Hell, why not?

As he left the city, a day game was on at Candlestick, the parking lot a sea of multicolored paint and windshield reflections. Sunlight danced on the bay, flashed off planes final-approaching SFO, bathed suburb towns: Burlingame, San Mateo, Belmont—station-wagon-with-wood-on-the-side names. Across the bay, the hills rose above the salt evaporator ponds and rolled east toward prison-town Dublin.

It struck him then how much had been lost in the killing of Angela Justine DeBray, the years of bitterness, grief, isolation, of things denied. Dead people and dead hopes. Deborah Ann Werneke. Field Marshal Z and whoever had fed him the idea. *Filthy lucre*. Stilted, doctrinaire rhetoric, but whose?

Following signs, he exited the freeway and found a gas station where he bought a fill-up, a machine sandwich, and a small-scale map. As he ate, he spread the map, Atherton showing up as an oddity. Instead of the spiderweb of lines typical of other towns, Atherton seemed almost undeveloped.

Crossing El Camino, he understood why: increasingly larger homes, lush landscaping, driveways disappearing around tree-lined bends, avenues running uninterrupted for long stretches. After a couple of loops, he backtracked, found a bookstore with an established look and an old-fashioned bell that tinkled when the door opened. Inside were an older man and a girl about nineteen. He approached the man.

"That thing in the papers," Wil said, "the Angela DeBray kidnapping. Would you have anything on it?"

The man looked up from a list he was checking. "Nothing in print right now. Thing like that makes you wonder, doesn't it? Even today."

"Sure does."

"If you're interested, the house is just up the hill. Kind of hard to find, but a real landmark."

"The family still there?"

"Nope. The DeBray Foundation gave it to the city. Heck of a write-off—twelve million, the last I heard."

Wil asked what the city was doing with it, heard tours, fund-raisers, garden clubs, "have to be creative where they get money these days."

The man found a sheet of paper, rough-sketched the directions. Wil thanked him, smiled at the girl, who smiled back, reminding him of Holly, the same coltish charm. In a few minutes he was turning through an open gate that spanned low stone wall on either side of the drive. Newish asphalt ran past a shuttered security hut, then curved by oaks, myrtle, pathways, and bridges over a creek. Farther on, slate roof showed through the trees.

The house was sandstone, its length widening to roundness at either end. Dark beams ran under eaves and supported balconies; tall windows reflected clouds and sky. Island in a sea of green, a pond sat marked by clumps of horsetail. Wil saw koi, splashy orange in the pea-soup water.

One other car was parked in the lot. As he walked toward the house, an older couple came out, nodded to him in passing. Wil heard car doors slam, engine catch, the pop of gravel under tires. He stepped up through oak doors.

There was an open entry and large rooms to either side, sitting room left, dining room right, natural wood in abundance. Stone hearths opposed each other; a long burnished table gleamed between high-backed chairs. Walls were free of decoration except for electric candles in hammered iron fixtures and a running band of geometric frieze.

Wil saw movement from the corner of his eye. He reached into his pocket and popped a ten into a glass bowl on the entry table where it joined a layer of other bills, ones mostly.

"Very generous, sir. We thank you."

"Such a beautiful home," he said, turning. She was small and dark-haired, late fifties maybe, dressed in red with a double strand of pearls. Latina face with large eyes, burgundy-rimmed glasses, hands clasped at her waist: *Felice Ornelas*, her name tag read.

"Frank Lloyd Wright designed it. At one time it was the private residence of the DeBray family. He was in media and publishing."

Wil looked past her, through open door to empty parking lot and back. "Angela DeBray?"

"Yes, although we're just the DeBray Community Center now."

"Would you be up for a tour of one?" Noting uncertainty, he added, "I'm quite serious."

Felice Ornelas smiled. "So I see." She went into another room; Wil could hear two women talking and then she was back. "Looks like you're in luck." She began her spiel: the house built in 1934 by a midwestern insurance executive, sold to DeBray in '59; the style classic Wright Organic, the architect designing everything from furniture to light fixtures and friezes.

"Hope you're paid by the fact," Wil said as they took carpeted stairs. "You know the house so well."

Felice Ornelas smiled over her shoulder. "It's why they hired me. That and I was still nearby."

"You knew all this before you were hired?"

She led him to a paneled sitting room, stunted pines and a Japanese stone lantern visible outside. "I used to work here," she said quietly.

Light chill, a feather on his neck; the feeling that without knowing it, maybe his luck had changed. "Well, no wonder," he said.

"September of sixty-two until they put Mrs. DeBray in the home, poor thing. I was maid, cook, whatever—five of us would trade off. Quite a place it was then."

"What about when Angela was taken?"

Her look became guarded. "I'm sorry, but they've requested I not get into all that. I hope you understand."

"Of course. You must have been very attached to the family."

"I was to Mrs. DeBray—at least the first one, Frances."
She led him into a large airy bedroom. "This room was
hers."

"I didn't realize there were two. What about Collette?"

"She was nice, but in a different way—less elegant, never
completely comfortable with the parties and all. She was in
show business before Mr. DeBray married her. Strange, you'd
think an actress would be very outgoing. But Collette was
shy."

Wil looked at the canopied bed, the span of dressing table
with silver brushes, mirrors, and combs laid out behind a vel-
vet rope separator.

"What happened to the first Mrs. DeBray?"

"Warm, isn't it?" Felice Ornelas opened a window, turned
back to face him. "Frances ended her life with pills. Her girls
were devastated. Mr. DeBray too, of course."

"Daughters?"

She nodded. "Michelle and Patrice were away at school
when it happened—early 1970."

Angela had been three in 1974: "So Elden remarried right
away."

A nod. "Demands were always great with so much enter-
taining. Rare that people weren't at the house for one reason
or another."

"What was he like, if I may ask?"

She hesitated. "Elden DeBray loved being with his family.
Very much the master of his castle, though. All of us, Collette
too, were extra careful when he was around." She seemed to
reconsider. "Not that he was hard to work for, just particular.
He was older than Collette—forty-five to her twenty-nine
when they were married."

"May I see Angela's room?"

"Certainly. Here I am rambling when you want to see the
house."

They moved to a room across the hall. Wil's first impression was surprise at the simplicity: child-size bed and

dresser, a chenille spread with rosebuds, small chairs and table at the window, armchair near the bed. He pictured Elden
DeBray with a storybook open, Angela drifting off, then noticed there were no photographs of the little girl and asked
about it.

"The council thought it best," Felice Ornelas said. "They
don't want curiosity-seekers."

"And you?"

"She was a beautiful child. Seems to me a picture wouldn't
hurt." She sighed. "They doted on her, particularly her father.
And Collette—she'd sit there all night sometimes when Angela got scared."

Wil handed her his card. "Felice, I'm trying to find a girl
named Holly Pfeiffer, you may have read about it. I know
you've been asked not to discuss Angela, and how hard it still
is. But I have to ask: Will you help me—please?"

Her eyes held no expression. "I thought the FBI was looking for Holly Pfeiffer."

"They're taking a different route than mine." Wil explained
his involvement, tracking Max.

"The man helped murder Angela, and you expect me to
help?"

"Max was going to lose his own daughter unless he went
along." Her look was pure disbelief. "Look, all I can tell you
is she doesn't deserve what's happened any more than Angela
did."

She walked to the door, glanced briefly down the hall, then
faced him, hands twisting. "What is it you want to know?"

"Anything you remember—where you were."

"The kitchen," she said. "We did our baking at night. All
of us were there except Tommy. He was upstairs. The De-
Brays were in the city."

"What time was this?"

"Ten-thirty. Suddenly they were in the house, five of them,
like soldiers, but with masks. Dorothy got hysterical—they hit
her, fired their guns, had us lie on the floor. The two guarding

us said more were outside and not to get brave. That's when I heard her."

She clutched herself as though feeling a chill.

"She was screaming and Tommy yelled something and there were more shots. Then they were downstairs, one of them with a hand over her mouth. Her eyes . . ."

A vein in Felice Ornelas's neck jumped, and her skin had the hard look of set paste. Wil asked if he could get her some water, but she went on as though not hearing.

"Before leaving, they said whoever came outside would be shot. Finally I went out a back window and got to a neighbor's."

Wil waited as she took a deep breath. "And Tommy Littlefield?"

"Poor Tommy, the blood was coming so fast we couldn't stop it. He died right there." She pointed. "I'd never seen anyone die before."

"Were you close?"

"Of course—we knew his wife and kids. The sad thing was he'd been given the night off. Tommy stayed late so we'd have somebody with us."

A voice called from downstairs.

"Right there," she called back. "Mr. Hardesty, I'm a religious person, but I was glad when those people died that way." She damped down on tears starting. "That was justice."

"What was it like here after that?"

"Like the house's heart was gone. Mr. DeBray just drank. Collette tried to keep busy, we all did, but it was pretense. She started getting migraines."

"And the older girls?"

"They didn't come back when their mother died, and they didn't after Angela."

Wil looked out the window at the koi pond, a gardener fishing something out with a net. "Did that seem odd?"

"Nothing people do surprises me, especially people with money. I think they blamed their father for what happened to Frances—Patrice gave me that impression. Hard to know Michelle's thoughts. What does that have to do with this?''

''Nothing probably. They live near here?''

''Hillsborough. Every year I send Christmas cards, even if they don't. I do it for their mother.''

The voice came again from downstairs; a tour was mustering in the foyer. ''Really, I have to go,'' she said.

''You ever see Collette?''

She paused on her way out the door. ''Collette's not well. Sometimes she thinks I'm Frances, sometimes I'm Angela.''

''And the other times?''

''Last week she asked if I still bake the pear tarts she used to like. There's no telling with a stroke.''

''Will you take me?''

''What possible good—?''

''I can't know unless I talk to her. My word: I'll leave whenever you say.''

''Felice,'' the downstairs voice more insistent.

''I'm off at three,'' she said. ''You want to meet where the bus stops by the front gate, I'll think it over.''

She heard the key in the lock, the click of the dead bolt. Quickly she put her feet up on the bed, her back to the wall, braced her knees into her chest. The door opened to a rush of unstale air, then *her* voice.

''Before we begin, Eve, I have a surprise. Do you understand?''

''Yes,'' she said in the proper tone. ''I understand.''

''Aren't you curious?''

She hesitated, wondering what such an admission would bring. Discipline? Another meal withheld? Approval from the voice, perhaps?

''Curious insofar as it serves the revolution,'' she said. ''For me alone, no.'' She felt the bunk springs compress, a presence beside her.

"That's well considered, Eve. You see? We're not displeased with you, even though that may seem the case." A pause. "Now the surprise—bearing in mind that your life is still in my hands. Is that clear?"

"Yes. I mean clear."

"Good."

She felt the blade of a scissors at her left temple and the blindfold fell away. Then she was rubbing her eyes, squinting into light from a single candle in some kind of holder. The candle was between herself and—someone, the brightness of it making her eyes water.

The face came gradually into focus: roundish, even-featured, smiling slightly. She was older, hard to say how much because her complexion was strikingly clear, with wide blue eyes that seemed to miss nothing and say less. Platinum-blond hair was swept back and upward; a few loose strands caught the candlelight. She looked like a magazine model, yet her clothes resembled battle fatigues.

"My name is Monika," the woman said simply. "I am you and you are me. We are one."

She blinked, her vision as unsettled as her thoughts. "Why?" she asked, all she could think to say.

"That will be clear soon enough. And I'm sure you realize there's no going back now, only forward."

She understood all right, the revelation equivalent to an open death warrant. Something inescapably hypnotic in the face, though; wanting more from it until she knew everything: *"Why me?"*

The woman reached out, touched her hand. "We have little time left. Soon you'll be on your own—meeting people who think as you do, feel the way you feel. People who have the means to implement those feelings."

A flutter went through her, fragile wings beating at a window.

"The unknown is always fearful at first. A brief separation, then reunion."

She said nothing. Impossible to process it all.

"Think how far we've come," the woman Monika went on. "This is just the next step. The logical progression."

"Progression toward what?"

"Something we're forging together. Remember about power, Eve? You'll not simply possess the power to influence events, you will *be* that power. All you need do is take it."

The dream is yours. "The tapes," she said. "You knew my father?"

The woman smiled. "Your father possessed extraordinary qualities, we agree on that. But you have everything of his and more." The blue eyes shone now. "You have the gift—and you have me. You'll honor his memory with things he never imagined."

The words seemed to apply to a different person. Like a dream that time had been, Holly Pfeiffer a fading shape in a closing scene—a glass float bobbing away on a dark and fast-moving tide. She fought the tightening in her throat by concentrating on the face.

"We'll begin with this," the woman Monika was saying. She reached into the pocket of her fatigues, pulled something out.

The pistol brought a flinch, then she steadied on it. It was like Hardesty's, only smaller. Chrome plated.

"Look at me, Eve, that's it. What do you see?"

"I—"

"Someone who believes in you, right? Who trusts you."

She nodded.

"Then you must trust me now. Take the gun."

She did. It felt compact, solid. Comforting in a strange way.

"Extraordinary, isn't it?" Monika seemingly capable of entering thoughts. "Even unloaded it conveys a sense of purpose."

As she held it, it seemed to become part of her. How could she once have disdained anything so perfect?

"Why do you think I've given you the gun, Eve?"

"We have enemies."

"That's right. And we do what with enemies?"

"We kill our enemies. They would destroy us. We kill to survive."

"Very good, Eve. I'm really quite pleased with you."

After so many humiliations, she felt a surge of pride at the words.

"Now, someone in my favor deserves more food. Are you hungry?"

She tried to curb the eagerness in her nod.

"I'll arrange for it. But first I want you to look at something." The woman Monika reached into another pocket, handed over a photograph. "This is the man who ordered you killed, who burned your home. Look closely. This filth wanted you dead before you'd even lived."

She looked at craggy visage, unruly hair, hot eyes. Somehow he was familiar, the ghost image from a past life. The gun felt big in her hands.

"What do you see?"

"I see an enemy."

"Tomorrow this man will stand before you. Tomorrow I'll load your gun and give you the pleasure of killing him." She read the shock and half-smiled.

"Do you remember your mother, Eve, the way she died?"

The blue eyes bored in now and her brain seemed to be firing messages at her from all directions. "The FBI—"

"No, Eve, not the FBI—not this time. *He* was responsible for your mother's death." She paused. "I say this in case you might be tempted to feel pity or mercy tomorrow. If you can't kill this dog for what he did to you, then kill him for her."

At first she sat stunned. Then tears of outrage welled and she was conscious of the woman Monika rising, holding the candle close, the light fragmenting until it felt like splinters entering her eyes. She closed them, saw her mother's face through a haze of red. She felt breathing, the touch of fingers on her face and then warm lips pressing hers.

Validation.

TWENTY-FOUR

The sign at Monte Verde Convalescent Hospital was weathered boilerplate from which the name had been cut in Spanish-style letters; whitewashed and thick-walled, the place reminded Wil of a sprawling hacienda. Tile roof, trees and flower beds, ivy. From the far side, the gray nose of an ambulance.

Wil parked, opened the door for Felice Ornelas. "I don't believe I'm doing this," she said. "I could lose my job."

"The foundation would fire you for this?"

She looked grim. "I know them. People in suits."

"Felice, I can drop you somewhere or you can wait in the car. But I have to—"

"You won't make it. Seclusion is all these people have left to buy."

They started up the walk.

She said, "I feel so sorry for Collette. No one ever comes. One other woman is all."

"No one from the foundation?"

Felice Ornelas shook her head. "It's a shame—when Collette's clearheaded, she loves the company. Which reminds me: I'll interpret, but no guarantees, and we leave if it isn't going well. At the desk, you're my nephew who used to visit."

Wil nodded, opened the entry for her. Trailing, he took in soothing colors, low-pile carpeting, soft music. And the rest: wheelchairs with sagging shapes, televisions playing without volume, shuffling feet. In one section, pinched men faced each other over checkers; down a hall, an attendant wiped up something as a bent woman looked down.

He felt like a truck driver barreling toward a cliff without brakes.

The woman Felice was talking to was younger than she was, but her expression wasn't. She regarded Wil closely, then wrote something in a book and handed Felice two passes. As they walked, he took peripheral peeks into the rooms, saw faces defocused or turned away. He asked about what seemed like color codes outside some of the rooms.

"No heroic measures," she said, stopping outside a door with one of the codes. "Sign of the times." She poked her head in. "Mrs. DeBray? It's Felice. May I come in?"

Wil stayed at the doorway. The room was small but larger seeming; sliding glass led to an enclosed patio with eucalyptus trees beyond. Flowers in clay containers brightened the patio.

She was facing that way, turned at the voice.

The incongruity hit him first: white hair with skin that was rosy and more or less unlined, the effect striking in someone still relatively young. Second impression: better overall than he was expecting. Then he fathomed the eyes, the confusion in them. Under the right one a faint tic responded to an unseen rhythm.

"Felice?" she said.

"You got sun today, didn't you," Felice said, smoothing wisps of white off Collette DeBray's face. "And they washed your hair, it's so soft."

She positioned the chair so it better faced the room, giving Wil a chance to compare Collette to her old UPI photo: high cheekbones, well-shaped mouth, graceful neck—the pieces there but not the whole. She was dressed in a housecoat something like Rose Pfeiffer's.

"Felice?" she said again. The voice was reedy, hesitant.

Felice took her hand. "I've come to visit—we have. See that nice-looking man?" She combined a point for Collette with a gesture to Wil to come forward.

He did, picking up hand lotion and hospital food smells. He pulled a chair over and sat down, watching closely for reaction from Collette DeBray.

"Felice? Who is that?"

Felice raised encouraging eyebrows. "That's Wil, Mrs. DeBray. He's come to visit. Can you say hello?"

A tremor rippled through Collette DeBray. "Elden?"

"Hello, Mrs. DeBray," Wil said. "I'm glad to meet you."

She looked at Felice, touched her hair.

"Elden can't be here today, ma'am. This is Wil."

The tic, then, "Not Elden?"

Felice shook her head slowly, the gesture for him to go easy.

"Have you been thinking about Elden?" Wil asked.

"Yes," she said. "Are you taking care of my baby?"

"It's all right," Felice said. She reached for a brush on the dresser, let down Collette's hair, and began slow strokes. Collette DeBray closed her eyes for a long moment, then opened them.

"Him," she said. "I want him to brush my hair."

Felice registered surprise, but handed over the brush. After initial awkwardness, Wil smoothed out the strokes, guiding them with his free hand. Collette DeBray sighed.

"Elden did my hair like this. My baby's too."

"They'd sit in front of the fire," Felice said to Wil. "Such pretty hair she had."

"Pretty hair," Collette echoed.

"Tell me about Elden," Wil said. "How did you meet him?"

She smiled. "In a play. I was Cleopatra. He brought flowers, took me home." Suddenly she stiffened and tried to rise. "I have to go. He'll be angry."

Felice put a hand on her shoulder, took the brush from Wil. "It's fine, Mrs. DeBray, we took care of it. The house is just fine."

"You know how upset he gets."

Wil said, "I'll talk to him if you like."

"Would you? If it's clean, he won't have to punish anyone. You'll tell him?"

"I'll do that, yes," he said, watching the relief spread like dawn.

A nurse appeared, told her how nice it was she had company, whispered something to Felice, then left the room. Felice began putting up Collette's hair with barrettes from the night table.

Wil said, "Mrs. DeBray, can you tell me about Elden's other daughters?"

"You remember Patrice and Michelle," Felice said.

Collette DeBray searched Wil's face. "Please. He wants everything to be perfect." Suddenly she yawned, and it was as though a fuse had blown behind her eyes. "Felice?"

"I'm here, Mrs. DeBray."

"Is this a friend of yours?"

"That's all right now, it's time for your pills. We were just leaving."

After Felice Ornelas gave him directions, neither spoke. Wil left the windows down as they drove, welcoming the fresh air. Finally she asked him to pull over in front of a red curb.

"You sure I can't run you home?" he asked.

"Miles out of your way," she said. "Besides, the four thirty-five'll be right along. You better have this." She reached into her purse, pulled out a worn leather wallet, opened it, and jotted something on a card. "Me with business cards. Something, huh?"

She handed it to him. Written was: 745 Chestershire, Hillsborough.

"If they ask, you never heard of me."

He leaned over and took her hand. "Thanks, Felice," he said. "Stay well."

She looked at him before getting out. "Sweet Lord, isn't that the truth," she said.

•   •   •

Narrow streets, high hedges, low oaks, old money: Hillsborough crept toward Skyline with a grace that spoke of concerns beyond the day-to-day. Following a spur off Black Mountain Road, Wil got lost, backtracked around a wooded creek, found access to Chestershire—745 an older, heavy-featured stucco two-story, with a curving tile roof and deep-set windows. Brick walk split a hedge of blistered eugenia to an arched door.

Wil knocked, looked around at empty flower beds, drought-affected fuchsia bushes, a NO SOLICITING sign. He tried the iron ring. There was a squeak as the door's small port was opened.

"Patrice DeBray?"

"The sign says no salesmen." Her voice was smoker-husky.

He passed his card through the port and told her the basics—himself, Max, Holly, jamming for breaks and time.

"Bit late to do the DeBrays much good," she said caustically. "Have a nice day." The port was shut, then latched.

He banged the ring against the iron plate, twice, three times. *Goddamnit, Max.* He was poised for a fourth when the port opened again.

"I'll call the police, don't think I won't."

"Fine, let *them* ask." Bluff better than nothing.

"What the hell are you talking about?"

"Life and death," he said. "Thinking of somebody besides yourself." Silence, figuring he'd blown it, then muted voices arguing.

"So ask," she said finally.

Wil found his license, held it up. "Couple minutes inside, then I'm gone," he said. "How about it?"

The port shut; Wil heard more arguing, then the door opened. She was tall and Bacall-blond: tans pants, denim shirt untucked; burgundy loafers without socks—more self-reliant-looking than attractive, as if she rode a mean horse. Behind her Wil caught a glimpse of black hair and blue robe retreating into dim light.

''My sister,'' she said. ''Michelle doesn't see people.'' Wil followed her to a room with small windows, the effect monastic—secure, perhaps, from another point of view. Worn chairs fronted a fireplace filled with wads of newspaper ash. Unmatching tables and lamps flanked a dated couch.

Patrice DeBray took the left chair, crossed her legs. ''You're thinking we could afford better,'' she said.

''Would it matter?''

''What matters is we could if we wanted, which we don't. You always come on like that?''

''Sorry, I'm a quart low on patience. Nothing personal.''

She looked him up and down. ''Maybe. So as not to waste time, why don't you tell me what you know about us.''

Wil filled in some things Felice Ornelas told him.

''No need to ask where you got that stuff,'' she said. ''God knows why she'd want to go back there.''

''What kind of man was your father?'' he asked.

She stretched slowly, watching for effect. ''I thought this was about Angela.''

''It is.''

''Then that depends on who you hear it from.''

''Collette said he was strict, that he had to have his way or punish—her word. She said he loved his family.''

''So you saw her, did you?'' Patrice DeBray went to a cabinet across the room, came back with a silver box and her top buttons open. She took a cigarette from the box and lit it. ''Some people have a strange definition of love.'' She took a drag, exhaled at the ceiling. ''He certainly did.''

''How so?''

She sparked off his eyes, found interest in the smoke. ''My father was the youngest self-made millionaire on record. He'd buy up unprofitable newspapers—bleeders he called them. Same with magazines, then radio stations. Used to say he could make a million dollars just by breathing. But love?'' She flicked ash toward a glass tray. ''That is obscene.''

''He hurt your mother as well as Collette?''

''You could say that.''

"She ever get help?"

Patrice DeBray forced a smile. "Who from, the courts? His lawyers? Charities he propped up? Money talks—we learned that before we learned to shit through a duck. Am I shocking you yet?"

Wil said nothing.

She leaned forward to tamp the cigarette, show him that she wore no brassiere. "Listen, daytime TV's got nothing on this family." Her eyes were bright but devoid of humor. "Now about—"

The first shot came from the doorway, enclosed-space loud and missing him by inches before routing plaster over the hearth. It froze him momentarily.

"No," the scream Patrice's.

"Get out of the way, Treece. I won't let you do this." She was framed in the doorway: blue robe from earlier, black hair disheveled, eyes wide-wild. She had a double-grip on a stainless-steel revolver. She fired again, just before adrenaline kicked in and he dove behind the couch.

"Shel, stop it. Right now. Give me the gun."

"You stop protecting him."

To distract her, Wil shoved the far lamp table over and it fell with a crash that drew two more rounds, rapid-fire holes in the wall. He flattened, inched back from the edge of the couch.

One more shot, deafening, like the others.

"Stop . . ."

Wil got up cautiously. "That's it," he said. "All over."

Bam. The unexpected round slapped through his coat before Michelle DeBray began dry-firing hammer clicks. He took deep breaths and came toward her, holding his hand out for the gun, when her eyes rolled back and she crumpled like a dropped sack, her head thudding the hardwood.

"Shel . . ." Patrice rushed to her.

Wil kicked the empty revolver under the couch. "Jesus. Where'd she learn to shoot like that?"

"Firing range. Where'd you learn to count?" Patrice was

on one knee, checking her sister, then looking at her hand, at blood running down it onto the floor. *"Shit . . ."*

"Let me see it." Wil checked the bullet-torn skin between her thumb and forefinger, gave her his handkerchief to press on it. Then he carried the unconscious Michelle to an upstairs bedroom, laid her on one of the beds, and checked for steady breathing.

"She'll be all right," he said to a white-faced Patrice. "What about you?"

"Terrific, thanks. *Damn*—no reason to report this, is there?" She slumped onto the arm of a chair.

"She ever do it before?"

"Never this bad."

"What's the matter with her?"

Patrice DeBray gripped her wrist and said nothing; her eyes shut, then opened. "Same as me," she said finally. "Elden DeBray, husband and father of the year. You need a paint-by-numbers?"

"No. That why your mother took pills?"

She nodded. "God, I hated her for that. Now I'm not so sure I wouldn't have done the same thing." She moved from the arm to the seat. "Would you get my cigarettes, please, this thing's starting to hurt."

Wil did, along with the ashtray and some ibuprofen from the bathroom cabinet. He lit one for her as she downed the pills, passed it over, watched deep drags and the color returning to her face.

"I finally told my father I didn't give a damn anymore, I was going to the authorities."

"And?"

"He said he had a better idea—he'd buy us this house and set us up for life. It worked for him because he was going to marry again."

Wil watched sunlight leaving the room. "Did you ever warn Collette?"

"Figured it was a waste of breath. You can imagine what Elden DeBray represented to a show girl."

"Actress," Wil said.

"Whatever. She'd visit us sometimes." She took a final drag, crushed the smoke.

"And Angela?"

"Angela was a genius, did you know that? Her scores were off the charts, even at that age." She folded her arms over her chest. "Cute little thing. You could almost set your watch by when it started."

Wil felt his stomach turn, Elden DeBray's presence thick as the smell of her cigarettes. "You must have said *something* to Collette."

"Oh yeah. Her answer was to get into little theater and civic work and other stiff-upper-lip bullshit. *Christ.*"

Wil blew out a breath. "So no one did anything?"

"That I know of. What did she say?"

He shook his head.

"Maybe he'd quit, we said, maybe a lot of things. Sounds awful, but maybe Angela was better off the way it turned out."

"You can't mean that."

"Beaten to death, suicide, what's the difference. In a few years she'd have been as dead as we are."

It was like viewing the maimed survivors of a long-dead wreck; Wil stood and walked to the window, leaned on the sill. "Did you go back at all?"

She nodded. "I'd never seen him that way—all broken up, barely able to function. He just stared."

"And Collette?"

"Collette surprised me, she held it together. Way better than I would have."

"You ever hear Max Pfeiffer's name mentioned then?"

She lit another cigarette, this time without help. "You implying some tie-in with my family?"

"I didn't say that."

"I should hope not, and the answer's no."

"What about Tommy Littlefield?"

"Thomas came just before we left. I liked him—enough to

call his wife and send her some money." Patrice felt her sister's forehead, stroked her cheek.

"Were you aware Littlefield was seeing someone?"

"My God," she said harshly. "Is that what you do all day, root around in people's trash?" She began buttoning her shirt. "Great job."

"What would you say if I told you it was Field Marshal Z's sister?"

"Unreal. You could have worked for my father, you know that?"

He looked at her, at the bloody handkerchief, then at Michelle passed out on the bed, and suddenly he wanted out—anywhere but this fucking house of horrors. It felt hard to breathe, not to smash a window and jump. "Look, lady, all I know is it's a damned shame to *let* Elden DeBray win. Thanks for the help."

"You won't report it?"

"Two conditions," he said, locking on Patrice DeBray's eyes. "One, put the gun where only you can find it. Two, get her to a head doctor, and I mean tomorrow."

"Your coat," she said as they went downstairs. "At least let me fix it."

"You have enough things to fix, and I have to be somewhere." He opened the front door, stepped outside on legs that felt like rubber. Through the hedge, he could see a man peering across his front lawn at the DeBray house. "Sorry about the noise," Wil said. "Just a loud, bad movie."

He drove fast, both hands gripped on the wheel, the open window forcing cold air down his collar and through his damp hair. Across the divider, southbound headlights winked on with the deepening twilight, then swept past in the torrent of cars. He could see a plane gliding in over the water toward the airport and, farther on, the glow of San Francisco.

Knowing he was late, hoping there'd be food before Lincoln Stillman came on, Wil checked the time again, barely saw it. Instead he pictured the same thing over and over like a repeating video. Pink bedspread with rosebuds, small dresser, an armchair looking oversize in a child's bedroom. A mother who kept vigil there often—Collette DeBray trying to save her daughter from her husband.

TWENTY-FIVE

Behr snapped the trigger on one of the guns, a tec-9 machine pistol, wiped excess oil from it with a dust-free rag, then reached into the carrying case for a pump shotgun. *Not long now*. With economical movements, he had the Winchester apart and was looking down the barrel when Monika walked in.

"Was ist los?" he asked, regarding her through it. "You don't look like a woman on the verge of triumph."

She said nothing, slumped into a chair.

He cupped his hands. "I said . . ."

"I heard you."

"Then where's the elation? A few hours and—"

"Phase one is ending, that's all."

Her tone brought him up short. "That doesn't sound like you, *Liebchen*. Want me to rub your back?"

"No. And don't take that tone with me, I'm fine."

He said nothing, the better part of valor.

She looked in the mirror. *"Scheiss,"* she said. "Who in God's name is that?"

"You're allowed a little fatigue—the pace you set."

"At my age, you mean."

"That's not what—"

"Never mind. Did you *hear* her today?"

"Part, not all. Sounded like a final exam." Behr finished with the shotgun, started on one of the handguns.

"Economic theory, geopolitics, calutron enrichment, plutonium separation—*phenomenal*. She's a computer, Behr, so good I'm almost afraid . . ."

"You don't want to let her go, do you?"

Monika smoothed her hair; her expression was neutral, but when she spoke, her voice was charged. "I can't think that way."

"No, I suppose not. Hand me that brush, will you?"

She did. "I'm aware of what's involved, if that's what you're thinking."

He shrugged. "Two years in a war zone with Ammad Nassir . . ."

"Learning, Behr. Preparing."

"Expensive lessons." He got another handgun, in seconds had stripped it down to parts.

"That's right. No sailors for bus fare, no degradation to survive. Just who and what she wants. On her terms."

Thoughts touched on before, but not like this—a jet of air on a raw nerve. "Has it been so bad?"

"Giving myself away, bit by bit, piece by piece? What do you think?"

"You *are* tired."

"I look that bad, do I?"

That absurd thing about her looks again. He sighed. "Your looks are not a problem. Being you might be."

She checked the mirror again. "The truth is, I feel half dead. Except with *her.*"

He began loading thirty-round curved magazines for the submachine gun. "What about us?"

"We're finished here, you know that. The FBI's not stupid."

"I meant *us*, Monika. You and me."

Monika withdrew the chrome-plated automatic intended for Eve. "What have I been telling you? There is no us." She checked the action and trigger pull, ejected the clip.

"All due respect, but I don't believe it."

"Really," she said with sarcasm. "And when will *I* know?

Tomorrow at breakfast? Ten years from then? When I'm dead?'' Sighting in the pistol, she looked very Monika, unyielding terrorist of Berlin days, the life and death puppeteer.

"Wolf Hilke's dead, Monika. Don't wait too long."

She lowered the gun, reinserted the clip. "Whores like us don't get to choose, Behr."

TWENTY-SIX

Tire squeals on the ramp, Wil descending lower and lower; from the looks of the underground garage, Stillman had pulled quite a crowd. Finally he found a spot alongside a Jaguar, parked, and took the elevator to the surface.

Union Square was blowy, noodle cups and newsprint whipping by him on the sidewalk. He dodged across Powell, asked someone in the St. Regis lobby where Lincoln Stillman was appearing, then followed the directions to a conference room upstairs. Inside, a dressy woman took twenty-five bucks from him, told him he'd missed dinner, waved him to an empty chair at one of the round tables. As waiters hustled out last dishes, a man at the podium read announcements, then launched into the introduction, mentioning how sorry they were Mrs. Stillman couldn't make it. More then about the evening's speaker, the man calling him synonymous with defense since before the 49ers got respectable. Laughs, then: "Ladies and gentlemen, Lincoln Stillman."

Wil heard the sound of forearm crutches, turned, and saw him—eerie, as though Stillman had stepped directly from the microfilm: the same rumpled-looking suit and bow tie, sandals, bulldog face, strong-willed hair—nearly white now. He was shorter than Wil expected—five-nine or -ten with a thickish upper body that made him look top-heavy. Deft with the crutches, he reached the podium quickly, settled into a chair the other man had readied.

Stillman sat the audience down with a gesture, tugged an ear, dropped half-glasses off his forehead, checked his notes, pocketed them, shoved the glasses back up again.

Wil could see a jury buying it. The spiel, too:

"Don't see a lot of my clients out there," he began. "Probably all those pinstripes—too damn close to what they used to wear." *Laughter*.

He did a slow scan, milking it.

"You think that's funny, you lawyers, try wearing prison stripes some time. Spending your days in a space where most people wouldn't keep a dog—looking over your shoulder for a blade or a billy or a hard-on. How many ever even visited a jail, let alone heard those big doors slam shut?" He scanned the audience, the few hands raised.

Wil checked the room, too, caught rapt, uncomfortable, patronizing as Stillman went on. "Most of you know my work, more or less. What you may not know is what keeps me at it.

"Outrage," he said after a pause. "Next time you're upset over some slob trying to drug-deal his way out of the ghetto, try seeing the real crime. War on drugs? How about war on freedom?"

Citing examples, Stillman dipped back into his cases, concluding with Berkeley Eleven, which became a plea for sixties-style activism. "Fight, get scarred," he said. "With luck you'll wind up like me—beat on and bloody, but ready for the next round."

The applause was genuine, as if some skeptics had crossed over, though afterward Wil noticed mostly younger people approaching the podium. He settled down to wait; forty minutes later the last one moved off. Stillman was getting set to leave as Wil handed him his card.

"Interesting talk," he said.

Lincoln Stillman eyed it. "The private dick who phoned my service?"

"Still hoping you had a few minutes, Mr. Stillman. For Max Pfeiffer's daughter." Up close, Wil saw the wear and tear: sags under the eyes, brown spots, tiny veins webbing the nose.

"Poor old Max, who knew? How about the hotel bar? That way I won't have so far to fall."

They took the elevator, crossed the lobby to the bar, dim and clubby and crowded with lawyers from upstairs. Stillman nodded to some, shook a few hands, then they were settling into a booth that two people were leaving, Stillman giving them the glad hand as well. The bar girl was at his elbow almost before he could rest it on the table. "Aren't you a sight," he said. "Double bourbon and branch for me. And for Mr. . . ."

"Hardesty," Wil said. He ordered a Calistoga, no glass.

"You a teetotaler?" Stillman asked as the girl moved off.

"Had my share already."

Stillman grunted. "Don't trust a man who won't drink, but that's your nevermind. I read about this thing with Max and the money, real turd in the tapioca. Him dead, his daughter snatched . . ." He shook his head. "What's your involvement?"

Leaving out the DeBrays, Wil ran through it.

"Monika mentioned your chat. Never lost a client that way myself."

Wil forced a smile as their drinks came; Stillman slugged some and exhaled sharply. "Lighten up, deadeye. You making any progress?"

"Working on it."

"You and the Feds," Stillman said. "Wouldn't get my hopes up. They couldn't find a broom in a broom closet."

Wil rolled the mineral water between his hands. "You still think they were responsible for Paulette Pfeiffer's death?"

Stillman took a smaller gulp of bourbon followed by a sip of his water. "Who told you that?"

"Man named Henry Shirmir, said you had proof. That you gave it to Max."

Stillman frowned. "If it's who I remember, that's one genuine certified loose screw. Proof? You don't think I'd have gone public with something like that? My heinie. Incidentally, what'd you really think of my speech?"

Wil eyed Stillman's whiskey, feeling its heat through the glass. "Interesting."

"So you said. Kind of horsepoop word, interesting. You agree or disagree?"

"With freedom, sure. But let's talk 'freedom from' to go with all the 'freedom to.' Seen too many victims, I guess. You were in jail?"

Stillman winked. "Who said that? You clear on this Shirmir thing? I might have told Max I could see the Feds behind Paulette, but that was it. Hell, he suspected them from the beginning."

"What was he like to work with?"

Stillman powered down the rest of his bourbon, waved to the girl for more. "Real pit bull. Turned Berkeley Eleven our way—I admit that from the one modest bone in my body. Was me hired him, though, and so much for modesty."

Wil watched the girl put down Stillman's bourbon, another Calistoga for him. "What made him quit?"

"Stress, burnout, who knows? Lot going on then."

"It wasn't some disagreement?"

"Not with me."

"How long did he work for you?"

"Let's see: February seventy-three until he left in seventy-four. Right when the ARV got themselves massacred."

"One interpretation . . ."

"Nine ragtags against a hundred cops—what would you call it?"

Stillman's tone was all mock righteousness; even so, Wil felt a button pushed. "Willful disregard comes to mind. And I admit, I'd have trouble defending it."

"Mr. Hardesty, I get the impression you think I'm in the guilt-or-innocence field. Hell, I'm not here to protect society."

"Maybe not, but you're part of it," Wil said, no food in eight hours fueling his response. "Who wins when it's all smoke screen and street hustle and to hell with the truth?"

"Law One-A: Lawyers are advocates. We start looking for the truth, we lose it."

Just what he needed, a pissing contest with Lincoln Stillman. He wondered how far he ought to take this one, but
Stillman seemed to be enjoying it.

"Well?" he said.

Wil had another swallow. "Well, what?"

Stillman smiled. "Give up or want some more?"

Fwoomp—the boiler kicking in. "You ever looked into the
muzzle of a gun? I have. All you can do is hope the head
directing the trigger finger gets a notion in time that it's not
worth it. People like you take that notion away." He looked
at Stillman's expression changing, wondering that he'd actually said it.

"Well, now. *Wellllll, now.* Don't stop on my account." The
grin was wolfish.

"No, that was out of line. Forget I said it."

"Forget, hell, I live to fight. What do you think a lawyer is
if not a hired gun? And tell me that isn't what you'd want."

"Moot point. Laws deter when there's respect for them. I
don't have the answer necessarily, but there're too many bad
guys walking around."

Stillman's laugh turned heads around the room. "*Sieg heil.*
And explain 'necessarily.' "

Wil tossed off the rest of the Calistoga, its sudden carbon-
ation making his eyes water. "Try having a care for what
you're building."

"Sorry, that ain't the way it works."

"My point is, it's not working," Wil said. "All that's happening is the house is on fire and the wrong people are getting
burned."

"Hey, talk to a fireman. Anything else?"

Wil spread his hands. "Yeah. Check your politics at the
door."

"You got something in mind, say it."

Wil measured his tone. "Cleon Chapman."

Stillman smiled, but his eyes blazed. "Field Marshal Z is
what you're saying. And your crystal ball is showing."

"If Chapman caps a career in sixty-eight with some well-deserved hard time, there is no Field Marshal Z. Speaking of outrage.''

''What Cleon got from me then was another chance. Did it turn out shit? Yeah. Would I do it again? Bet your ass.'' Stillman's eyes searched for the girl. ''Two more here,'' he said before turning to Wil. ''God*damn*, you're high and wild, but you got heat. You hunt?''

''Not in years.''

''I like doves myself, evasive little bastards. Trick is to anticipate where they're headed and put your spread there.'' The girl put down the order; Stillman hefted his. ''Drink up, deadeye.''

Wil asked the girl for peanuts, something he should have done when he sat down. After she brought them and left, he took a deep breath. ''How well did you know Chapman?''

''Before his trial, not at all. Afterward . . .'' He hesitated. ''I knew some people in the Mambas I thought could help him. And I helped his mother once.''

''Beyond that?'' Wil could see the mind working. His bet: Stillman trying to shade and dodge.

''Nothing I recall.''

Wil drank a silent toast to Arnella Chapman. ''Had you any idea Max was going to leave the way he did?''

''No, but I wasn't surprised either. He missed Paulette. Hell, who wouldn't have, the looker she was.'' He drank. ''You believe he committed suicide?''

''So far. His note said, 'Trust me,' as though he was doing the right thing somehow. Know what that might be?''

''Nope.'' Stillman dabbed at condensation with his napkin.

''Did you know he was involved with the ARV?''

''Max was the *last* person I'd have figured for something like that.''

Wil ate a handful of peanuts, thinking the pissing contest had turned into a tennis match—less exciting, but at least they weren't being stared at anymore. ''Do you remember a friend of his named Joel Beck?''

''Sorry. Anybody else in your bag of tricks?''

"Rafael Canizares?"

"Uh-uh." Stillman bottomed-up. "Qualification: I meet a ton of people, most of whom I don't remember. Let alone the time factor."

The bar girl reappeared, said she was going off if they wanted to settle up. As she checked with another table, Wil reached into his pocket. "My party," he said.

Stillman put a hand out. "Not this time. Put it away."

Wil threw two twenties down; Stillman leaned closer. "What do you make a year, deadeye, forty if you're lucky? Tell you a story: My old man was a hard SOB, raised spuds on somebody else's dirt outside of Moses Lake, Washington. The one *good* crop he brought in was the year I get polio. Doc tells him I need this therapy, it costs money as you might expect. Instead my father buys DDT to fight the bugs. Crops come first, he says, and it's God's will about my legs." He rattled the crutches.

"So my ma leaves him, takes me, and lands herself this millionaire meatpacker—they die on some socked-in runway, and I get the money. I go back to this miserable farm where my father still lives—as usual, he's up to here with the worms and the blight and the owner squeezing his ass. I say, 'Pa, I've got money now. You want this land so much, I'll buy it.' He looks at me, and you know what he says? 'That's all you ever wanted, you and your ma, was filthy lucre.' So I leave and a year later he's dead. And every time I spend a buck or a hundred, that's what it is, because he said so. Take your cash, deadeye." He pushed it at Wil, thumbed a fifty out of his wallet. "It's only lucre, right? Daddy's filthy lucre."

Wil just stared as he slid out of the booth, hoisted himself up.

"Know your problem?" Stillman said. "Deep down you know there isn't a damn spit of difference between us." He winked. "Keep in touch, I might have work sometime."

Stillman was up and gone by the time Wil's heartbeat throttled back to normal. He sat in the booth while the pieces whirled:

Deborah Ann Werneke; *filthy lucre*, Z getting the term and the idea from somebody smart; Stillman dealing with Z even after the ARV were robbing banks, something the lawyer just denied—Stillman hooked into everything when you thought about it. Yet who would, because the question was *why*. Monumental what the man would be risking.

Another waitress came by and Wil ordered coffee; the bar was emptying and she brought it right away. As it cooled, reality set in. What he had on Stillman was nothing—two words remembered as odd by one of the conspirators, plus circumstantial appearances by Stillman in the lives of key players.

Just the kind of thing the cops loved.

Wil looked around the room and recognized the man who'd introduced Stillman, sitting with two men and a woman. He walked over. "Sorry to interrupt. Just wanted to say what a great evening."

The four looked at each other, then at Wil.

"Thanks," the man said. "Stillman's a draw when we can get him, which is rare."

The woman said, "Yours sounded exciting from here. Hope it's not how your coat got ripped."

Wil grinned. "That obvious, huh? I'm going to send him a letter with everything I thought of after he left."

"Always the way, isn't it?"

"Any idea where I should send it?"

The introducer responded. "L.A., some P.O. box—Stillman's real private. You a lawyer?"

"Writer," Wil said. "You wouldn't happen to know Mr. Stillman's plans, would you?"

"This for the rematch?" Snickers around the table. "Be up early. He's got a seven-something out on United, I'm driving him to the airport. We buy you a drink?"

"No, thanks, enough excitement for one night." He smiled with them. "In your opening, you mentioned Mr. Stillman's wife."

"Right. She came along last time—German girl, quite a

package. I think old Lincoln liked showing her off." He rolled his eyes, turned to the woman. "Her mind, I mean."

The other men laughed.

"You don't remember the year?"

"Eighty-two or -three, in there. Stillman's been turning us down until this gay-Army thing with the Supreme Court got him some *grande* press. I tell you about her posture?"

Wil left the men cracking up, the woman throwing peanuts at them.

Wil's call to the airport confirmed a United flight to L.A. leaving 7:22 A.M. He checked his watch, made a decision, then roused Canizares on the fifth ring.

"Sorry about the hour."

"No big," the lawyer said through yawns. "How was Stillman?"

Wil explained, told Canizares not to expect him.

"Pretty shaky stuff. Mincemeat in court."

"For now it's what I've got," Wil said. "How's Rose?"

A pause. "Rose has had a change of heart."

"Meaning what?"

"Meaning she feels badly about the way she acted. You find Holly, she'd be welcome at the house."

"Why now? Any idea?"

Canizares cleared his throat. "I've been working on her. Maybe she's paying attention. Wants to hire you, she said."

"I assume you're kidding."

"Nope, and she pays well. You interested?"

"Thanks, but no thanks."

"Well, don't say I didn't try. Good luck."

Wil placed a credit-card call next; an answering machine clicked on. He heard the receiver lifted, then Mo competing with his recorded message.

"*Goddamn this thing.* Hang on, it'll finish in a second. All right: Lieutenant Epstein, I think."

"Hey—you're up, everybody's up."

"I read midnight here, Pedro. You ever hear of common courtesy?"

"Dinner on me next time, your choice."

"Be still my heart."

"Mo, I need back in—somebody to talk to who'd know this guy Behr. Somebody German. Somebody tonight."

There was an audible sigh. "God."

"It could save her life, Mo. I'm close."

"What about the Feebles?"

"Special Agent Vega got the word on my finer qualities from your boss."

Epstein perked up. "Freiman? How'd Vega put it to you?"

"Desist now or open a fruit stand."

"So which is this?"

"The usual—trying to make lemonade from the lemons." Wil gave him his number, and after Mo hung up, got another coffee, brought it back to the booth, and pondered his moves. Tailing Stillman would be dicey, the lawyer out of sight for varying times. The choices: one—sleep in the car, follow Stillman to the airport, take the same flight; two—be at SFO already. Both risked being spotted or Stillman's leaving before Wil could get a rental in L.A. Night flight seemed the answer until he called for departures and found the last one gone.

Which left a hell of a drive, Larry King and No-Doz.

Epstein phoned then: "The German agency is the BKA— Bundes Kriminal Amt. Schenk is who you want, my source met him during the Olympics." He spelled the name, dictated a number.

Wil finished writing. "Saint Mo—last favor? Call somebody you know in INS records. I need a check on the date and place a couple was married. German woman, possibly a citizen by now—this would've been eighty-three or earlier. The name's Stillman, first name, Lincoln."

Silence, then: "Your idea of a joke, right?"

"Dinner and a weekend for two at this nice place in La Conchita just happens to be available."

"Tomorrow after ten, and we'll see. Now buzz the fuck off."

TWENTY-SEVEN

Monika watched the shapes come into focus: furniture, light fixtures, her paintings. She checked the clock radio—almost two—yawned, swung her feet into slippers, and used the bathroom. Finished, she splashed water on her face, looked into mirrored eyes as she toweled.

Almost by themselves her eyes tracked the curve of breast to belly, hips, and what lay between: this thing that men did anything for. Her middle-school Nietzsche surfaced, something about love being transfiguring power. The line formed and hung there: *When a man is in love he endures more than at other times; he submits to everything.*

She lit a cigarette, thought about what was soon to end, this thing with the three of them. Balanced power, classic Walpole: Behr extending the force of her will, protecting her against Lincoln; Lincoln providing shelter and deep cover for her operations; herself and what she gave. Carousel horses came to mind, each eyeing the other's back. Circling endlessly . . .

Not endlessly.

Once more she went over tomorrow, anticipating, envisioning. Imagining herself without Lincoln's wit and intellect, his attentiveness, little things he did to please her. How it was in the beginning. The thought caused an odd sensation before passing, like the chill from a sudden cloud shadow.

She flushed the cigarette down the toilet and on her way back to bed paused to crack the window for air. She took in cricket hum, night wildflowers, Big Dipper through the trees, garage with its tile roof and hooded windows, one showing faint light. The passageway to Eve's room.

And then there were two.

Standing there, she pictured it: governments dropping like dynamited buildings, nuclear weapons in the hands of the perfect terrorist—a female, beholden to no one, loyal only to her intellect and to Monika.

One and the same.

In her closet, she found dark pants and top, espadrilles, a small flashlight with a red filter lens. Down the stairs then, out the French doors and into night air, through the garage's side entrance, up the narrow stairway to the second landing. Past Behr's quarters to the end of the hall.

Being careful to make no noise, she released the dead bolt, inched open the door; illumination from the hall light revealed Eve on her side, breathing rhythmically. Monika closed and locked the door, twisted on the flashlight. Watching Eve sleep, the strange feeling swept over her again, and she eased down next to the bed. For a moment she thought her creation would awaken, but after a deep sigh, she was still.

Monika twisted off the light, let the blackness envelop her, senses adjust. She could smell the rough soap from Eve's bath, feel the rise and fall of her body, hear the rush of air from her lips—all she could do not to reach out and touch her. Suddenly she longed for sweet heather and warm springs, sheep grazing junipered moors, and no tomorrow.

TWENTY-EIGHT

Traffic was light, trucks and a few campers with APVs out to get a jump on Memorial Day. Stars showed; a hint of summer wafted in, blooms and the fragrance of drying grass. Through the windshield, Wil made out orchards, row crops, eucalyptus dividers, here and there fields of artichokes—spidery shapes in the night.

Lisa thoughts surfaced: her with someone else, sweat like battery acid on his skin. *Nobody you'd know.*

He dialed up a jazz station, lost it to static, tried another talk show, then turned it off and sipped lukewarm coffee as he drove. Stillman thoughts now: his sucking in a vulnerable Max, stricken over Paulette—the car bombing not too big a stretch to think Behr, the link to Stillman that he needed. Stillman lying about his involvement with Cleon Chapman after Cleon's trial. Pulling Chapman's strings, working Max into the ARV, Max's military training crucial to future operations. Holly crucial leverage to ensure Max's cooperation on Angela DeBray.

Why?

Not money—Stillman's inherited lucre enabled him to defend whomever he chose, including those without it. Lashing out at the wastrel oppressor ruling class represented by Angela's father? Elden DeBray and Lincoln Stillman likely supported the same charities.

Always more questions than answers.

At Paso Robles he stopped for gas, the twenty-four-hour station surprisingly busy at that hour. After a trip to the head and fresh coffee, he found a phone, dialed the overseas operator and got a line, then punched in the number Mo gave him.

"Bundes Kriminal Amt. Büro Oberst Schenk."

Wil told the woman his name, where he was calling from. Her switch to English was rapid and barely accented.

"May I tell Colonel Schenk which law enforcement agency?"

"Just tell him Ernst Jürgen Behr."

She repeated it, put him on hold; seconds passed, then the line was picked up. "Schenk here." Clearing of throat, a crumple of paper—office lunch if he had the time differential figured correctly. Then: "You mentioned a name?"

"I need your help, Colonel. I'm the one who made Behr."

"You are not FBI?"

"No. Private."

"Why my help? And how did you get this number?"

Wil told him; over line hiss, he heard the creaking of a chair. Outside the booth, a big-rig jakebraked, brapping noise intense until the truck passed.

"You always have trucks in your office, Mr. . . . ?"

"Hardesty. I was told you linked Behr with the Locusts."

"Die Heuschrecke, yes. Behr came to our attention during a double murder—a banker and his mistress in nineteen sixty-eight. He had a different name then, one of several he used." Wil heard him gulp something. "Mr. Hardesty, I hope someone not in law enforcement knows the danger here."

"Thank you, I've seen him in action. I was told Behr wasn't a member of the group."

"That's correct. He worked for the group's leader, who disappeared, unfortunately."

"But you knew who it was." Bugs seeking light fluttered against the glass.

"No. Our fault, I'm afraid—we killed everyone who might know. We did get a subordinate's confession, however. Apparently there was a core group to which the leader imparted ideology and issued standing orders. But always there was an intermediary.''

Wil heard muffled German, then: ''I have meetings, Mr. Hardesty. Is there something else?''

''When did the leader disappear?''

''Judging from a lull in activities, fall or winter of sixty-nine. By summer, the gang was finished.''

''How extensive was their range?''

''Berlin, then West Germany—Stuttgart, Wolfsburg, Essen, Bonn.''

''Can you tell me which incident preceded the lull?''

Pause-hiss, more shuffling of paper, impatience in his tone. ''Lars Doitsch, industrialist—kidnapped, ransomed, shot in the knees, dumped on the steps of the Bundeshaus, twelve November, sixty-nine, Bonn. The following June they attacked a Berlin *Vopo*. The final incident I was referring to.''

''*Vopo* . . .''

''*Volkspolizei*, Mr. Hardesty—a police station. And now I must go.''

''Was Behr seen at the *Vopo*?''

''No. He vanished also during the lull.''

''Last question: Your take on the leader—man or woman?''

Schenk paused, expelled breath. ''Man, but that reminds me. The one who confessed mentioned their ongoing concern for creating the perfect terrorist, someone the leader could train to take over. Someone young. And now, goodbye.'' He hung up.

The perfect terrorist.

Someone young.

An air horn sounded from the roadway. Fighting his thoughts, Wil slammed the car door, then spun the rental away from the all-night station and up the ramp.

Seven A.M.: gray light turning brown, San Fernando Valley traffic creating a throb of stop-and-go red. Wil checked his watch, imagined Stillman taking off about now, making better

time from San Francisco than *he* could to LAX. Half mile in
ten minutes; Wil made a decision and a right on Topanga
Canyon, gambling on Pacific Coast Highway. Traffic was
somewhat better here, the coast road to Santa Monica moving
steadily, if not fast. Cutting in on Route 10, he picked up the
molasses stream at the San Diego Freeway, then exited and
caught the airport loop. By eight-twenty he was parked against
a curb, the terminal he wanted a shallow angle ahead.

He got out, stretched, raised the trunk, and feigned unload-
ing. Spotting a phone, he confirmed Stillman's flight had left
after a forty-minute fog delay and would be landing momentarily. Next he tried Mo Epstein, despite his admonition to call
after ten: Lieutenant Epstein was not in yet, was there any
message? Wil declined, fumbled through his wallet for the
Chronicle clipping, and dialed the number listed at the bottom.
Two screening voices came on, then Vega.

"What is it, Hardesty?" Fatigue came through clearly.

"I haven't seen today's paper. Any luck?"

"You called for that? Christ Almighty!" Vega breathed au-
dibly. "No," he said finally. "We've got a hundred things
going and none at all, not since the blood in the junker. Where
are you?"

"Out of your hair. I was hoping it'd buy me a question."

"One—and make it brief."

He did, was hanging up when a Rolls Royce swung in. A
uniformed man stepped out, around the car and into the building. Ten minutes passed, fifteen; a motorcycle cop cruised
past, eyed Wil hurrying to close his trunk, then ticketed the
Rolls. A minute after she'd left, Wil watched Stillman exit the
terminal with the uniformed man, bags in hand. He put them
in the trunk, held open the car door and shut it behind Stillman, then tore up the ticket. The Rolls eased away from the
curb and out into traffic.

Wil followed, allowing cars to dart in between; several
lights and the Rolls was turning onto the San Diego north-
bound. From two lanes over and a dozen lengths behind, he
munched gas-station trail mix and eyed the car's distinctive

lines, darkened windows. Past Wilshire, the car slipped over
to the right, Wil with it: left lane, Sunset exit. The Rolls turned
then, maintaining a pace neither fast nor slow through Brent-
wood and into Pacific Palisades. At that, Wil nearly missed
the car's hard right.

He approached with caution, preparing to U if the driver
had made the tail and was waiting. He wasn't, and Wil horsed
the rental. Tricky here: no cars ahead for cover, winding upward into hills showing fewer homes and more trees—scrub
oaks and sycamore, green with spring growth. Washboard
ocean showed through the decaying overcast. Free of smog,
the air held the pale scent of yellow broom.

Gradually the Rolls slowed before a narrow gate that began
opening automatically. Wil swung off the road and down a
spur on the water side, parked, and walked back up to where
he could see the gate. Closed now, it was flanked by high wall
fronting a large property.

He looked around: no other houses on this section of road,
a few roofs showing well below where he'd parked. No hab-
itation on the steep hill behind the wall, nor on its crest.
Sounds: birds twittering and the low hum of insects; faint and
far away, the moan of a foghorn. Sunlight morsed off a pleasure boat heading upcoast toward Malibu.

From what he could see, the house was big and multistoried.
Matching its Mediterranean style was another building, garage
most likely. Wil walked back to the car, took a left at the lip
of the road; driving slowly past the gate, he saw bougainvillea-
lined drive and a hint of courtyard. Wall-mounted video cameras caught opposing sides of the entrance.

He accelerated around the curve, past NOT A THRU STREET,
up to where the road ended. Beyond the barrier, two trails
took off through the brush, one looking promising. Wil turned
around and drove back down to a service-station pay phone
on Sunset. Waiting, he swallowed two more No-Doz with
vending-machine coffee.

"Lieutenant Epstein."

"Anything yet from INS?" Wil's fingers tapped the coin slot.

"God forbid a 'good morning.' "

Wil stopped tapping and took a deep breath. "Sorry, Mo—morning."

"You sound like a long hard night."

Wil said nothing; pages turned in his ear.

"You never heard this, got it? Lincoln Everett Stillman married Lilith Monika Unseker November seventeeth, nineteen sixty-nine, Bonn, FGR. Place of U.S. entry: New York. She became a citizen August fourth, nineteen seventy, L.A., now their place of residence." Another page turned. "Stillman vouched for a cousin, one Jürgen Schmidt, who came in as an employee. Schmidt died in seventy-seven—"

"Hold a sec. Died?"

"Drowned off Catalina. This what you're looking for?"

"Not exactly. Schmidt can't be Behr if he's dead."

"Assuming it was him they fished out."

Wil allowed the possibility, and another. "How hard is it to get in here, Mo—say, like this Schmidt did?"

"Biggest hurdle'd be the Germans. If Schmidt *was* Behr, he'd have had to acquire new ID, then with the forgeries get legal documents to emigrate—all with the *Polizei* on alert. Be tough. Long as he was legit from there, though, he'd probably skate."

Rapid-fire thoughts, aided by recall and his Schenk notes; *Bonn, November 12, '69: industrialist Lars Doitsch, shot and dumped. Five days later Stillman marries Lilith Monika Unseker. Behr and the terrorist leader vanish—lay-low time.*

1972: Cleon Chapman, Stillman defendant and hard-case project, founds ARV, becomes Field Marshal Z—intros with bank robberies, moves up to kidnap-ransom schemes, both Heuschrecke m.o.

Filthy lucre. Max Pfeiffer. Angela DeBray.

Stillman. Behr. Monika. Son of a bitch.

"You there?"

Wil snapped out of it, his pulse racing. "I'm here."

"Me and somebody hot, pal, you and Lisa. Later."

Lisa's name was like ice on a cracked filling; he shook it off, made two more calls, one to San Francisco, one to Atherton. Then he started the car and gunned it back up the hill—past the gate again, around the curve to the end of the road. Locking the car, he noticed something under the passenger seat and slipped it into his pocket.

Fresh air and just moving around made him feel better; blooming ceanothus left pollen where it touched. On both sides of the trail, yucca spiked upward. Swallows darted ahead of him like stones being skimmed.

He was sweating by the time the trail joined a fire road at the ridgeline; twenty minutes and he was at the hill he figured must be the right one. Leaving the road, he crossed an area thick with foxtail, then he was high above red tile roofs—the house and garage. Ten minutes, twenty, thirty: A hundred yards from the bottom, he stopped among a grouping of small oaks that lined a ravine, the best available vantage point.

Perhaps four acres in all, the estate sat in the notch made by the hills and the curving road, wall controlling access only from the front. Lawn contoured under big trees to a patio at the rear of the house. Below him, his ravine became a stream-bed that was ushered through the grounds, then out a culvert.

The house he'd seen as Mediterranean now looked merely restless. Balconies jutted, walls stepped forward and receded, windows wore heavy molding. The garage was simpler, a long rectangle with four bays and inlets of glass above. Servant's quarters, he guessed, though he still saw no one.

What now? When to do it?

Waiting for darkness meant losing the better part of the day, but increased his chances of entering unseen. Compromise: wait for dark, go in before if the opportunity arose. Wil ate the last of the trail mix, folded the shetland under him for comfort, and settled himself on the dry ground.

TWENTY-NINE

Lincoln Stillman told Henning to screw the eggs, he wasn't hungry. He opened the doors to his office, poured himself a hair of the dog, then sank down in the leather chair. Someone had left the drapes open, the lawn in full view, but he was too tired to get up and close them, make The Insatiable Thing go away. Was it ever going to rain again in this godforsaken country?

He drank and poured another, thinking he really ought to cut down. After last night's run-in with the peeper, he'd slept poorly despite the two belts ordered up afterward. And what did this Hardesty know, anyway? Trying to get a handle on it in the bar, he'd come off as merely evasive. Then baiting the man, wasting more time—real shitdrool performance. Pooped with the long day, he'd been caught off guard.

Have a care for what you're building ... pure slop! He wondered how the man survived two go-rounds with Behr.

He was wondering how it went with Monika, forced to eat it on her deal with the Scourge of Jerusalem, when they entered. Behr nodded his usual greeting, but her kiss and smile surprised him.

She took the chair beside the desk, draped a lug-soled boot over one knee. She wore khaki trousers, steel-gray shirt open at the collar, silver choker and ear studs, the effect typical Monika—industrial-strength sex appeal—with something added, a brightness.

"And how was our adversary?" she began. "Did you see him?"

"Nothing to worry about, pet. The guy's dead in the water."

"I see. And the event?"

"Same old crapola," he said warily. "Talking to corporate titsuckers. And speaking of money . . ."

Her fingers twisted spun gold.

"Deal's off, I take it?"

"Behr and I worked something out."

He shrugged, trying to read her tone: nothing beyond the ordinary. Their brief glance was no problem. He knew what existed between Monika and Behr, had long since ceased to let it bother him.

"You're enrolling her in law school, I *knew* it." His wink at Behr drew a polite smile. Monika's also seemed genuine; maybe this thing was copacetic and the other night nolo contendere. Okay by him.

"Thinking over what we discussed, the answer was obvious," she was saying now. "Still, I'd like you to see how things stand with Eve." She rose. "You're tired, I know, but can you come now?"

Eve, shmeve. "To see you reap what you've sown, pet? Always time for that."

Behr handed him the crutches and they stepped out onto the patio, Monika in the lead. Without overcast the day was turning hot; sunlight skittered off the oak and eucalyptus leaves. A squirrel tore up the oak, then chattered down at them.

"Where is everybody? I wanted some things done. Tear out the lawn to start with—thing's got a drinking problem." He laughed, savoring the humor. His victory.

She looked back. "I gave them another day off. Henning just left."

Stillman shrugged off a twinge of apprehension. He'd shown her all right; mess with ol' Linc, you took on a wild boar. So why the nerves? Hell, the power had been his from day one, he had it back was all. "That land I was telling you about, Monika? It's in Washington state, spuds so big you have to roll 'em to market. Hell, Daddy used to cut up the culls like T-bones.'' *You lose, pet—take it up with Daddy.*

She held open the side door to the garage, her hair flaring white sun. Then they were up the stairs and down the hall, Behr at his elbow. ''So what is this, show and tell? PTA?''

''In a way, Lincoln.'' She found her key, snapped the dead bolt, swung the door back, and followed him in.

The girl was in jeans and the long-sleeved pink shirt she'd arrived in, the bloodstains faded or by now crudely laundered out. She sat on the opposite end of the bed and regarded him singularly, her face tense and devoid of expression.

''Hey, little sister,'' he said to be pleasant.

Behr unfolded the metal chair he'd brought in, then left the room. ''Sit down, Lincoln,'' Monika said. ''Eve has something to show you.''

Eve, my ass. Was he the only one didn't need a reality check? He sat, looked around. ''Bit tight in here for demonstrations, isn't it?'' The feeling came again, something about it not right: her body language, Monika's folded arms, the way they were staring at him . . . *Fuck this*. He reached for the crutches, but she'd positioned them against the sink.

''All right, Eve,'' Monika said, and in spite of himself, he had to look as the girl brought out a chrome-plated automatic pistol from behind her back.

For the moment no one said anything; Stillman saw flush rising on the girl's face and neck, felt his own sweat pop. ''Monika, I'd question your sanity if I thought that was loaded.''

''Not as yet,'' Monika said. She produced a piece of paper, unfolded it. ''Lincoln Everett Stillman, you have been found guilty by this tribunal of the crimes of murder and attempted murder. The penalty is death. Have you anything to say?''

With difficulty he found his voice. ''Are you out of your *mind*? Just who am I supposed to have murdered?''

''Paulette Miles Pfeiffer. It's all here.''

''This is insane,'' he said in a voice not sounding like his.

"You understand me? Fucking lunacy. Hand me those canes."

Monika stepped forward and took the gun. She withdrew the clip, thumbed in a single cartridge, reinserted the clip. Then she worked the slide and pressed the loaded weapon back into the girl's hands.

"What the hell have you been telling her?"

"The truth, Lincoln." Monika straightened, put a hand to the girl's shoulder as she raised the pistol. "Finger inside the guard, Eve, like I showed you. Now aim for the heart."

"The heart? For God's sake." Too far from the girl, too far from the door, too far from his crutches, too far from . . .

"Behr . . ."

The door remained closed.

"Behhrrr!"

Stillman swung his eyes back to the gun, pointed at his chest. But it was as if the girl's resolve was melting, the muzzle moving in circles now, her face a maché mask down which tears were starting.

"Shoot him," Monika said.

Cords in the girl's neck stood out and her whole body trembled. *"I . . . can't."*

"Yes you *can!*"

The circles increased in size.

"She can't," he blurted. "She knows better. Something you haven't leached completely out of her."

"Now, Eve." But the gun was already on the way down.

Monika stood rigid, fists clenched as the girl sagged. Suddenly she yanked back the gun and ejected the cartridge, which went spinning away on the floor.

"I'm gravely disappointed, Eve," she said. "You betray not only the revolution but my faith in you, our future. Everything we worked for." She tossed the empty gun in the girl's lap. "You leave me few options."

Stillman's sigh came all the way from his colon; he wiped his face with his sleeve. "Look, why don't we just forget this ever happened?"

Monika called Behr's name, and this time he appeared, a black revolver shoved into his waistband.

"Nassir's people are coming," he said matter-of-factly.

"Never mind that. We have a problem."

Stillman said, "What about it, Monika? Forgive and forget?"

"After trying to steal what's mine?"

"*A fucking joke.* You can have the money."

"I intend to." She gestured to Behr. "Kill him."

"Wait . . ."

For a long moment she hesitated, then her eyes hardened. "You're right, Lincoln," she said. Then to Behr, "Kill them both."

On the bed, the girl had brought her knees up and was clutching them, her eyes wide. *"Oh, God, no . . ."*

Monika bent and held the girl's face in her hands, kissed her fiercely. "Without trust there is nothing, Eve." Abruptly she turned away. *"Now!* Before I change my mind."

Behr drew the revolver and cocked it.

Jesus God, so that's how it looked. One chance left, courtroom ice summoned from the blizzard raging inside: "Ask him how it felt to blow up your precious Wolfie."

Behr's face reflected disbelief. He leveled the revolver.

"Blew his shit right up. Just a job at the time, nothing personal. Until he met you."

Sweat glistened on the big man's forehead.

"Hold," Monika said. "What did you say?"

Behr's eyes went to her as though not comprehending.

"Inquiries I made turned it up—Behr did nasty things for the union then. Like eliminate a rabble-rouser spouting reform, even after he'd been warned. Ask him, pet."

Monika turned on Behr, the color gone from her face now, lips a pinched line. Tears were forming in the big man's eyes. *"Please . . ."*

"You killed my Wolf?" she said. *"You?"*

Behr's voice was part whisper, part whimper. "I'll always love you, Monika," he said. Then he raised the gun and fired.

THIRTY

Stiff from sitting, Wil was trying to guess where the chauffeur had gone when he heard the popping sound, unmistakable even at this distance.

Garage.

Fear for Holly blew off his caution; he stumbled down the ravine, over rocky ground and low knoll, then sprinted across the grass, following a line of trees. No one in sight still. He leaped the stream, skirted the patio. Ten more steps and he was at the short side of the building, lathered and flattened beside the door. Listening to nothing. Unholstering the .45.

Heart pounding, he twisted the handle, swung the door wide, jerked a look at empty stairwell; halfway up, still no sounds. Then . . . something. Gun hand braced, his back against the wall, Wil eased upward. And heard it again.

Moans.

He inched forward down the hall: one door, two, the sounds coming from the room by the far stairs. He edged out, saw nothing and flattened again; from inside, the moans rose and subsided. At the door frame, he risked a look, caught his breath.

It was not a big room for so much chaos, stagey except for the genuine horror of it. Blood patterned the wall and the bunk lay on its side. Red handprints stained a dripping sink while a bloody towel backed up water in the basin. Behr sat on the floor, cradling a woman's head. Her chest was an apron of blood, the eyes hooded in death. Behr rocked and moaned. With another towel, he wiped the woman's face.

Something on the floor beside the overturned bunk: Keeping the .45 on Behr, Wil bent and picked it up—nine-millimeter unspent round, new blood on the brass. Instinctively he pocketed the bullet as Behr ceased moaning and became aware of him.

The big face clouded; he said something in German.

Wil shook his head, gestured with the gun. "That Mrs. Stillman?"

Grief flooded back, incongruous on Behr's thick features. "Not Stillman," he managed to say. "Not ever."

Wil could see the grip of a revolver. "All right, on your knees," he said. "Hands behind your head. Now."

Behr just looked at him; Wil heard a car door slam.

Backing toward the window, he watched Behr lower Monika Stillman's head gently to the floor, then rise to his knees, the man huge even then. He locked the .45 on the big chest and risked a look: Lincoln Stillman tossing a briefcase into the Rolls Royce; beside him, Holly Pfeiffer looking dazed, Stillman's clawlike grip on her arm.

Wil felt a surge of elation, then anger as Stillman began shoving her in after the briefcase. He smashed a pane in the glass, yelled, *"Run,"* saw her twist left-right-left in Stillman's grasp, and then he was out of time, swinging back to see the big man still kneeling. Lifting the revolver.

The shot lanced through belt-loop high, just as his own shot went wide. For a second he hesitated, then the sight of Behr rising spurred him and he was through the broken window, rolling down steep tile in a shower of glass, flailing for purchase and off the roof. Landing hard, he felt pain in his ankle, saw the .45 spin away under a utility truck, and Behr coming through the smashed frame.

Up and limping, not seeing her, hoping she'd made it as the Rolls gunned out the drive, Wil pushed off for the house, looking back once to see the big man land. *Move, move.* He reached patio tile and jumped a lounge, his ankle and side stabbing him.

Shots came, the air near his head buzzing. Shouldering through French doors, he rolled on thick carpeting—desk, chairs, bar: a study. He made it through the inner door, banged it shut behind him. Hall, foyer, stairs—conscious of no other details than his lack of a weapon and a route of escape.

Stairs.

He limped toward them, then up, expecting shots at any second, pausing for breath at the top. Still no Behr. He picked a corridor, began opening doors, searching for some means to defend himself: bathroom scissors at least a possibility; guest bedroom—sparsely furnished, no help. He was in a third bedroom when he heard the bursts.

Into the hall, understanding the brief hiatus now: Behr retrieving the submachine gun that nearly finished them at Tahoe. Noise level said he'd removed the silencer—more efficient that way in close combat.

Another burst, this one louder as Behr climbed the stairs. "Nowhere to hide," he shouted. "I see your blood." More rounds ripped down ceiling and light fixtures.

Wil heard him eject the magazine, slam another in, work the action; he headed for the last bedroom, the door closed and locked. Ankle hurting, his side on fire, he stepped back and took a hobbled run at it.

Once . . . twice: The door gave before his shoulder did, but just barely; through it then, followed by another burst that raised splinters and drove him back. Into the muzzle of an automatic pistol.

Her eyes were shut tight, lips drawn back. Breathing hard, she pulled a dead trigger, flinching each time.

"It's Wil, Holly. Give me the gun." Her eyes opened; she stopped jerking, allowed him to pry her fingers loose from it. Nine mil, unfired.

"Where'd you get this?"

Nothing.

"Where . . ."

"I couldn't shoot him." Thready, as if her throat were too small.

Playing off it: Monika wanting one of them shot, a test of some kind. But she'd never have given up a fully loaded gun—rather put a round in, ejected it when Holly'd failed. The bullet . . . He searched the shetland, felt it there, chambered it. The round fit: life and death for both of them. He worked the slide.

Two bursts tore the door completely off.

"Lock yourself in." He shoved her toward the bathroom, turned to face the opening. Through a crack in the shattered frame, through plaster dust and blue haze, he saw Behr moving down the opposite side of the corridor—graceful, controlled steps like the afternoon at the stone house, the assault weapon a deadly extension.

"Not then, not now, you asshole." Wil whipped the pistol around the door frame, saw the big form duck into one of the bedrooms before he jerked it back. There was a moment of quiet, then a laugh as Behr poked his head out. Buying it.

"A gun with no bullets, a stick in the forest." He stepped back into the hall, started forward. "Time to pay."

Wil swung around and fired. For a moment he thought he'd missed, so negligible was the reaction. Then the big man's shirt began to redden and he slowly dropped the submachine gun. Behr looked down at his chest, then at Wil, then his eyes drifted upward to things unseen.

It seemed as if he took forever to fall.

She held tight, shaking, until he had to sit down, all of it catching up. When the shakes stopped, she wrapped the wound in his side, Wil wondering how a two-inch in-and-out could bleed so damn much. As she worked, he told her things about her kidnappers, leaving out the why, still thinking about what he was going to tell the FBI. She told him then about how it had been for her: the tapes; Monika's calling her Eve; her failure to obey orders and execute Stillman. Monika's passing sentence on her too; thinking she was going to die, praying to her father for help. Knowing then she'd always love him.

She began to cry softly; Wil held her again until it stopped.

"Nearly forgot," he said. "I brought you something." He pulled out the sprig of bay leaves, leathery and broken, but still fragrant. "Wouldn't want your next dish to lack flavor."

She took them, sniffed, then a smile started and took over.

"Sorry about their condition. I know where to get more."

"No, they're perfect. What do we do now?"

"For starters, my car's about a mile up the road and Stillman left the gate open. Feel like stretching your legs?"

"Are you kidding me?" She took his keys. "Don't go anywhere."

"You, either."

When she'd gone, he started going through the upstairs, discovered nothing much, and tried the study: ornate desk, law books, the open floor safe with nothing—not even a stray bill. Behind shutters, he found four locked vertical files and with a paper clip opened the first and plunged in, hitting on the memo right away. The rest of the cabinets yielded nothing he was looking for.

Finished with the house, he started on the garage, downstairs first, then up: nothing in the horror room or the storage quarters on either side. Last room—from the chain-saw case, knowing immediately whose it was: ammo, grenades, fuses, boxes marked EXPLOSIVE, pump shotguns. And behind the locked closet door he sprung open, a gray metal legal file.

The taped cardboard box was long and flat and stacked in the bottom drawer under a case of double-aught shells. Wil broke the seal, looked at report papers listing Holly Pfeiffer as patient, Joel Beck as physician, then X-ray film underneath the typed reports. He took the box and shut the drawer, then headed back to the study, where he put the memo file inside and resealed the tape. He was gulping Tylenol from a bottle he'd found, working his ankle gingerly, when the desk phone rang. He picked it up, heard a familiar voice driven by urgency.

"You get him, Behr?"

"Not Behr, Stillman."

Silence, then: "Deadeye? Saw you charging to the rescue, figured I'd let Behr handle it. Son of a bitch sure is slipping." His speech held the hot slur of liquor.

"Slipped," Wil said, searching for identifying background noises, hearing none.

"Just as well I hedged my bets, then. You want money?"

"It's over, Stillman. Where are you?"

The lawyer drank from something, expelled breath. "What did we talk about before? Now's when it gets interesting."

"I found the medical records. And I know why Monika wanted her."

"Aren't you the busy one."

"She mentioned people were coming for her, and a name—Nassir. *Ammad* Nassir?"

"Could be."

"When?"

"You got me," Stillman said. "Man, I'd forgotten what Monika was like when her back was up—my fault, trying to take her down a notch. Shoulda known." Another gulp and bottle sounds. "Got two-and-a-half million big ones here I'd split, plus a job now that Behr's dead. Who needs the law, right?"

"Talk to me, and I'll think it over."

"How about some odds on my chances?"

"Slim but breathing."

There was a pause. "Hell, any gamble's better than none, I s'pose."

"Why *you* in all this?" Wil asked.

"You in the study? Somewhere in the Louie there's pictures. Have a look, then you tell me."

Wil slid desk drawers, found them finally in a manila envelope, old snapshots, portraits, nudes. She was blond and perfect and he told Stillman he saw what he meant, which wasn't far from the truth.

"She used everybody and nobody cared," he said, "espe-

cially a lonely old crow like me. I'd have done anything for
her and did.''

"You knew what she was?"

"Didn't give a flying fuck. Hell, I got off on it. We did
some banks, then some more—that was the deal, see. She and
Behr needed cover, I needed cash. By the time we met, I was
through the meatpacker's bundle and then some. Always was
shit with money, and none of my clients had any. Made more
enemies than lucre.'' He drank.

"Then it was her idea."

"Yep. Took half for her thing and left me the rest. Ol'
Monika—not bad for a lost-cause lawyer with no illusions
about his talent or future, a cripple with this face anyway."
He paused. "I am damn straight going to miss that woman. I
truly am."

Favoring his good side, Wil eased into the big chair. "She
set up the DeBray thing too?"

"Let's just say she saw the possibilities. Chapman, for instance. Here's this street kid I kinda liked because he was a
battler, like me. I land him in the Mambas—she sets him up
as a field marshal with his own army. But that was Monika.
Sad she never liked Cleon and he never took to being dictated
to by a woman. Finally got too big for his britches, so she
turned him. Bye-bye Z. She knew he'd fight." He paused.
"Now what about the cops?"

Wil parried. "Why did Behr kill her?"

"Your girl didn't say? Hell, she was going to have him
shoot *me*, till I told her about him blowing up her first husband. He had no choice after that, she'd have skinned him
with a butter knife." Sounding drunk now: "Truth—you
haven't called the cops, have you?"

"No. What about Max?"

"Him she met at Berkeley Eleven, all intense and smart as
a whip—that she *really* loved. Next thing I know, she's having
me blow up his wife and blaming it on the Feds. Max was
already predisposed to hate their guts."

"I found the memo."

"Amazing what money can buy. Voilà Max and me. Voilà Max and Cleon Chapman. A million and a quarter, Jack, what do you say?"

Wil rubbed eyelids that felt lined with scouring powder. "Was it Monika's idea, using Holly to keep Max in line?"

Stillman laughed sourly. "Credit where it's due. Six fucking weeks my guy Cleon can't hold it together. Even at the end he blows it."

"Why *her* after all this time?"

"Simple—none of the others Monika found worked out, not sharp enough or something. Personally, I thought all of it was a crock."

"And that's why you ordered the Tahoe hit."

"Damn—gotta leave *some'n* for you to figure out. Nothing's worth shit unless you earn it. Look how I turned out."

"Not too late." Wil shifted positions, the movement like rope burn on his side. "At least you'd have confidence in your counsel."

"Bad day all around, deadeye, no lawyer in his right mind represents himself." Another gulp and whiskey gasp. "Out of booze—speak now or forever hold your dick. You reached a verdict?"

"Yeah. Give it up."

Stillman grunted. "How long to earn one-and-a-quarter mil, let alone the wages?"

He surveyed the room, patio, expanse of lawn, the hillside rising behind it. "How long to wash out the blood?"

There was a belch and a buzz.

Wil sat behind the big desk until he heard a car in the drive. Holly entered, flushed and alive, pushing hair off her forehead—despite everything looking like something out of a Reebok ad.

"I *ran* up there. God, it felt good."

Wil smiled back, gave her the taped box, told her to lock it in the trunk of the car. Then he called Vega.

•   •   •

LAPD units got there first: patrol officers—one of whom retrieved his .45 from under the truck—then detectives in plainclothes and vanilla cars. Then Vega with Doty, other FBI agents and a CIA man. Wil was blocking it out for them when the vans arrived: crime lab techs and coroner's people, a medic unit. Lurking outside the gate, media teams.

One of the EMTs redid his makeshift bandage, recommended a tetanus shot and stitches. For a long time everyone looked at everything, then Wil gave his statement, Holly hers. Prevailing theory: money to drive a domestic terrorist operation as motive, bank jobs the means. Monika's fevered dream was responsible for Holly, Behr for Monika, Stillman for the rest. Stillman, they hoped, would add details when he was apprehended.

Inevitable, they all agreed.

Harder would be apprehending Nassir's people, but the CIA man voiced optimism before leaving to spread his net. Around seven the bodies were wheeled out on gurneys and driven away. Wil told Vega where they'd be the next few days, then they left.

He took Pacific Coast Highway along the ocean, past Malibu and Trancas where he used to surf, the late sun adding gold tint to green waves curling up the beach. At Point Mugu, they stopped, threw rocks in the water, and watched the sun break the horizon, wispy clouds turning pink then gray in the afterglow. Her questions, which had started with a kind of manic intensity, quieted with the fading light, and by the time he was making the turn for La Conchita, she was head-against-the-window, *thank-you-Max* asleep.

THIRTY-ONE

After a restless night on the couch, Wil got up at five, made coffee, and watched the oil-rig lights give way to predawn. By eight, he'd showered, had breakfast, sorted through mail, then cleaned up as much as he could without waking her. Before he used the phone to set up an appointment, he played back messages, hearing Lisa's voice on the last one, shutting it off before . . . what?

He didn't want to know. Not yet.

He poked his head in, saw her sleeping, debated waking her. Instead, he left a note telling her where things were, that he'd be back in two hours.

He nearly was, twenty minutes in a supermarket line and his sore ankle the kicker. She was in the kitchen waiting for him as he limped in. He put down the bags, saw she had on clothes Lisa had left, an appliquéd purple sweatshirt and jeans. Her feet were bare, hair still damp from the shower. She held a coffee mug that she set down to hug him.

"I never said it yesterday. Thank you."

Don't you want me?

He smoothed her hair, thinking how soft it was, how good his shampoo smelled on her, her body in Lisa's sweatshirt. Feelings he didn't even attempt to catalog.

"De nada," he said finally. Then, "How about a walk on the beach? Thing to do in La Conchita."

"No shoes okay?"

"No shoes rule." He led her slowly downstairs, across the street, and through the access tunnel, where she helped him climb down onto warm sand.

"Where are we, anyway?" she asked.

"Eighty-five miles north of L.A., twelve south of Santa Barbara. Over there's where I surf—Rincon del Mar."

She squinted, held a hand to her eyes. "Maybe I could try it sometime."

"Name it," he said.

As they strolled, he filled her in on the Rincon—the right point break and rocky bottom, takeoff spots that during big swells merged to let you rip all the way down the length of the point. About the banana plantation just up the street, how the fruit ripened in blue plastic bags. Small talk that felt right.

He moved to dry sand where they just sat for a while. Joggers passed with their dogs; off to the right, small birds chased retreating waves, then were chased as the water surged back.

"It's beautiful," she said. "No wonder you like it here."

He let a minute go by. "Remember when we made our deal, I told you I'd do everything I could to find the truth? Well, I think I have."

She cocked her head. "What was that yesterday?"

"Part, not all. You know from the beginning I've had questions: Why your father killed himself, why someone wanted you dead. A few days ago, I learned that Holly Pfeiffer's medical records had been stolen. Yesterday I found them, along with the X rays. Behr had them."

"The box I put in the car."

He nodded. "This morning when I got sewn up, I asked the doc, a friend of mine, to look them over."

Her toes dug into the sand. "And?"

"After the bombing, Holly was treated for concussion by a doctor named Joel Beck." Confusion in her eyes and a hint of fear—Icarus seeing first feathers fly off the wings. "Beck found a hematoma, bleeding inside the brain; draining it, he discovered compression damage. His notes show a guarded prognosis, then increasing concern. When seizures started, he put her on phenobarb, then Dilantin, then both. Quite a lot at the end.''

''What do you mean *at the end?*''

''You remember me saying Max had to cooperate because it was the only way he'd see his daughter alive?''

She picked up a fistful of sand, threw it down. *''What are you telling me?''*

''Here's what I think happened: After he took Holly, Z kept up her medication, Max would have made sure he got it. After a while, though, Z got careless—she'd have seemed normal to him, doc said. But skipping it would have triggered a major seizure. Z tried to revive her, but it was too late.''

''I won't listen.'' She stood and kicked sand, stormed away.

He followed, spun her around; she struck out at him, blind windmill fists. He grabbed her arms and held on: ''Max did everything Z said to get his daughter back. But Z screwed up—then, and when he heard the FBI jumped in at the airport. In a rage, he called the media, told them Angela was dead. But Max already had Angela, he'd picked her up from where she was being held and was on his way to catch the charter, exchange her and the money for Holly. Then he hears what they found . . .''

She just looked at him.

''Imagine how *that* felt. Change of plans, he tells Clayton when he gets there—nobody going south, just the case. Max takes *you* and bolts.''

''No! . . . NO-NO-NO-NO!''

''Angela DeBray becomes Holly Pfeiffer. You even looked similar.''

She slumped to the sand, her expression making him want to stop. ''Why didn't he just go to the police?''

He sat beside her. ''I'll tell you now if you want, but I'm asking that you wait.''

''My God, why?''

''Because a lot depends on it. Okay?''

She brushed away tears. ''Angela was identified. Why doesn't anyone else know about this?''

"Vega told me yesterday what they found: decomposed remains wearing clothing and a bracelet the DeBrays identified. It was too late for footprint matches, and she'd had no broken bones or dental work—things they could verify. And Z had taken no chances, crushing the skull."

"The ringing in my ear . . ."

"Tommy Littlefield was shot while they were taking you, I talked to someone who was there. The gun would have been close to your ear."

Stricken replaced hopeful. "So my father—*oh, God!*"

"Max knew you weren't safe. So he chucked everything and atoned by being a father to you."

"Then why did he *leave* me?" She was crying openly now. Noticing, a family moved down the beach to where they could play untroubled.

"My guess is, he was hoping to end it there, take the heat before they put it together, any of them. He wanted to protect you. Or maybe he knew he couldn't anymore."

"Protect me from *what?*"

"From all the people he knew could hurt you if the truth came out."

She put her head on her knees, rocked until the crying stopped. Finally she said, "I don't understand why they tried to kill me."

"That was Stillman. He wasn't sure what you'd learned from Max, what you might tell the FBI. Dead you were no threat to him." He touched her hand. "Look, I know this is hard—I even debated whether I should tell you. But more than anyone's truth, it's yours." He paused.

"When you find time, think about what you'd like me to call you. Will you do that?"

She looked up, eyes puffy but pinning him. "I don't have to think about it, I'm Holly Maxwell. It's who I was at the lake, and it's who I am now."

A flock of pelicans glided over; Wil watched them dive and re-form, then move on while she stared at the horizon. Trucks rumbled by on the roadway.

"I'm hungry," he said to ease away from it. "How does clam chowder and cornbread sound?"

"Typical male," she said, the sarcasm welcome for once, her smile without saying.

As they were walking back, he said, "The part I asked you to trust me on? It's up north. You decide not to come, I'll report back what happens."

"Stay here?"

He shrugged. "Nice here, you said."

"Sad when a private eye doesn't know his own client."

He watched her scramble up the revetment toward the tunnel. "Just wanted to hear you say it."

They left at noon, stopping first in Santa Barbara to buy her some clothes and incidentals, pulling into San Francisco around dinnertime after a largely silent trip. Wil checked them into separate rooms, a small place in the Marina district where they ate Italian deli that he foraged up on Chestnut Street. A call to Canizares set up the reunion for next morning.

Wil was dozing with a paperback when she knocked and let herself in. He sat up, stunned by the transformation: green dress cut to the knee, stockings, light makeup, gold earrings. That hair.

"Be honest with me," she began haltingly. "Does this look okay for tomorrow?"

"Turn around," he said. Then, "More than okay. How are you feeling about it?"

"Scared."

"It's not an audition, Holly. If anything, she's the one who has to prove herself."

"I keep telling myself that."

"What, then?"

"I guess . . . I don't know." She sat on the bed, her face a question mark. "I don't know where I'm going or what to do next. I'm not even sure who I am. Do you have any idea what that's like?"

"About every other day," he said. "Just trust yourself. Seems scarier than it is."

"It's all so new. I keep wondering . . ."

He leaned over and touched her cheek. "Don't stop wondering, okay?"

At the door, she turned around. "You always make me feel better."

Just wait till tomorrow, he thought as she said good night and shut the door.

THIRTY-TWO

The big Tudor looked the same to Wil; Holly just stared at it. Sun was beginning to show through the morning overcast, flare off the diamond-shaped panes of glass. He took her arm and they crossed the street, past Canizares's Mercedes and up the walk.

"You look great," he said.

Her smile disappeared as fast as it came.

Kenneth met them at the door, then Canizares in the entryway. The lawyer took him aside. "Mrs. Pfeiffer wants a moment alone with us first, Hardesty."

"Five minutes," Wil said, glancing at Holly, seeing no reaction.

Canizares nodded and excused the two of them, then they were in the big living room, Rose Pfeiffer holding a cigarette as she turned from the window.

"She's really very lovely, isn't she," Rose Pfeiffer said in her smoky voice. She had on a housecoat of Chinese design: mandarin collar, frog buttons over scarlet and cream brocade, matching slippers. "I wanted to take a moment to thank you, Mr. Hardesty, and to apologize for my prior actions. I hope you understand."

Wil took the hand she offered. "I think I do. You'd like this to work out."

Something resembling a smile appeared; she drew in smoke.

"Was she harmed?" Canizares asked. "We saw the news reports."

"She's been through a lot. But she's strong and—"

"Mr. Hardesty," Rose Pfeiffer put in, "I sincerely hope there will be no surprises today. Your support for my wish to have the girl rejoin her family would mean a great deal. Both to me and to you, if I make myself clear."

"Transparent," Wil said.

"Excellent." Rose Pfeiffer crushed out her cigarette, glanced at Canizares, pressed a button on the table phone. Almost immediately the door opened, Kenneth retreating, then shutting it behind him.

Wil went to Holly and drew her into the room. Rose Pfeiffer gave the girl a perfunctory kiss and, "Oh, my poor dear, you're so thin." They sat then, Wil and Holly on one couch, Canizares and Rose Pfeiffer the other. Kenneth knocked, entered, put a coffee service down on the low table between them and poured a cup for each, smiling at Holly before leaving.

Canizares began. "I've been going through your father's papers, Holly. I'm sure you're aware he left you a substantial amount of money."

She nodded.

"I have also been directed by your grandmother—"

"I can speak for myself, Mr. Canizares. My dear, I would like to put any differences we may have had behind us and to offer you a home here. After all, we do share the same name."

"No," Holly said without emphasis.

Rose Pfeiffer lit another cigarette. Sunlight illuminated the nuggets of stained glass in the windows and brought shine to Canizares's scalp. The lawyer sipped his coffee.

"No, what?" Rose Pfeiffer said at length.

"I'm sorry. No to your offer is what I mean."

"My offer is not something—"

"Perhaps it would be best if we were all on the same page here," Wil put in. "That way you won't have to pretend Holly is your granddaughter, when the truth is she's your niece."

He heard Holly's intake of breath, watched expressions freeze on the other two.

"I saw your sister, Mrs. Pfeiffer, her mother. Maybe it was the coat that did it, the one like yours you'd given Collette. So I did some checking, found the maiden names matched and put what happened together from there."

Rose Pfeiffer took a deep drag, her intake seeming to suck the smoke completely from the cigarette. "Are you responsible for this, Mr. Canizares?"

"Absolutely not."

"True," Wil said. "Your Mr. Canizares has been a rock."

"I had better not find out otherwise."

Wil turned to Holly, told her about seeing Patrice and Michelle. Then he said, "Mrs. Pfeiffer, Holly is unaware of some things. Do you prefer explaining to her what her biological father was like or should I?"

Rose Pfeiffer seemed poised for something; instead she blinked, tamped ash from her cigarette. "That won't be necessary."

"You don't have to say anything, Mrs. Pfeiffer," Canizares said. "As your attorney—"

She silenced him with a wave. "My sister's husband was a degenerate bastard monster. Collette barely knew Elden DeBray. Even after they were married, she saw everything he was and nothing. Only when Collette actually saw what he was doing to Angela—and how he reacted when she confronted him—did she come to me."

Holly froze. "What are you saying? That this man you say is my father, *did* things to me? *Molested me?*" She turned to Wil. "My God, is that what she's saying?"

Wil waited. "Mrs. Pfeiffer . . ."

"I knew what he'd done to Patrice and Michelle, to their mother. I knew he'd crush Collette if she tried taking Angela. Then it came to me, so simple. A kidnapping—take the little girl away from the abuse, send her someplace where Collette could join her after she'd gotten a divorce. Elden would never know."

"So you talked to your lawyer," Wil said to Canizares.

"Mrs. Pfeiffer, I'm advising you to say nothing further."

"And he took it from there. Let me guess: Canizares knew Stillman already through Max, knew that Stillman associated with people who'd do it. Only it got out of hand, didn't it? Max got sucked in, something neither of you planned, maybe Stillman even assured you wouldn't happen. Some choice he has to make: lose his daughter or kidnap his cousin."

"He didn't even know my sister. In our family, we didn't discuss our black sheep."

"Mrs. Pfeiffer, do me a favor and cut the crap."

She looked at her hands as if they belonged to someone else. "It's true. Among other things to show her independence, Collette made pornographic films—that's how Elden met her. He got it hushed, but not before she'd sent our mother and father to early graves. How do you forgive that?"

"You did."

"Nobody deserved Elden DeBray." Rose Pfeiffer's cigarette burned untouched; pallor had replaced skin tone against the richly colored housecoat. "I'd have done anything for Holly. Max said nothing about that filth having her."

"That I believe," Wil said. "The irony was, all Max had to do was have his mother put pressure on Stillman to get Holly released."

"He *swore* no one would be hurt," she said. "And what was two million dollars to Elden DeBray? All Collette had to do was arrange for her and Elden to be away."

"Just a nice little business deal," Wil said. "Then somebody gets excited and shoots Tommy Littlefield, who wasn't even supposed to be there. His mistake was getting seduced by Z's sister, Z probably threatening to cut off her coke supply if she didn't scout for him. Then Z screws up Holly's medication. Enter Monika Stillman, who somehow learns about Angela's IQ tests and who's already obsessed with genius and what it can do for her. Holly—whom she never intended to return to Max anyway—is dead. But Angela's fair game.

"No one knows this yet, not Max, not Rose, not the De-

Brays. Meantime, Angela is where her mother can slip away to see her during the ordeal—Collette's role of a lifetime. Everything turns sour then. The FBI tries to save Angela, Z freaks, and suddenly there's a body everyone thinks is hers. But Angela's right here, isn't she? That's why you didn't want your 'granddaughter' in the house, for fear she'd recognize things. You, for instance. Must have been a tense moment at the funeral.''

Rose Pfeiffer lit another cigarette, matching the one in the ashtray. ''To this day, I see my son's face.'' Her hands twisted. ''Max had no idea—when he got here, he went crazy. I begged him not to take Angela, told him what we'd arranged. Instead he shoved me, knocked Kenneth down, yelled something about having to get Holly back. When I heard they'd found the grave . . .'' She leaned back against the couch.

Holly sat rigid. ''Why didn't you *do* something?''

Rose just looked at her; Canizares fidgeted.

''They couldn't,'' Wil said. ''Even if the Feds found Angela, she'd be sent back to Elden and everyone else to death row. Rose and Collette could only hope Max would relent, at least let them see you. But Rose already had fought him for custody of his own daughter. She and Collette exposed Holly to being killed. Stillman exploited him, his friends betrayed him.'' He gulped coffee. ''All he had was you—not his own, but somebody he could make it up to.''

The scene played surreal, humans turned into mannequins. Then Holly swiped angrily at tears. From his coat, Wil pulled out a folded piece of paper and handed it to Canizares, who opened it slowly.

''Where did you get this?''

''Stillman's files. Looks authentic until I remembered your old man worked for the Justice Department. Stillman told me all it took was money. How much, counselor? Enough, I hope.''

Canizares regarded his coffee. ''What do you know about it? Seeing your father die by inches, not earning enough to keep your family from bleeding to death. A fucking memo to help convince Max the FBI was responsible for Paulette—why not, I figured. Working for Stillman was probably a good career move for him.''

"How much?'' Holly said.

Canizares was silent.

"My God, he would have given you the money.''

"He always had everything,'' Canizares shouted back. "I owed him enough as it was. Any more, I'd have hated him.''

"So instead you sold him out. Congratulations, Mr. Canizares.''

The lawyer stood and walked to the window; behind his back, fists clenched and unclenched. "How did you know?''

Wil leaned forward. "Just something about you dribbling me information, not mentioning Henry Shirmir or Joel Beck, someone else you'd have known. Wanting me where you could see what I was up to, convincing Rose I might be getting close to her sister. That for appearances she ought to reconcile with Holly.''

"Is it true?'' Holly asked.

Rose Pfeiffer's expression was the answer.

Holly stood up. "Mr. Canizares, now that it's clear who I am, I'd like to know where I stand with the DeBrays.''

Canizares thought. "I suppose if Hardesty's willing to go along, we might make a case for a share of the estate. Depends on the sisters.''

"I see.'' She turned to Wil. "Perhaps someday I could talk with them. But if there's nothing else now, I'd like to go.''

"Please,'' Rose Pfeiffer said. "Stay . . .''

Holly looked at her, then straight ahead as she left the room. Outside on the walk, Wil took her arm.

"Is this really what you want?''

"You heard them. How can you even ask?''

"They made mistakes. When Max died, they didn't know what your showing up would mean. What little they saw only convinced them to stonewall.''

"And what about after I'd been kidnapped? When coming forward, even just to you, could have changed things.''

"Good point," he said. "You okay with what was said in there?"

"I'm not sure it's hit me yet."

"Elden DeBray's not even a blip on the screen anymore—don't let him do to you what he did to Patrice and Michelle. Live your life."

They paused at the car. "Do me a favor," she said finally. "No more revelations for a while. I'm sick of secrets."

"Right." He reached to open her car door, caught himself, walked around to his side, and got in. "Don't say it," he said. "Don't even think it."

She grinned at him.

"You know if you decide to press this DeBray thing, I'll take it as far as you want."

"People will get hurt, won't they?"

He started the car, put it in gear.

"The answer's no," she said. "But it's not them I care about. It's you."

"Thanks." He eased past the entrance to VistaMar, then pulled over. "We haven't talked about where you want to go."

She smoothed the green dress. "Tahoe. I decided last night to rebuild, get to know my neighbors. Holly Maxwell, too." Her face clouded suddenly.

"What is it?"

"Shouldn't I have remembered something? What he did, I mean. I don't recall any of—"

"From what I've read, blocking's common in that kind of trauma," Wil said. "If it hasn't come up, count your blessings. You ready?"

"No," she said. "Not quite."

Wil went in first. "Hello," he said. "I've brought someone to visit. Would you like that?"

Collette DeBray looked up from a place mat she was fringing, colored burlap strands arrayed in her lap. She wore the same navy blue housecoat, the same confused expression.

"It's Wil, Mrs. DeBray. I was here with Felice."

"Wil," she said.

He beckoned to the doorway and she came forward, biting her lip. "This is Holly," he said. "Holly has come a very long way to be here."

"How nice," Collette DeBray said. Then her eyes cleared and she searched the girl's face. "Strange how you remind me of someone. I'm so forgetful. Please, what was your name again?"

"Holly," she said, taking the woman's hand.

"That *is* a pretty name. Do I know you?"

The girl stared at Collette DeBray, then turned to face the patio and the swaying trees outside. A hand went to her forehead.

"Oh dear, something's wrong. Did I say something?"

After a moment, Holly turned back from the window. "No—it's just that we were friends once," she said, her eyes shining. "May I sit with you for a while?"

Wil excused himself and went out to wait in the car.

There were tears, initially, and long periods of quiet, but the day was fine, warm and clear and feeling like summer. By the time Wil stopped the car, it was twilight. Yellow tape still hung across the road to her house and the burnt sides of the pines looked thin and ragged against the sky. For a while she poked through charred framing and rusted metal. Evidence that someone had been watering the daisies brought a smile.

They checked into the lodge then, had dinner on the deck. She told him ideas she had for the house and to hurry up and send her his bill before she ran out of money. After conversation wound down, they just sat looking at the moon on the lake, at lights moving across the night sky, Wil wondering if she felt the same ache he did.

In the morning he drove her to a neighbor's, parked in the drive with the motor running.

"I hope everything works out," she said. "With your wife and all."

"Thanks."

"No—thank you."

"Anytime." First-date awkward, trying not to say the wrong thing. He tapped the steering wheel, ticked at himself but stuck. "Guess I'll see you around."

"I hate this," she said. "Don't be a stranger, okay?"

"Your housewarming, just let me know." Wondering if he'd actually come; knowing the answer. "And don't forget the Rincon. You'd look good on a board."

"I won't. She kissed him then, a tentative one he didn't resist, followed by a second with more enthusiasm. Then she opened the car door and ran toward the house without looking back.

Wil drove away slowly, barely noticing the road, boats and their water-skiers, view spots starting to draw the first big crowds of summer. At South Shore, he turned in the rental car to a clerk who got wide-eyed at the amount, then caught his flight and was home in a few hours. He took a pillow out to the deck lounge, watched the ocean for a while, and fell asleep. It was cool and dark when he woke up, fog moving in from out in the Channel. He made coffee, pressed the phone message he'd postponed, heard Lisa saying she was glad he hadn't been killed, that she'd heard about it on the news and been worried. Relieved, he called to tell her he was back and missing her, but no one was home.

Four months later, she filed for divorce.

Coincidentally, a card from Lake Tahoe came the same week the newspaper ran a story about a box turning up at FBI field office, Los Angeles. In it was a human head packed in dry ice, with a piece of paper noting the Revolutionary Command Council, in the spirit of international cooperation, was pleased to serve in the apprehension of the criminal, Lincoln Stillman. In conjunction with the case, Federal District Judge Harold "Bucky" Carper was credited with alerting FBI investigators that Stillman attempted to bribe him in exchange for safe haven. Agents had been waiting for Stillman to appear at the judge's residence.

No body was found.

The card from Tahoe said HOLLY MAXWELL IS HOME in bold lettering. Inside, it had a date to christen her new place and a personal invitation to please come. Before he could think it over, figure it all out, Wil wrote her a polite note saying he was tied up, walked it to the mailbox. Then he started in on the house, cleaning and throwing stuff out, one pile for the trash, one for the Goodwill. As he worked, he thought about doors. Doors closing, doors opening.

Around sunset he took his cassette player and some other things to the beach, where he gathered pieces of driftwood into a large pile. The long flat box containing Holly's medical records he put in the center of it.

Thinking Max Pfeiffer would approve, wishing his tortured soul peace, he spent several matches igniting the wood, then punched up an old tape with Country Joe and the Fish, Buffalo Springfield, Hendrix, Richie Havens, and The Byrds on it. As "Chimes of Freedom" made a dent in the night, he watched the box catch and take hold, colored flames turning the X-ray film into black curling shapes that broke apart in the swirl.

He piled more driftwood on, then sat back, hoping Max could see the glow from wherever he was.

Still, if nothing else, it made a damn nice fire.